OF THEIR OWN FREE WILL

Fort Mims to New Orleans

(A Novel)

By

L. E. DENTON

CONTENTS

Chapter 1

August 30, 1813

The few trees still inside the fort were lifeless again that morning. No breeze stirred their leaves. There was no relief from the stubborn rays of the sun and the sticky, uncompromising heat that enveloped them all.

It didn't just come from the blazing sun as it made its way across the sky, but the air itself, which suffocated and surrounded those huddled inside Fort Pierce. It seemed to strangle them with its cloying dampness, as if to smother the very life out of them.

The whole compound had been up since before dawn. Those who had been manning the gunports cut into the sturdy timbers that comprised the fort's outer walls had been relieved of duty, but they did not sleep. Instead, they scraped up what food and water they could to sustain themselves and found a place to stretch out on the fort's churned, muddy ground. Sleep would not come to them, though. It was impossible considering what was expected.

Lieutenant Montgomery, who was in charge of the forty militiamen who had been sent over from Fort Mims, paced nervously inside the compound. Sweat poured from his forehead as he contemplated what would happen to the hundred and fifty civilians that shared the squalid interior of the fort with him and his men. They were a motley mixture of black slaves, half-breeds and whites. They were dependent on him, and he wasn't quite sure he had the wherewithal to help them in their time of need. Reports had been coming in for two weeks of roving bands of Creek warriors, dressed in the accoutrements of war. These warriors were armed with muskets as well as clubs, painted red to signify what they wished to do with them, and their numbers were growing. Nervous scouts had been reporting their presence to the north, and as each day passed, the garrison's anxiousness increased.

Montgomery did his best to calm those around him, a pasted half-smile on his face. He tried not to dwell on his ill luck at being assigned to defend this stockade, which had less than half the men and muskets of Fort Mims. Some of his men had called it a suicide duty. And the heat was oppressive. If only it hadn't been so unrelenting these past weeks. He was sure it increased the tension in the fort, agitating those enclosed in the walls.

One thing he was sure of was that the Red Sticks had a mind to eradicate Fort Pierce. Why wouldn't they? There were people of importance seeking shelter here. Farmers with large land holdings and half-breeds who defied the wishes of the warriors. These half-breeds wanted to live at peace with the white man, not go to war with them. Some were large landowners themselves, with their own slaves, and a vested interest in getting along with their neighbors. The clans they represented were important, too, and had provided vital information to the Mississippi Militia. They, just as much as the whites, were an impediment to the will of the rampaging Creeks.

Jacob Worley, 17, sweated and fretted along with all the others. He knew full well the dangers at hand. They had all witnessed the carnage and rage of the Red Stick war parties. It had started as a tribal conflict, with the Upper Creeks demanding war, egged on by their prophets and the Shawnee Tecumseh, while the Lower Creeks were content to live alongside their white neighbors. The Red Sticks had initiated the hostilities by destroying crops and burning down the farms of the peace-seeking members of their tribe. But then came the battle at Burnt Corn Creek. Red Stick warriors had been on their way home from Pensacola, where they had gotten guns and ammunition from the English and

Spanish, when they were ambushed by the Mississippi Militia. This action had ignited the fuse, and the warriors then turned on their neighbors and own recalcitrant people with a vengeance.

Jacob wiped his face with an already wet handkerchief. He and his family had been cloistered within the walls of the fort for more than two weeks, and its confines became more claustrophobic with each passing day. But as more and more sightings of war parties were announced by the scouts sent out daily by Lieutenant Montgomery, the fear he felt – the raw, uncompromising kind – had overwhelmed his sense of safety in numbers. Were they prepared for the inevitable – a full-scale attack on their compound?

Along about 10 o'clock, a lone black boy was spotted sprinting into the clearing surrounding the fort. Jacob watched as he came, his small feet beating a rhythm on the packed red earth that encompassed the fort. As the young boy drew closer, a look of panic and terror could be seen on his face. The fort's gate slowly opened and he staggered in, panting and sweating from exhaustion. He fell on his knees and began to cry.

The Lieutenant approached him. "Here, here, what is all this about?"

The young boy gulped. "They're coming, sir! They're everywhere!"

"Calm yourself. Hey, you!" he pointed to Jacob. "Fetch this boy a cup of water."

Jacob did as he was told. He ran to the well and grabbed a hollowed gourd, dipped it in the bucket of water that rested on the rim of the well, and hurried back to the boy, who grabbed it and drank thirstily.

"Now," the Lieutenant said authoritatively. "Tell me why you've come."

"Me and Sam was tending some cows in a pasture close by the fort."

"Which fort?"

"Mims, sir. Anyways, we done saw lots and lots of Indians, sir. They was painted for war, it looked like to us. We ran back to the fort." The tears began streaming down his cheeks again, making more tracks down the reddened dirt that dusted their surface. "But they didn't believe us, sir. Said we must have seen some cows." He began blubbering.

"So how did you wind up here?" the Lieutenant asked sharply.

"They grabbed us, sir. They grabbed us and tried to drag us into the fort. They got Sam, but I'm a mite smaller than him, and wiggled away. I hoofed it over here. Saw lots more Indians."

There was a collective gasp from the crowd that had gathered around the boy. The event they had been expecting was now at hand.

"It's fine, boy. You're safe now." The Lieutenant tried to speak with confidence, but his mind was racing. He spoke to the gaggle of women that had joined the men gathered around the boy. "You women, see that he gets some food, will you?" He paced off to the center of the compound and raised his voice.

"It appears, ladies and gentlemen, that the time is at hand. What we have been dreading has now come to pass. I expect all militia members to post themselves at the gunports. The other men need to be prepared to take their places if necessary. Be sure all firearms are loaded and able to fire. I expect the women who can load or shoot to be prepared as well. The rest of you – be sure all fires are stoked. We need as much water drawn from the well as we have buckets for. What food we have needs to be prepared and ready to eat. All children confined to the buildings." He stopped and glared. "We are not slaves or free. We are not black or red or white. We must work together and prepare for the worst. No bickering. Am I understood?"

There was no reply, only the sound of scurrying as his orders were carried out.

Jacob took his place beside his father at the northern wall of the fort. He checked his musket nervously, fumbling with the lock and breech, inspecting it to be sure it was ready to fire. His father had bought it new for him in Mobile for his sixteenth birthday. He had never fired it at another human being, only used it for hunting. Would it be different, he wondered, aiming it at something other than a deer or raccoon? He glanced over at his father Thomas, stoic and detached as always. Jacob thought to himself, could this incident cause his father to show some emotion, some drive, some reaction? It didn't look as if it would.

His Uncle John was stationed nearby, close to the next gunport. He was dressed as most white men were, with breeches and a buckskin shirt. But the paint on his face, half black and half red, designated his Creek ancestry. This gave his countenance a fierce look, and Jacob could tell by his body movements that his uncle was not the least bit impassive about what was expected to come rushing at them on the other side of the wall.

Jacob glanced around and saw his stepmother busily helping draw water from the well. It was unlike her. She usually allowed everyone else to do the work as she imperiously directed. He assumed his three half-brothers were somewhere within the confines of one of the buildings of the compound. Just as well, he thought. They were too young to witness what was about to happen.

About eleven o'clock they heard the drums from Fort Mims. The timing was suspicious. Jacob was used to hearing them at noontime, when the fort called everyone together for the midday meal. Why were they summoning everyone at an earlier hour? Jacob looked around and saw that he was not the only one questioning those pulsing, throbbing sounds of drums. His uncle had cocked his head and glanced over at him, tipping his rifle up to signal his concern over the sound. His father, musket at the ready, did not move a muscle.

The jarring sound of gunfire began a few minutes later, coming from the northwest. Along with the shots, faint human voices could be heard – war cries. Even though Fort Mims was over a mile away, the sounds drifted through the sultry, steamy air, unmistakable to all. It was under attack.

A hush fell among the women, busy before campfires and hauling buckets of water. They stopped what they were doing and looked nervously toward the men stationed along the fort's walls. A low murmur rose after a few moments. Jacob's stepmother put down the bucket she was carrying and rushed over to her husband.

"What will we do now, Thomas?" she wailed.

"Hush, Sophia. We're as safe here as anywhere."

Sophia was not used to being addressed so by her husband. "Safe?" her voice raised. "We are not safe! Those red devils will be upon us next!"

The Lieutenant strode toward her. "Ma'am, get back to the women. Now is not the time. Your husband does not need to be distracted."

She turned and huffed off, her ever-enlarging backside signaling her displeasure.

The sounds of gunfire increased. The militiamen peered nervously through their gunports, keenly aware they must not be caught off guard. The whole fort depended on them.

Noontime came and went. The sounds emanating from Fort Mims did not slacken. The Lieutenant had a few women bring water to the men. They drank thirstily, their throats parched and dry, as much from the strain of fear and dread as from the blazing sun at its zenith.

After another hour, the militiamen stationed at the gunports were swapped out with other men. Lieutenant Montgomery handpicked those who took their place. Jacob's Uncle John was picked; his father was not.

Jacob moved and placed himself at his uncle's back. John was his mother's eldest brother, and as such had been tasked with the teaching the ways of the Creeks to his nephew. The rules of the Creek culture were clear. A mother's eldest brother had a greater influence on the raising of the boys of the tribe than even their own fathers. Jacob understood this. He had a great fondness for his uncle.

The sound of gunfire continued to echo over the distance between the two forts. Sometimes sporadic and sometimes fierce, it signified a great struggle. There had to be hundreds of Red Sticks to generate such fire, and the fire from Mims in response. The men along the walls of the fort did their best to maintain their bravado for the sake of the women, but on closer inspection one could see the dread etched on their faces. Many of those housed here had relatives and friends inside the walls of Fort Mims. What would become of them?

The strain intensified as the minutes ticked by. Then suddenly, about two o'clock, the firing came almost to a stop. Now the stress almost exploded among them. Some of the women sent up a howling wail, their anxiety giving way to an almost animal sound. Would they be next? Mims was a far stronger fort, with more men, and for that reason attracted most fleeing homesteaders, more men who could pull a trigger and women who could load muskets. If the Red Sticks were repulsed at Fort Mims, the horde would surely descend on Fort Pierce, a smaller and more vulnerable prey.

Lieutenant Montgomery redoubled his efforts to encourage the men on guard at the walls. He strode among them, offering a word here, a pat on the shoulder there. More water and a little food was brought to keep their strength up. This was the crucial moment for the inhabitants of Fort Pierce and they couldn't slacken their vigilance. Defied at Mims, it would take the Red Sticks less than a half-hour to come tearing at Fort Pierce.

The lull did not last long. After an hour or so, the firing of muskets in the distance began again in earnest. Jacob was startled by its return.

"What could that mean, Uncle? Why have they started back up?" he asked.

John turned. "Wish I knew. Can't mean anything good," he replied grimly.

Finally, as the sun waned to the west, the firing stopped. An eerie silence filled the fields and forests, bayous and streams between Fort Pierce and Fort Mims. At last, the apprehension and unease among them lessened somewhat. It would be highly improbable for an attack to be launched after dusk, especially since a most epic battle had already occurred that day.

Men at the gunports were swapped out again. The Lieutenant ordered that all within the walls partake of the food the women had prepared. The children streamed out of the shelters, most running straight to their parents when spotted. All gathered around the fires. Some of the women brought bowls of stew to the men still manning the walls and they ate, hungrily and gratefully, happy they had been spared for at least one more day.

When darkness had settled, the Lieutenant called out for his best scouts. Jacob followed his uncle as he joined the gathering at the center of the fort.

"Men, we need to know what happened at Fort Mims. I'm afraid the situation will not be a good one or Major Beasley would have sent me word by now. The Red Sticks may still be outside the fort."

The men around him shuffled their feet and murmured their agreement.

"It will be a difficult situation. Better than a mile between here and there, it'll be very dangerous to cross. I need six of you to volunteer to undertake a scout. You all are very aware of the capabilities of the enemies we face. Take a moment and consider if you are up to the task."

Jacob tugged at his uncle's sleeve. "Are you going? Can I go with you?"

John looked at him sternly. The paint on his face made his countenance seem even more grim. "No, you cannot, Jacob. You aren't ready. Besides, you aren't a scout."

"I know these woods, Uncle. You know I do. The two of us have hunted this land many times," Jacob pleaded.

"You aren't ready." His uncle placed his hand on Jacob's shoulder. "What you ask is more than I can grant. It's best you stay here with your parents. The Lieutenant will still need men to guard the fort."

Jacob was disappointed. He hung his head but had to admit his uncle's advice was wise.

John strode up to the Lieutenant. "I will volunteer, sir. I know this area well and have hunted and trapped with many of the warriors who oppose us. I understand their ways and believe I can slip through."

"Well, you are most certainly painted for it, John. I suppose the Red Sticks would have a hard time determining if you are friend or foe, especially in the dark." Five others quickly volunteered. They gathered around the Lieutenant as he gave his instructions.

"Wait a couple more hours, then slip out. Get as close to the fort as you can without making yourself known. If you're caught, the scalping knife will be your fate. Then rush to the walls yelling, they'll let you in. When you find Major Beasley, ask if the Red Sticks are still near in force, and if not, see if he can spare any men for us. If they've been beaten at Mims, they'll be hitting us next. Report back as soon as you can."

At the appointed time, the men slipped through the gate and made their way northwest, keeping to the cover of woods as much as they could. Those that remained in the fort were not idle in their absence. Lieutenant Montgomery kept men posted at the gunports and the women managed the fires and saw to it the children were put to bed. Most of the occupants of Fort Pierce were silent, tense, as they waited for the scouts to return.

It was past midnight when they did. Calling the password, they silently slipped through the gate, one by one. The Lieutenant had grabbed a snatch of sleep but was quickly roused at their approach. He could sense the news would not be good when he saw the scouts' faces, and he waited, pacing in a circle, close to the center of the fort. Finally, when the last man was safe inside, they made their report. All the awake adults

– black, white and red – gathered around. Jacob's Uncle John was the first to voice his report.

"It's bad news, Lieutenant."

"Tell me. Tell me what you found," the Lieutenant spoke impatiently.

"I got as close to the fort as I was able, sir. There was fire inside. The woods surrounding were full of Red Sticks. I was challenged more than once but answered. They couldn't tell the difference in the dark. I was able to cross the clearing in front of the gate and took a look inside."

He paused. "All dead. The buildings put to the torch. I saw white people on the ground, women too, all covered in blood, clothes ripped off. There were still a few warriors inside the walls, taking scalps and rifling through the rooms, looking for loot and trophies."

The crowd surrounding the scouts gasped. All dead? How could that be possible?

From the light of the fires inside Fort Pierce, their flames dancing and crackling in the still, hot air, their smoke billowing skyward, the crowd saw Lieutenant Montgomery shake his head, then raise his fist. Then his voice was strangely quiet, almost a whisper, like a hiss. "Damn them to hell!" he said.

Chapter 2

On The Road

As soon as John made his report, he pulled Jacob and his parents aside.

"Listen, we're in a bad position here. The woods are full of warriors, and it will be very difficult to get out of this situation. You must prepare yourselves for the worst."

Sophia grasped his arm and started blubbering, "What about my boys?"

"I don't have any wisdom to share with you, Sophia. The Red Sticks made it very plain at Fort Mims that they aren't above slaughtering anyone who opposes them, including women and children."

Thomas spoke up. "What do you think we should do?"

Jacob found his parents' reactions odd. For the last few years, ever since his mother died, his father, and most certainly his stepmother, had shown no interest in listening to anything John had to say. Their sudden reliance on his opinion could only indicate they had the same gripping, paralyzing fear that Jacob himself was experiencing.

"We'll wait and see what Lieutenant Montgomery has to say. I'm not sure he will be able to extricate us, but we'll wait and see."

By that time, all the scouts that had returned from Fort Mims had given their reports. One of them talked of captives, women, in the forest. Another had seen Red Stick bodies, and wounded being succored by other warriors. There was, at first, stunned silence at the news. Then, a sort of howling and sobbing broke out among the women, as they returned to their assigned places in the fort. They gathered their sleeping children close to them and rocked them in their arms.

The men stayed at the center of the compound and peppered the Lieutenant with questions. "What are your plans? What will we do? Do we have enough men and ammunition to withstand an attack? What about our women and children?"

The Lieutenant raised his hand. "For now, there is nothing to be done. I will keep men posted at the gunports. The rest of you, get some rest. I will do my best to come up with a plan. We are in a dire position, no doubt. But the good Lord has watched over us thus far. I have faith He will see us through."

Before daylight, he roused a handful of his most trusted men. Others, he roused to take a turn at the gunports, at which time those who had been standing watch grabbed their blanket rolls and found a place in the compound to lay their weary heads. The women rose and began to rekindle the fires and tend to the needs of the children. This time Jacob was assigned a gunport. He looked nervously through the opening, his finger on the trigger of his newly primed musket. He hoped he would be ready if an attack occurred. He was unsure if he was.

John made his way to him, through the jumble of men and women, the cluster at the center of the compound. The animals – beasts of burden, pigs, and chickens – were being fed and cared for, though there was not much feed left. Because of the turmoil of the last few days, they had been penned up inside the fort to prevent the Red Sticks from taking them. No grazing outside the compound had been allowed, on orders from Lieutenant Montgomery.

"I'm off, Jacob. We're to scout our way to the river to see if there's a means of escape by water."

Jacob looked at him quizzically. "Would there be enough boats for us all?"

"I don't know. We will take a look see, just in case."

"Be careful, Uncle."

"I will. I promise." He gave Jacob a brief smile, a welcome sight after the days of stress. Jacob noticed he had re-daubed his face paint. If one didn't know any better, one would think John was an enemy instead of a friend. He wore the traditional leggings of the Creeks and a small loincloth with the long tail of a cow attached to the rear. He hung his bullet pouch, powder horn and knife at his waist and nothing else. His chest displayed traditional Creek markings. Because of the paint on his face, it was difficult to notice John's white features – the lighter eyes, the flared nose, the paler complexion.

As the scouts drifted off into the tangle of the woods, their muskets resting comfortably in the crook of their arms, those that remained in the fort did their best to keep busy. Some of the women occupied themselves with washing, using dirty water over and over. Men who were not assigned a detail gathered together and argued about the best way to proceed. The militiamen rested as best they could among the clutter and noise of the fort. Some of the children scampered about, playing the games that all children do, while others clung desperately to their mothers' skirts. Lieutenant Montgomery made his rounds of the gunports, checking on each to be sure the man was vigilant and had not spotted anything unusual.

As Jacob stood watch, he could hear the querulous and grating voice of his stepmother, as she berated his father over one thing or another. She was unhappy over the spot they had been assigned within the walls of the fort. She disliked having to work with the other women, insisting that all her labor be done by their slaves, Sally and Moses. She insisted that the heat prohibited her from tending to their three young sons, Jacob's little stepbrothers, Michael, Joshua and Matthew.

"You must do something, Thomas. I cannot go on like this," Sophia exclaimed.

Jacob could not see but could almost feel his father's response. He would be nodding along, dispassionately as always, in agreement with all her complaints. Jacob tried to stay focused on the treeline a hundred yards away from his gunport, but it was difficult. He wondered if perhaps his life would have been easier these last seven years if his father hadn't decided he needed a new wife after Jacob's mother died. He decided it would have been.

The sun was well risen before the scouts returned. They came swiftly and silently through the heavy underbrush that cluttered the treeline, the vines and jumble of scraggly bushes clinging to the bases of the tall pines. As they entered the fort, their faces were grim.

The Lieutenant strode forward to meet them at the gate.

"I take it you don't have good news," he stated firmly.

"We don't," Josiah Freeman said. He looked around at all the folks gathered around them, with a look of regret and almost pity. His demeanor set the crowd to murmuring, their worst fears realized.

"Tell me what you found."

"The woods is crawling with Red Sticks, sir, between here and the river. John was able to make it all the way to the shore, but there weren't no boats. No way to safely get us down river."

"John?"

"Josiah is correct, Lieutenant. I saw no sign of a single boat. Not even a canoe. There's no way to get away from here by water."

The crowd groaned. The women set up a high-pitched chorus, their men trying to comfort them as best they could. Jacob, still posted at his gunport, glanced at his family. His stepmother was at the point of hysterics, pushing away her husband's hands as he tried to comfort her.

"Let's stay calm, everyone," the Lieutenant reprimanded the crowd. "We are in a fix, but I mean to find a way to get us safely out of this situation. Your distress will not help matters."

"But what are we to do?"

"There's only one solution. If we can't go by water, then we must go by land. Hurry now. There is much preparation to be done."

The Lieutenant raised his voice above the rumble of the crowd that pressed all around him. Women, with tear-streaked faces and raised hands, men with fists pumping in the air, their faces worn and worried from the weeks spent within the fort's walls, waiting and wondering what their fate would be.

"Listen to me, folks. We must make haste while the enemy is scattered. We cannot overcome a strong force. We just cannot. So I propose we do the following: gather what wagons and buggies we have and head southwest, to Mobile. The youngest children will ride with what food we can carry. Everyone else will walk. We have a shortage of conveyances and draft animals, but we will have to make the best of what we have. We leave tonight, as soon as it gets dark. We'll destroy what we cannot bring with us. Anything that we will not use on our flight is expendable. The enemy will be within these walls after we leave. We must leave nothing that would be of use to them. Is this understood?"

A low murmur greeted him. His jaws clenched, his brown eyes flashed. There was no doubt those gathered around him knew he meant what he said.

"What about the livestock I brought?" Mr. Henderson asked. "I have half a dozen good cows here, and some pigs as well."

The Lieutenant lunged at him. "I said, if we can't use it we destroy it. We will not be herding your livestock to Mobile." He stopped and glanced around. "I know many of you have brought your valuables with you. You need to abandon anything you can't carry. There will be no room for them in the wagons.

No dishware. No furniture. No farming tools. The only thing we'll bring on the wagons is foodstuffs and powder. Any extra muskets. There is no room for anything else."

There was grumbling, especially among the women, as they went about preparing for the journey. Leaving behind what they held precious was difficult. But destroying it was another matter entirely. But they understood the need well enough, even if they didn't agree with it.

The wagons and buggies were looked to by the men. Some needed minor repairs, which was done without much difficulty. The horses, mules and oxen were fed and watered. The squeals of the pigs being slaughtered was difficult to hear, but there was nothing to be done about it. Some of the carcasses would be used for meat, the rest would lay where they fell, to rot in the hot summer sun. The cattle suffered the same fate, though with less noise. Chickens were trussed up, to be slung along the walls of the wagons and buggies, dangling on the outside.

Jacob, since relieved from his post, helped his father dispense with the farming implements and furniture his stepmother had insisted on bringing with them when they came to the fort. They used axes to break apart what they had carefully packed just a few weeks before. Moses, their field hand, helped with the work, silent and morose as always. The chock, chock sound of their axes was greeted by the same noise all around the compound, as the dwellers of Fort Pierce followed their instructions.

The women were busy before the fires, preparing what food they could. There wasn't much flour left, but they used what they had to prepare bread before nightfall. Stews were set to boiling, using what few vegetables they still had available and meat from the recent slaughter of hogs and cattle.

While all these preparations were taking place, the Lieutenant made his rounds. There were still men posted at the gunports, keeping an eye on the straggly woods for any signs of life. This was a most critical hour, as the majority of those who inhabited the fort were busy making preparations for their departure.

The posted men knew this, and the responsibility lay heavy on their shoulders. The searing rays of the sun gave them no relief as they mopped their brows and peered through the slits, tense and edgy at the prospect of an attack at that moment.

As the sun began to sink in the sky, they began to load the wagons. Foodstuffs were piled at the sides, leaving room in the middle for the most important cargo, the children. There were six wagons, two pulled by oxen, and four buggies in all. Forty or so children and a few older women to tend them would make their journey south in their confines.

Jacob and some of the younger men hitched the horses and oxen. The animals were spooked by all the unusual activity that had taken place that day, and it was not an easy task. Jacob struggled with a single mare assigned to a buggy. He wondered to himself if all the effort put forth that day would make any difference. He understood, more than some, the fierceness of the Red Sticks. He knew for a fact that his uncle was by now considered a bitter enemy, as he had sided with the Creek National Council in support of the Lower Creeks' desire to get along with their neighbors. He knew that if John were to be caught he would meet a slow and painful death.

As for his own father, Jacob knew what his fate would be if caught. Being white, he would be killed outright with no hesitation on the part of the enemy. That was the way of the Creeks. His own fate would most assuredly be the same.

Final preparations were made shortly after darkness. The Lieutenant made his way among the people. "It will be all right, folks. My men will see to it. I am placing most of the militia at the head of our column and a few to our rear. Scouts will be sent ahead, and I will have a few at our backs, to make sure we aren't followed. The rest of you men, be sure to have your muskets at the ready. Womenfolk, those of you who can shoot, please be available if we need you."

There were murmurs and whispers among the crowd, but most seemed satisfied with his reassurances. After all, the Lieutenant had kept them safe so far, hadn't he? He had maintained a cool head during the madness of the last few weeks. His commanding presence had prevented panic from taking over the fort and resulted in getting them this far.

Jacob found a place to station himself along the line of the wagon train. He had his bag of bullets and his powder horn at his waist, his musket tucked in the crook of his arm. He shouldered a small pack that contained a few necessaries – his razor, a bit of lye soap, an extra pair of stockings and a clean shirt. He glanced at his father, whose load was much heavier. Sophia had not been willing to divest herself of all the belongings she had brought to the fort, despite the Lieutenant's clear instructions. She had given her husband a much larger bundle to carry, including some candlesticks that had belonged to her mother and several pieces of pewter. This, however, was none of Jacob's concern. If his father was unable to tell her no, that was his responsibility. For a moment, Jacob wondered why Sophia hadn't tasked their slaves with carrying her fancies, and then he realized she was most probably afraid they would steal them. She, of course, carried nothing.

His uncle was nowhere to be found. Jacob assumed, rightly, that his skills as a scout were being utilized by the Lieutenant. John was well known for his abilities to track and reconnoiter. He had spent his adult life as a hunter, a lucrative trade in the wilderness that surrounded the neat farms and plantations that dotted the area along the Alabama River.

The gates of the fort were flung open, and the train moved out. The scouts at the front had been sent ahead and gotten word back that all was clear for the moment. With a collective sigh of relief, the two hundred people that had been confined for so many weeks moved forward. Despite the blackness of the night, Jacob could still see the tall, stark timbers of the walls of Fort Pierce when he glanced over his shoulder. Then the rain started to fall.

CHAPTER 3

A Difficult Journey

It was one of those dense, soaking rains that poured down on the plodding column as it left the fort, the type that often falls that time of year in the Tensaw region of the Mississippi Territory. It drenched them unmercifully, along with the narrow path on which they struggled. It mired the horses and wagons in deep, thick mud, and slowed to a crawl the terrified people who accompanied them. The women hiked up their skirts to make their way easier. The men jammed their hats further down on their heads in attempts to keep their vision clear. Canvas was stretched over the children huddled in the wagons in the hope of sparing them from the deluge, without much success.

The refugees were forced to stop regularly to gather and help heave wagons and buggies through the mud, while the men at the front of the column did what they could to widen their path. The minutes and then hours slipped by as they struggled onward, uncertain of what lay ahead but full well knowing what they were leaving behind.

The downpour, in its own way, was a blessing despite the difficulties it imposed. It muffled the sounds of their departure and lessened the likelihood that any who had designs on them would be able to attack them as they struggled south.

It was past midnight when they came to the first creek they needed to ford. The torrential rains had left it roaring and tumbling southward, headed to its eventual demise into the Mobile River. The column halted.

The scouts had reported that the creek had widened but was still not deep. Lieutenant Montgomery briefly spoke to those at the head of the wagon train.

"It's fine, folks. Your conveyances should make it safely across without difficulty. Just take your time. We will continue on as soon as we cross. We haven't put enough distance between ourselves and our enemies yet. We have many miles yet to go, and this is just a small inconvenience."

The word spread down the line of the straggling train. As each wagon crossed, the roaring waters passed through the spokes of their wheels, as the men and women who marched beside them did their best to maintain their footing on the creek's slippery bottom. Before long, all were safely on the other side.

The rain had slacked off, and was now falling softly in large, fat drops that splashed and danced on the leaves and foliage of the underbrush that choked the path before them. Jacob breathed a sigh of relief. He had wrapped his extra shirt around the firing mechanism of his musket in an attempt to keep it dry. He hoped the rain would soon end. His gun would be useless if wet. His only protection would be the sheathed knife strapped to his belt. He aimed to go down fighting if they were caught.

He knew as well as anyone the dangers of fighting the Red Sticks. He had spent many days of his youth among the Creeks. He had journeyed with his mother and uncle as a young boy to her family's village of Woccooche for the annual Green Corn Festival, a celebration of the nearing harvest. During the summer and winter, they would travel for important ceremonial days and participate in rituals important to their culture. Although he had a white father, Jacob was considered a Creek among the tribe. His mother also had a white father, but according to tradition, she was still a full member of the Beaver Clan, as was Jacob.

As he tramped along, the squelching sound made by his boots in the mud periodically interrupting his thoughts, he recalled the high-risk stickball games regularly enjoyed by the warriors of his mother's clan when they visited. At the edge of the village was a large, rectangle of trampled dirt, with two posts at each end. Cheering crowds would greet the two teams of competitors. Using two sticks, the point of the game was to get the small, leather ball through the posts at each end of the field. Each stick had a leather pouch at the end, and this was used to scoop up the ball and catapult it toward the posts.

Two teams would square off and the battle would ensue. There were few rules, and often the game would turn into a vicious, violent melee. Bystanders were often bowled over by the combatants, and injuries were inevitable. Cracked skulls and broken bones were common, but the game continued despite it, until one team was declared the victor. Jacob was always taken aback by the savagery displayed, and whenever he was invited to join in with other boys to take their own turn on the field, he refused. He saw no sense in it. He could see, however, that these games were little more than preparations for hand-to-hand combat. Any fool could see it. The Creeks had, in their own way, prepared their young people in the ways of war. The skills they had learned were being used now, only against members of their own tribe. Jacob shivered at the thought of being caught by any of the men or boys he had watched on the ball field. It most probably would not end well for him.

After many long hours, the rain came to a halt, and a weak looking sun appeared in the east, shrouded by the haze caused by the shimmering ground mists that rose all around. Heat emanated from the soaked earth, flushed as it was from the warm rains of the night before. As they approached another creek, the slow-moving train came to a halt. They all did their best to gather around the Lieutenant, who had positioned himself on the tailgate of a wagon, his arms comfortably folded as he stood silently and patiently for his charges to quiet.

"It has been a long night. We are thankful for the rains, even though it greatly slowed our progress. It seems to have discouraged our enemies from following us. That, and their exhaustion from the attack on our friends and neighbors, which surely cost them dearly. Our scouts, both front and back, have not seen any signs of the fiends, for which I thank Providence."

He raised his hand as a murmur rose. "We still have a long journey ahead, my friends. I promise that in two hours' time we will stop for a short rest. First, we must cross this creek in front of us. It's deeper than the last one and will take more effort to cross. We will string rope across to help us. Do your best to keep your weapons dry. There may be a use for them before our trip is done."

Despite their weariness, some of the militiamen got busy tying stout ropes to the chestnut and oak trees that lined each side of the fast-rushing creek. Slowly the wagons were helped over, with men on either side to guide them, while the water lapped up to the horses' chests. The women crossed, grasping the guide ropes. Before long, all were safely on the other side.

They continued onward. They were in a deep pine forest now, the long straight trunks rising majestically above the littering of straw that covered the ground. Here the rain had not been as intense, the ground firmer and easier for the wagons to traverse. The path they had been following was no more discernible than before, but the tangle of vines and bushes that had grasped and clawed at them as they struggled in the dark were fewer. When they reached the edge of the pines, they stopped.

The children were let out of the wagons and the beasts of burden were freed from their hitches and led to a grassy area to feed. The women, despite their fatigue, busily got small fires started to warm up the victuals they had prepared the day before. The scouts made their way to the campfires, flinging themselves down before them and hungrily attacking the food that was offered them.

Jacob found his three younger brothers gathered with his parents at a small fire near the center of the camp. Sally and Moses were seated a short distance away. They all seemed none the worse for wear, although he had no more gotten himself seated among them than his stepmother began questioning him as to his whereabouts since they had left the confines of the fort.

"I looked for you, Jacob. Where were you? Your father could have used some help with his bundles," she admonished.

"I was busy."

"Busy with what?" she replied sharply.

"Someone besides the militia and the scouts needs to keep a lookout for the hostiles."

"Hostiles? I thought they were your family," she replied maliciously, slyly looking up at him as he stood before her.

"I just stopped by to make sure you are safe. I will take my leave now and find my uncle."

With that, he turned and left. It was not the time to explain the vagaries of his Creek heritage to his stepmother. He had tried before but to no avail. She persisted in her belief that all Creeks were the same. There was no talking her out of it.

He found John at the fire of the Thompson family, hungrily consuming some of the fine stew Mrs. Thompson had simmering over the small fire. As he squatted down beside his uncle, she offered him a bowl and a weary smile.

"I saw you Jacob, with your musket at the ready on our march. It was nice to see a young man intent on doing his duty."

"Thank you, ma'am."

Mr. Thompson spoke up. "Yes, it is nice to see some of the young folks take an interest in protecting us. Our own son William would have done the same if he were here."

"I don't believe I know your son."

"He's a few years older than you. He has himself a trade in Mobile. He works at the docks, supervising the loading of the ships at the port."

"So you'll have a place to stay once we reach there."

"Yes," Mr. Thompson replied with satisfaction. "It's been awhile since we've seen him. He hasn't dared travel north since the troubles started."

John stood. "Thank you for sharing your meal with us. We are most grateful." He indicated for Jacob to follow and led him away from the fire, to the edge of the clearing.

They walked past their exhausted fellow travelers, most of whom had finished their meals. The children were lackadaisically idling before the fires. There was no skipping and frolicking about. Many had plastered themselves to their mothers' sides, tired red eyes, glazed with fear, stared about their surroundings with little interest.

Once they'd drawn themselves away from the crowd, John put his hand on Jacob's shoulder. "We will start back on the trail soon. I have been thinking . . . would you be interested in joining me as a scout?"

Jacob gasped. "I thought you decided I wasn't ready."

John laughed. "I don't think you are entirely ready, but we are desperately in need of a fresh pair of eyes."

"You know I would, Uncle."

"That's settled then. You will not be on your own. You must stay by my side."

"That's fine."

"Find a place somewhere to store your pack. You'll have no need of it, at least for the next few hours."

The forward scouts gathered around the Lieutenant, who by that time had a vacant look of exhaustion around his eyes, no different than all the others.

"Take care, men. I know you haven't had much time to rest, but we must move forward. I don't need to tell you how to do your duty. Keep in mind that at sunset I plan on halting for the night."

"Is that wise?" one of the scouts asked.

"We must, despite our fears, Jonathan. Our party is in a weakened condition, and our pace has slowed considerably, despite the more advantageous terrain."

John spoke up. "I'm bringing my nephew along. He is a good tracker and handy with his musket."

The Lieutenant looked at Jacob warily. "He seems young, but I will take your word for it, John. He is your responsibility."

John nodded and the scouts dispersed.

Jacob and his uncle headed southwest at a slow trot, their heads swiveling back and forth, scanning both near and far.

"Have you seen any signs?" Jacob asked.

"Not a one. Not since we left the fort. I think our brothers are busy recovering, off licking their wounds."

"What did you see, exactly, at Fort Mims?"

John stopped and looked at him. "I can't describe all the horror I saw. I would prefer to forget as much of it as I'm able. But if you must know, there were hundreds of dead in that compound. In piles, stripped, scalped. Only covered by blood. All had been scalped. The women's bodies had been desecrated in such a way…" He paused. "It doesn't bear repeating. But there was more. I saw dozens of bodies of Red Sticks outside. Heard the sound of their wounded. They took heavy losses as well. I believe that has made our escape possible."

"So the prophets were wrong."

"Yes. But we knew they were wrong, didn't we? It has been told for months that our gods would see to it that the enemy's bullets would have no effect on us, that the spells they cast would see to it. How can people believe magic can stop the power of bullets?"

John shook his head. "Our people were deceived. Foolishly deceived. People wanted to believe they were invincible. That madness has cost many lives. Many more will be lost before people come to their senses."

As they ranged through the stands of pines and hardwoods,

interspersed with fields of tall grasses, they could find no indication that any man had tracked through the area in many a year. They did find some old mounds, built no doubt by their ancestors, their purpose lost to time. As the sun began to sink, they headed back northeast to find their fellow travelers.

They reported immediately to the Lieutenant. As the other scouts straggled in, they all agreed. No sign of the enemy.

A halt was declared in a small clearing, on high ground. The wagons and buggies were drawn into a circle to provide what protection they could in case of an attack. Water was drawn at a nearby stream, the draft animals tethered to leads outside the circle to graze. Children were lifted out of the wagons and the women began preparing the evening fires.

As darkness set in, the Lieutenant sent out pickets in pairs. One would watch and one would sleep. Ten men in all, three pairs in an arc to the north, two more positioned to the south. This was to ensure there would be no surprises in the middle of the night.

Food was dispersed and prepared. There was mostly silence as they all ate ravenously. Except for the whimpering of a few of the younger children and the occasional snorting of a horse tethered outside the circle, all was quiet.

Jacob fetched his pack from the Thompsons' wagon and used it to rest his head upon, a short distance from his slumbering parents and siblings. Sleep did not come as easily to him. He stared skyward and contemplated the dangers that still lay ahead.

He couldn't help but wonder if the Lieutenant had made the right decision to head south, to Mobile. Surely there were other fortified positions closer by they could have fled to. Heading through a trackless wilderness when the lives of so many were at stake seemed somewhat foolish to him. He arose and found his uncle, asleep with a group of militiamen near the center of their circle. He nudged him awake.

"Uncle."

John woke with a start.

Jacob whispered, "I have a question, Uncle."

John propped himself up to a half-seated position. "Now you have a question? Couldn't it have been addressed earlier?"

"I hadn't thought of it then."

John sighed wearily. "What is it, then?"

"From my reckoning, Fort Stoddert is but a few miles straight west of here. Why is the Lieutenant taking us all the way to Mobile, when we could almost as easily make it to there in the morning?"

"What you say is true. But I have a question for you – do we know in what condition we would find it? What if the Red Sticks have attacked there as well?"

Jacob thought for a moment. "I suppose we don't know for certain."

"Yes," John stated patiently. "We cannot know whether it would be a safe place for us. If we were to go to Fort Stoddert and then discover that it has also come under attack, we would be that much further from safety, and it could put us all in danger. The Lieutenant has made the best decision under the circumstances. He knows of only one truly secure place for us – Mobile."

Jacob thought for a moment, then nodded. "I see that now." He rose. "I'll let you get back to sleep."

John rolled over as Jacob made his way back to his own resting spot. He lay down, much relieved at John's reasoning, and fell into the deep sleep of the truly exhausted.

CHAPTER 4

MOBILE

Thomas Worley awoke the next morning to the sound of his wife puttering around their campfire. Sophia was in a foul mood. He supposed it was to be expected, considering the circumstances. She was imperiously hectoring Sally in the preparation of their morning meal. His son Jacob was nowhere to be found, and he rightly assumed he was off somewhere with his uncle. His three younger boys were huddled together, close to their mother. He had some sympathy for them, an emotion mostly foreign to him. He supposed it came from his own experience as a young lad, the shock and turmoil he had experienced when the news of his father's death at the Battle of King's Mountain was announced to him at the tender age of ten.

Those had been difficult days. His father was a farmer in Hillsborough, North Carolina. Unlike some of his neighbors, he had clung to his allegiance to the King and the mother country. Perhaps it was pure stubbornness that drove him, but Thomas could not be sure. He remembered when his father enlisted in the Loyalist militia as if it were yesterday. He abandoned his wife and four children and rode off with barely a look over his shoulder. Thomas had been the oldest of the children, and he could still feel the sting of what he considered his father's betrayal.

Then the dark day arrived when they heard the news of his death. His mother cried piteously, his younger sisters clung to each other. Thomas remembered thinking. "What is to be done now?"

There was no way to retrieve his father's body. Life had turned hard for the Worley family. The small patch of ground his father had cultivated didn't provide much, and the distance to the battlefield was too far away for the widow to travel by herself. So they depended on other Loyalists to properly dispose of his father's remains.

The next ten years of his life were a blur. He recalled the arduous struggle to keep his mother and sisters clothed and fed. It was too much to bear for a mere lad, he thought. And it wasn't just the backbreaking effort of providing for them, but the sneers and cruelty of his Patriot neighbors that cut very deep. After the war, he and his family were outcasts in the community. They had picked the wrong side, and the people of Hillsborough would not let them forget it.

He saw to it, as best he could, that his family was taken care of. By the age of twenty, his mother had passed away and his sisters had been married off. With a tremendous amount of relief, he sold what he had and headed southwest, where the promise of a new beginning beckoned.

As he passed through Georgia, he heard of the rich and fertile lands further west. Lands that were still virgin and pristine. He had a mind to make a living hunting and trapping. Not that he had any experience, but the thought of carrying on with grubbing a living off the land was not what he desired his future to be. He traveled to the rich, lush lands between the Tombigbee and Alabama rivers and decided that would be his home.

It was a wild country then, with very few white people. A few stray traders and an occasional hunter were the only white companions to be found. He was lonely, after having come from a home filled with women and the comforts they would bring. He also soon discovered he wasn't a very good hunter. His large frame bungled through the forest undergrowth and he usually chased off whatever game he could find. There had to be a better solution.

It was the golden age of Creek culture back then. Small villages dotted the landscape, with fertile fields of corn, beans and squash surrounding them. They were a friendly people in those days and didn't mind the blundering white man who occasionally showed up at their village circles.

As much as he disliked the prospect, Thomas knew he had no other choice but to fall back on the one skill he had – farming. There was a catch, however. His trader friends told him the best way to get clear title to a piece of land was to marry a Creek. Lands among the tribes were assigned to the women, not the men.

The Indian women he spied in the towns were comely enough, to be sure. But he spoke no Creek and did not relish the thought of marrying a woman who could not understand his directives. That would take too much time and effort, and Thomas did not believe it would be worth it.

After six or eight months, Thomas headed south on an old Indian trail to sell his rather small bundle of hides and furs to the traders in Mobile. He could have easily bartered them away to the white traders he already knew, but if there was one thing Thomas was, it was tightfisted. He thought he could make a better trade himself at the docks and wharves in the city.

Before he reached the city, he stopped in the small hamlet of Alvarez Station. There was a community well there, and as he refreshed himself he noticed a rather pretty young girl making her way toward him, buckets in hand. She could not have been more than fifteen, with black hair and eyes and a lighter complexion than common among the Creeks. He soon learned her name – Elizabeth. He decided, right then and there, that she would be his wife. He did his best to ignore her Creek mother and soothed himself with the fact her father was white. He now had a way to get hold of a piece of land and begin making his fortune.

Things had not worked out exactly how he had hoped. True, he did acquire a fine piece of bottom land within a half mile of the Tombigbee, a full hundred acres. But life with a woman who persisted in following her Indian culture was difficult. Perhaps if he had been more stern he could have put his foot down, but that would have required more of an emotional attachment than he was willing to give.

Instead, he had allowed Elizabeth time with her family, to travel and participate in those rituals and customs that he found, on the whole, to be repugnant. After two stillborn children, Elizabeth had produced a son, Jacob, and Thomas was satisfied. It was a shame, ten years after their marriage, when she died producing a third dead baby.

He was alone again. Impulsively, he had deposited Jacob at his brother-in-law John's cabin and headed south, in search of a new Mrs. Worley. John had accepted the responsibility for Jacob's care. As was the Creek custom, the oldest brother of a woman of the tribe had a duty to see to the raising of her children.

After arriving in Mobile he found Sophia. She was visiting her aunt and uncle and had sailed there from South Carolina. She was not the prettiest of women, he judged. But she was willing, and in Thomas' mind, that was all it took. And so, just like that, he found himself married again.

Lieutenant Montgomery interrupted his reverie. He stood in the middle of the circle of wagons and began loudly proclaiming it was time to load up and continue on. Thomas rose with a sigh. Sally and Moses got busy packing up their belongings and saw to it the children were once again safely ensconced in a wagon.

He had not wanted to purchase the slaves, but his wife insisted. Thomas was a very frugal man, and he detested the thought of spending his hard-earned cash in ways he thought unnecessary. He had made his way to Mobile, to the slave market, with a mind to use his money as wisely as he could. Sophia was insistent on her need for help around the house and gardens. She harangued him on the need for an extra pair of hands in the fields.

"Thomas, if you had a field hand, you could make even more money! Just think – you could finally clear those thirty acres near the creek. Our neighbors all have help. I don't understand why you haven't availed yourself of the opportunity to make our lives easier," she would pout in a most unpleasing way.

Two years ago, he gave way to the pressure. Moses was his age, at least, and had a bad limp from a childhood accident. Sally was young but unbecoming and did not hold any interest for her previous master. He got them for a very reasonable price. Once purchased, he brought them home and installed them in the shed out behind the house. There was a sturdy lock on the door to keep them from trying to escape during the night. There were four slits to let in some air, which Thomas decided was a concession they should be happy with, particularly during the heat of summer.

As the slow-moving train lumbered on, Thomas finally spied his son Jacob up ahead, in lockstep with his Uncle John. Thomas didn't like John. He resented his close relationship with his son, but couldn't figure out how to do anything about it. Deep down, he was a little afraid of him. Being a half-breed, there was no telling what he was capable of. So Thomas kept his resentment to himself.

Early that afternoon, a couple of scouts came back and warned the Lieutenant of a large boggy area ahead. They recommended the train move to the east to avoid it, as it would cause a delay if they tried to move the wagons through. Wearily, the Lieutenant halted the train and explained the detour to the east. There were grumblings among the people at the news. They were tired and footsore. He patiently explained what was ahead, and the grumbling ceased.

They turned off the trail, and by John's calculations that put them a further four hours away from their destination.

"I suppose there is nothing to be done," Jacob said.

"Not a thing. Montgomery is making a smart choice."

They marched along, mostly in silence. Jacob thought about the differences between his uncle and his father. On the one hand, his father provided for his day-to-day needs but did little to counsel or encourage his son. He was a silent hulk, in Jacob's mind. John, however, was engaging and gregarious. He knew everyone and was well liked by all. He had become somewhat of a leader among the Creeks for his skill and steadfastness on the hunt. He spent many hours teaching Jacob about the wild world that surrounded them. He instructed him on the best ways to track animals in the forests and the vast fields of swaying grasses found along the banks of the rivers, and the medicinal properties of the plants found there. He was proficient with bow and arrow as well as the musket, and freely imparted that knowledge to his nephew.

Jacob was only ten when his mother passed away. She had been a guiding light in his young life, and he was heartbroken at her death. His father gave him little comfort and almost immediately started planning on finding his next wife. John had understood Jacob's grief and consoled him as a father to a son. This act of kindness by his uncle even further cemented the relationship between uncle and nephew.

As the day wore on, the heat once again took a toll on the weary travelers. The searing rays of the sun and the hot dampness of the air slowed their progress. There were small bogs and marshes they were forced to cross, with the men at times having to help push the loaded wagons through. To top off their misery, they were all soon spattered with the foul stench of longstanding mud, filled with the rotting carcasses of all sorts of dead creatures. Occasionally they could hear the thrashing of alligators, who, spooked by the sounds of the train, headed to deeper waters.

Lieutenant Montgomery had by this time pulled most of the scouts from the head of the little column. He understood that the only threat they now faced was from the rear, as they drew closer to Mobile. This gave him a certain sense of relief, although he could not rest easy until they were all in the safe confines of the town. He was as weary as the others but did his best not to show it. His tall frame could be seen by all at the head of the column, just as spattered by mud as his companions.

He was not afraid to put his shoulder to a wheel of a wagon when it was necessary. It was part of his duty, he decided.

All in all, his Mississippi militiamen had performed well. In fact, they had done better than he expected, like true soldiers. They had been called to service and had sacrificed their needs only to find themselves on the edge of an unexpected catastrophe. He did wonder if any of their comrades at Fort Mims had been spared. According to his scouts, it was highly unlikely. He was saddened by their loss. But for the grace of God, he would have been there himself if Major Beasley had not decided to post him to Fort Pierce. The thought of what he missed sent shivers down his spine. He refrained from expressing those thoughts to anyone else, however. He had to turn his fear into resolve if they were going to make it through. He instinctively knew that spreading doom and despair would only impede their progress and could jeopardize the safety of the column.

Darkness had begun to fall before he found a suitable place for them to rest. They sheltered under a grove of live oak, the huge, ancient limbs spreading out over a soft bed of long-dead leaves. The women busied themselves before fires while the men inspected the condition of the wagons. One was found to be in such disrepair it was abandoned right there rather than wait for it to collapse on the trail. In future years, when discovered, it would be a haunting reminder of their desperate flight.

The next morning dawned, hot and muggy. They had not traveled far when a soft, misty rain began to fall, only adding to their suffering. Canvas was pulled over the tops of the wagons again in the hopes of shielding the children at least. The men and women who marched beside them slowed their pace.

Moses had been ordered to march in front of his master, so that he wouldn't have it in his head to take flight. A laughable proposition, Moses thought. This was not the time or place to escape his misery. He had other plans.

He had been born and raised on a plantation on the eastern side of Mobile Bay. He never knew who his father was but was close to his mother until he was separated from her as soon as he was big enough for the fields. She was a kindly woman, and did her best to nurture him despite their circumstances. When he was young, she regaled him with stories of their homeland that had been passed down to her from her mother, who had been captured on the coast of far distant Africa and sold to the highest bidder at Charleston. Once they were separated, he rarely saw her again.

His early life had been difficult, even more so when he fell out of a barn loft at age fourteen and broke his leg. It never healed properly and gave his gait a permanent limp. This did not stop the overseers from driving him hard. In fact, he was often given the most difficult assignments and worked longer and harder than the other hands, with the logic that his handicap prevented him from keeping up with the others so he must therefore be kept longer in the fields.

As a young man, he had burned with the desire to break free. But the few farms and plantations on the eastern shore broke up a vast wilderness of lush, deep forests of pines and oaks and magnolia trees. Bounded on one side by water and all the others by the mysteries of the vast woodlands, he had nowhere to run. He had taken a wife, but after a short while she had perished from a mysterious fever, one that took the lives of several of the slaves on his plantation. By then, he was nearly a broken man.

As he aged, he grew less restless and consigned himself to the same fate that had befallen all those with whom he lived. There was no free life to be had, only the drudgery of the fields. The hoeing, and planting and harvesting, the backbreaking labor that controlled him from the moment he awoke in the morning until the time he rested his weary head after dark.

The master of his plantation was a flighty, frivolous man. He was the subject of much gossip in the slave cabins. Sometimes word of his escapades would filter down from the house servants to the field hands.

Moses rarely took part in the idle talk of his peers. It was mostly shared among the women, and he had no use for women since the death of his wife. He had consigned himself to a solitary life.

And then one day, just like that, he was rounded up with five other hands and shuffled off to the bay and loaded onto a boat. It seems his foolish master had lost an enormous sum on cards, and in order to pay his debt he was forced to sell off some of his property. He and his companions were rowed across the bay and led to the slave market in Mobile.

Treated in the same manner as cattle, he and the others were shackled and forced to stand on a low platform, while they were inspected by a handful of buyers who pushed and poked at them. Moses did his best to look straight ahead and remained silent.

Before he knew it, he was in the back of a wagon, tied hand and foot, with Sally. She was a good twenty years younger than he, although neither knew their exact age. When they pulled into the swept front yard of their new master's farm, they were greeted by the sullen countenance of their new mistress.

"Thomas. What have you brought home?" she declared.

"You wanted slaves. I've brought you two," he replied.

Moses and Sally were untied and forced to stand for their new mistress' inspection.

"The man is a cripple."

"No he isn't. He has a limp, but other than that, he is quite serviceable. Besides, I got him for a good price."

She harrumphed.

"And the girl might not be much to look at, but I was assured by her last master that she is very good with children. Isn't that what you wanted?"

She crossed her arms and glared. "Well, I suppose they will have to do. I had hoped you would have been more discerning." And with that, she turned on her heels and flounced into the house.

Moses and Sally were locked into their shed that evening. There, plans began to hatch for an escape. They were not prompted by Moses, to be sure, but by Sally, who was younger and had a stronger will.

As the days, weeks and months passed, Sally and Moses listened. The mistress Sophia was a grumbler and provided much-needed information about goings on amongst the white settlers. Although master Thomas was not much of a talker, the neighbors that visited him in the fields were. Both spoke of the Creeks and their Negros, and how they were too easy on their slaves. They learned there was a growing community of free blacks in the swampy forests that surrounded them. Moses and Sally reasoned that if they were captured by the Creeks, their lives would be no harder than they were now. There was a chance, perhaps, that they would even be easier. Their best hope was to find other blacks who had managed to escape their shackles. And so they took comfort from each other at night, in the chill of winter and the withering heat of summer, locked in their shed.

That evening, the ponderous wagon train rested together for the final night. They had been traveling to the east of what had become the Mobile River, formed when the Tombigbee and Alabama joined some miles north. There was an air of excitement around the campfires, knowing their journey would soon come to an end. Prayers of thanksgiving were offered, and food gladly shared among them. Lieutenant Montgomery offered a speech, praising their dogged determination and courage in the face of lurking death. For the first time since they departed Fort Pierce, the children scampered and played among the campfires, buoyed by the optimism of the group as a whole.

Before daylight, scouts were sent south. They soon returned with the welcome news of a small skiff moored on the shore of Mobile Bay. The

Lieutenant immediately sent three civilian men ahead, and by the time the train had reached the spot in the early afternoon, there was already a covey of small craft to take them safely across to the city.

Jacob sat in the bow of a large dinghy and was one of the first to catch sight of Mobile. At last, safety was ahead, he thought. He watched the seagulls swirling overhead and the pelicans diving into the choppy surf of the bay, searching for food. His thoughts were filled with questions – what would the future hold for him and his fellow travelers? Would there be safety in the city? They had left behind all they had known. Would they ever be able to return?

CHAPTER 5

THE CITY

Fort Charlotte sat at the southern end of Mobile, its earthworks and red brick and stone facade the most prominent sight in the city. Its sprawling structure overshadowed the neatly whitewashed buildings that comprised the rest of the town, its black cannon thrusting out at various points threatening death and destruction to any who would gamble a confrontation.

First French, then British, then Spanish, the fort had changed hands over the decades until now the stars and stripes of the American flag hung limply on its flagpole, the fetid air unruffled by even a whiff of breeze. It had only been since April that the fort had finally given way to the formalities set out by the Louisiana Purchase. The Spanish had abandoned the fort, peacefully but petulantly, under the direction of American General Wilkerson, and had withdrawn to Pensacola. Mobile was now an American city, whether the inhabitants liked it or not.

The skiffs and other small craft that brought the weary Fort Pierce travelers to the piers jutting out into Mobile Bay left their loads and returned for more. The first smells that hit them were those of rotting fish and other foul odors that wafted up from the marshlands at the foot of the city. For those whose lives were lived on the solid ground of the interior, these smells were unfamiliar as well as unpleasant.

The city itself had been laid out in neat squares, thanks to its French founders. The main street along the bay itself was Royal Street, with a tavern, a Catholic Church and some businesses, mostly dealing with the Indian trade. People had gathered along the street in small groups, discussing the arrival of these hardy souls, and as soon as they stepped off the pier, they were bombarded with questions. A confusing mix of French, Spanish and English greeted them. The news of Fort Mims had traveled fast, even faster than the refugees from Fort Pierce.

The city had already been overwhelmed by a flood of refugees seeking shelter from the Red Stick menace to the north. It sighed and accepted these newly bereft visitors. It would find a way to house them, even though it would be difficult. The story of how these people had evaded a sure death and survived the trip to their port city swept through the streets like wildfire. It tugged at the heartstrings of Mobile's men and women alike. They accepted the responsibility to see to their welfare.

Thomas Worley sought out his son, who was standing with his uncle in the middle of a throng of men questioning and gesticulating wildly while John stood patiently, trying to answer their questions as best he could.

"Jacob!" he exclaimed.

Jacob untangled himself from the group and replied, "Yes, Pa?"

"Your stepmother has grown fatigued. We will be making our way to her uncle's home. They live on Conception Street." Thomas hesitated.

"Don't worry about me, Pa. I'll stay with my Uncle John. There is no doubt little room for us there, what with the two of you and the children, plus Moses and Sally."

A visible look of relief crossed Thomas' face. "That's fine." And with that, he turned to go gather up the rest of his family.

Jacob was relieved to see him go. There was no love lost between he and his stepmother or her family. From the very beginning, Jacob knew she had no use for him. He was, in her mind, tainted by the blood of his mother and her people. She was most vocal about her feelings when his father wasn't present. When he was, her attempts to be cordial were forced and unnatural. Jacob understood her resentment of him all too well. It had been expressed to him in a myriad of ways over the last seven years. He knew his company would not be missed.

Just then John broke loose from the crowd and sprinted over to Lieutenant Montgomery, who was leading his troops toward Fort Charlotte.

"Lieutenant! Sir!" he called.

The Lieutenant turned. "Ah, John!"

"I just wanted to express my gratitude to you, sir, for getting us safely here."

"Well thank you, John," the Lieutenant grinned. "You know, of course, we couldn't have done it without you and your fellow scouts."

John grinned in return. "Perhaps. But I want to thank you anyway. It took great foresight to keep us all together on that journey. I don't know of any other man who could have done it."

"That's a great compliment. Thank you. But I only did what my duty called me to do."

"What are your plans now?"

"I'll report with my men to whoever is in charge here, and then we'll make our way back north to Fort Stoddert. The last reports are that it wasn't attacked, and General Claiborne is there, our commander. How about you?"

"I don't know. I believe I'll head west for a bit, with my nephew here." He paused and clapped Jacob on the shoulder. I know of some rich hunting grounds in that direction. The Red Sticks burned me out last year, you know, so for now there's no going back. At least at present."

Before they left town, John and Jacob made a stop at Campbell's store, where John had an account. They purchased extra gunpowder and shot, brand new hatchets to wear on their belts, a half dozen steel traps, salt pork, flour, salt, a small cooking pot and various other supplies. Darkness had begun to settle when they headed west.

They spent their first night on the banks of the Dog River, from which the town of Mobile drew fresh water during dry spells throughout the year. Its waters were clean and pure, draining the surrounding countryside as it made its way to the Gulf.

The following morning, once they had crossed the river, they found a few faint trails heading westward. They picked one and followed it.

The trail they had chosen soon petered out. The undergrowth that surrounded them was dense, and they had to use their new hatchets to hack through clinging vines and the grasping arms of the ferns and yucca plants, and the crowded canebrakes that they stumbled upon. By mid-morning Jacob was thoroughly exhausted.

"Uncle, do you know where we're going?"

John paused for a moment. "Yes, I do. I was out this way last year. I have my mind set on some clearings not far from here. They're well-watered, and there were several beaver dams. Good hunting grounds for us."

In mid-afternoon, they came upon a stretch of lush grassland, a slight breeze swaying their greens and golds back and forth. By this time, there was no one happier than Jacob at the sight, as it meant they could move freely without having to use their hatchets to make a path.

As is often the case in the wilderness, the first sight of the meadow was deceptive. As the two of them explored it, they found it pockmarked with swampy areas with rivulets and small streams coursing through. Jacob let out a happy yelp at the first sight of a beaver dam.

"You were right, Uncle."

"Let's set up camp and then get our traps set just at dark."

They found a spot at the edge of the meadow and built a small fire. As darkness descended, they quietly made their way downwind of the dam and distributed their traps close by. Happily they went back to camp and set some salt pork to boiling on the fire.

They were well rewarded the next day, with each trap yielding a prize. They stayed at that spot for several days before moving on to another a mile or so further west.

A week, and then two, soon passed by. When they weren't skinning the beaver they caught, they were busy with their muskets. There were bear and fox and wildcat aplenty, and they had a growing pile of skins to prove it.

They eventually found themselves on the edge of a vast swamp, riddled with the decaying stumps of bald cypress trees, the ragged edges of their once-proud trunks providing a hiding ground for the alligators that preyed upon the other creatures there. John determined the best course of action was to move several hundred yards away from the muddy, odorous waters to a grove of large, towering oaks. They set up a semi-permanent camp, using the immense, low-lying limbs to shield themselves and their cache of hides from the intermittent rains that plagued them. A small strip of canvas was slung among the limbs, under which they could keep a fire going. The heat of summer was dissipating, and the nights grew cooler as the month of October progressed.

In the evening, John would regale Jacob with tales from his youth. His father, he said, was a Wilson, straight from the old country, near a town in Scotland named Greenock. "He was a wanderer, he was. He would have kept on traveling if he hadn't met my mother."

"Was she beautiful?" Jacob asked.

"Yes. Very. She was also kind, and patient almost to a fault." He paused. "I suppose that's where I got some of my own peculiar habits. I most certainly got my wandering foot from my father. I have never been satisfied with staying in one place too long. I built my cabin as a home base. I never had any intention of settling down."

"And what did you garner from your mother?"

John thought a moment. "I suppose I got the desire to get along with my neighbors, to accept them as they are and not stir up trouble." He jabbed at the fire with his poker. "That, of course, is what led Billy Weatherford and his followers to burn me out."

"I met Billy once," Jacob offered. "He seemed at the time to be a reasonable sort of man. What happened?"

"As you know, he's not much Creek. His father has a large plantation not far from your father's place. Billy was raised by the standards of the white man. The only Creek blood he has comes from his mother, who herself isn't even half-Creek. Didn't you notice when you met him that he looks like an ordinary sort of fellow? I mean, none of his features would ever lead you to believe he is an Indian."

"So what happened?" Jacob asked quizzically.

"I suppose it came from two things. His mother was a member of the Wind Clan, which in turn made Billy a member. The Wind Clan is the most powerful among us. All our village chiefs are of this clan, as well as the most important warriors and medicine men. As a member, Billy would naturally be looked upon as a leader."

"So why did he choose to be a leader among the Red Sticks rather than among those who got along?"

"I blame it all on Tecumseh."

"I remember when he came, a couple of years ago."

"Yes. Tecumseh was a powerful orator. I heard him more than once among the council fires. He was a very angry man, dead set on removing all whites from Indian land. He came down from up north, from his own people, the Shawnee, to stir up trouble. He's the one who convinced our brothers to turn against each other. I can understand it – he is very beguiling. He is tall and handsome, and a mighty warrior.

"But our kin are vulnerable, Jacob. They allowed him to coax them into starting something that will only bring death and destruction. There is no way our people can overcome the power of the whites. Most of our people have never seen the true nature of what they're up against. They haven't viewed the resolve of the forces against them. You saw

Fort Charlotte, Jacob. How can those who construct mighty fortresses with cannon be defeated by muskets and bows and arrows? I did my best to speak my mind among our people, and some listened. Many did not, however. That is why the Red Sticks would love to have my scalp. Many who agreed with me were behind the walls of Fort Mims. They were slaughtered right along with the whites."

"Pa said the Federal Road from Georgia to Mobile started it."

"He's correct. Our people got restless, seeing the hordes of whites traveling that road. It might have worked out if they had kept on traveling, but when more and more decided to settle rather than move on, tempers among us flared. And then when the Red Sticks started traveling to Pensacola to get arms and ammunition from the Spaniards and English, the militia had to step in. Up to that point, there had been no open confrontations to speak of. Those who wanted peace were harassed and tormented, but lives were not taken. When the militia tried to stop the import of arms at Burnt Corn Creek, that is what lit the fire."

Jacob thought on these things as he lay on his blanket. He saw his uncle's profile in the firelight, his troubled frown creasing his normally calm countenance. His uncle was a handsome man, he decided. Dark haired, but with a lighter skin than one would expect, and eyes not quite brown and not quite green. He was well muscled from years spent in the woods. He wondered aloud, "So what is to be done?"

"I don't know. That is what is most distressing. After what I saw at Fort Mims, something will have to happen. I fear it will not be in the too distant future. Retribution will have to be made, and it will be a sad day for the Creek nation."

Jacob nodded. The fear he had felt when they were huddled in Fort Pierce, facing the unknown, began to creep its way back. He knew they faced no imminent threat at the moment, but who knew what dangers they could face in the coming days? The struggle he had always felt between the two cultures he straddled was a real one. He thought of his mother and her happy reunions with family when they traveled to her hometown, and the joy and happiness he felt at the sight of his Creek clansmen. And yet, there was no denying his white heritage. Was there a happy medium? That night, under the spreading ancient limbs of the live oak trees that surrounded them in the dark, like protective sentinels, he had doubts of a reconciliation of any kind.

His future was unsure. He knew, however, that he could trust his uncle above anyone else. He was the one who had taught him how to survive, even thrive, in the woods. How to handle a musket, a hatchet, a knife. How to defend himself from the threats of the forest, of the wild beasts that roamed them. He decided, at that moment, that there was no going home for him. His father had taught him how to plow the land and harvest a crop, but to Jacob, those skills were of little importance now. Here, in the wilderness, was where he belonged, beside the uncle who had nurtured and encouraged him.

"I will stay with you, Uncle. I will follow you in whatever direction you decide to take."

They fell asleep that night to the sound of a soft rain, drizzling down from above.

CHAPTER 6

RESULTS OF THE HUNT

As October turned into November, Jacob was the happiest he had ever been. There were no worries out in the woods. Both he and John had all their immediate needs met. They found safe shelter and had a steady supply of food, furs to sell and each other's company. What more could a man want, thought Jacob?

He had given up on his razor soon after they left Mobile, and a full brown stubble had grown into a nicely shaped beard. His father had always insisted he be clean shaven. It was a relief to know he no longer had to follow those rules. He felt free, and very much his own man.

One evening, the two of them were huddled close to the fire. The weather had grown intermittently cold, as was usual for that time of year. They had just finished eating their evening meal of a good stew – bear meat accompanied by fruit from a nearby PawPaw tree, with a few dandelion greens thrown in, when they heard a shout emanating from the woods behind them. It was the first human voice they had heard in several weeks, and they both instinctively reached for their muskets. Soon two figures, with their hands raised, emerged from the darkness. John smiled and withdrew his hand from his musket trigger.

"Miko! Sabe! What are you fellows doing out here?"

"John! We would ask the same of you!"

John stood and waved for the duo to join them. They readily squatted down on their haunches and stretched their hands toward the warmth of the fire.

The two newcomers fell into a rapid discussion with John. Jacob had a difficult time keeping up with their conversation, as it was a mixture of French, English, Chickasaw and Creek. From their dress – buckskin from head to toe – and their hair fashioned into top knots with feathers intertwined – Jacob ascertained they were Chickasaw from further west. He was not sure how they had become acquainted with his uncle, but it was obvious from their gestures and the warm tone of their voices that they were old friends.

The taller one, Miko, pulled out a pipe, and after filling it and lighting it, passed it around. They all took turns puffing before passing it on.

Before long, Jacob grew drowsy. He gleaned that much of the discussion had to do with Fort Mims. How there was no certainty as to the number killed but was likely 500 or more whites, half breeds and Lower Creek. That the women had been brutalized beyond imagination. That the defenders had killed a goodly number of Red Sticks while defending themselves – upwards of 200. The black slaves, for the most part, had been spared, but were stolen away by the Red Sticks for their own purposes after the killing had finished. He nodded off, despite the grisly tale being told. It was difficult for him to decipher all that was being said, but he knew his uncle would share what was necessary the next day.

When he awoke the next morning, his Uncle John sat alone before the fire. Their two visitors had slipped away at daylight, he said. Jacob sat up, still groggy. He untangled himself from his blanket and moved closer to the fire. It was a chilly, windswept morning. The wind whistled through the scattered leaves of the oak they had sheltered under for the night. But the sky was clear and the sun threw out its early morning warmth despite the cool temperature. It would be a productive day, Jacob thought.

John poked up the fire and added wood as they sat together before it. They were both silent for a time.

"More news, Uncle?" Jacob said after awhile.

"Yes," he answered. "I suppose you gathered much of it on your own."

"Just that there were many killed."

"A few miltiamen escaped out the back and made it through the swamp and down the river. It is remarkable that they lived to tell the tale."

"Any you know?"

"I'm not sure. But I had cousins sheltered there. I doubt any survived," he replied soberly.

"I suppose we should consider ourselves lucky. Pa insisted we go to Fort Pierce, as it was closer."

"Lucky indeed. I myself chose the same, seeing as that is where you were."

They grew silent for a moment, staring at the fire.

"General Claiborne has gathered all the Mississippi militia at Fort Stoddert. They're busy patrolling and rounding up the warriors they can find, but it seems the bulk of them have moved north."

"I suppose Lieutenant Montgomery is with him there."

"Most probably."

"I wonder where Pa is."

"Don't know, Jacob. Miko and Sabe said many of the settlers have returned to their homes, depending on the militia to protect them."

There was silence for a moment.

"What's to be done?"

"I don't know. I haven't decided. According to my friends, the whole world is on fire over it. There's a force of militia and volunteers that have traveled down from Tennessee to help. They said the man in charge, General Jackson, is a very determined fellow."

John rose at that point and sort of shrugged and shook his head, sucking in a breath. "I need some time to decide what to do. Let's spend the day as we normally would, checking traps and skinning what we find. I'll put some thought into what is to be done while we work. Surely a solution will come to me."

Very few words passed between them that day, as they busied themselves with the chores of a trapper – gathering what they had caught and resetting traps along a small ridge they had found not far from the large swamp. They returned to their temporary camp and gutted and skinned their catch. It was tedious work, the skinning, though Jacob had grown much more adept at it since they left Mobile.

They staked the skins of the three foxes they caught on temporary frames they had built to help dry them out, and then leaned the frames against a nearby tree. Fox furs paid well, and in a few days, they would add them to the pile of skins they had already gathered, wrapped neatly in the hides of deer to keep them as dry as possible. Their cache had grown steadily. It would take some work to get them to a trader.

Their stored meat was lowered from where they had stockpiled it – in a large pouch made of deerskins in the upper reaches of a nearby tree, to keep any preying animals away from it. John skillfully spitted a large chunk of deer meat over the fire, while Jacob fetched a kettle of water from the nearby creek they were using to keep themselves in fresh water. Soon the water was boiling, and Jacob added some fresh greens to it, as well as a pinch of salt from their precious supply.

They ate hungrily, as all men do who spend their days in the woods. Darkness had descended by the time they finished their meal.

The flickering firelight gave a somber glow to John's face, as he spoke up.

"I have thought long and hard all day about what our next move should be." He cleared his throat. "I have struggled with what would be the best path forward for you and for myself, Jacob. I have come up with several possibilities."

Jacob waited.

"The first one is rather simple. I take you back to your Pa and your stepmother. That would be the safest course for you. I'm sure they will head back home before long, if they haven't already. The militia will be about, to protect you."

Jacob started to protest. John raised his hand.

"Hold on. Let me finish," he said sternly.

"There are two other possibilities. The first is that we join up with the Mississippi militia at Fort Stoddert. We could stay close to home that way, and be a help in protecting our friends, neighbors and families. There are good men in charge, and it would be an honorable thing to serve with them."

"And the other?"

"The other is a little more complicated. My friends expressed an interest in joining up with General Jackson and his men from Tennessee. They say he has already won some victories against the Red Sticks and has shown himself to be a great warrior. The bulk of our enemies are north, where they have gathered to confront him. They have no shame for what they did at Fort Mims, and more likely are planning on repeating it as often as they can. Now, you have grown into a man, Jacob. I believe we must come together and decide our fate as one. Let's get our rest tonight and allow ourselves time to decide what is best for both of us. We can talk more about it tomorrow."

With that, John moved a short distance away from the fire, bundled himself in his blanket and fell fast asleep.

Jacob stared at the stars, pondering. He glanced across the smoldering embers of the fire to the still body of his uncle, peacefully slumbering. What would be their fate? He understood now that their escape from the rampaging horde that had decimated the good people sheltered in Fort Mims had been a gift – a gift he should not squander. But for God's mercy, he thought, they would have shared the same fate.

He had never truly contemplated the spiritual. He knew of the gods of the Creek – the Master of Breath, the Creator, and the Horned Serpent, who imparted his knowledge to the wise young men of their people. But he had often gone to Sunday service, at the behest of his father, and understood the Christian God and the saving grace of his Son. As he lay there, he was not sure who to thank, but he decided to thank them all, just to be safe. He was young. There was time enough to decide which ones were responsible for the world and all who were in it.

He contemplated the three choices John had offered him. Without hesitation, he knew he would not be going home. Life there had been difficult ever since his mother's passing. His father's choice for a bride had not been a good one, in his opinion. Sophia had made life difficult from the day she arrived at the farm. Her obvious disdain for him had only grown over time, her sharp tongue employed most often behind his father's back. She had spoken ill of his mother often enough, sourly stating she could not understand why any white man would entangle himself with a savage who could not understand him or his ways. She was especially harsh after Jacob returned from spending time with his uncle, who would stop by regularly and whisk him away for brief hunts or to take him for overnight visits to their home village.

For a moment, he considered the next option, which was to join up with the militia at Fort Stoddert who were scouring the countryside near his home, seeking out the small groups of Red Sticks who had stuck close by. He quickly ruled that out. That would still put him too close to Sophia for his comfort.

Suddenly, a yearning came over him, one so intense as to almost take his breath away. He studied this feeling that burned within him. He examined it in his mind, turning it over and examining it from every angle. It came to him quite clearly then – he needed to be free. Free of the struggle of deciding who he was and where he belonged. He needed the freedom to decide his own path in life, to make his own decisions about his future and what it could hold.

It was decided, then. He would vote to head north, to confront those who had threatened him and those who sought peace. He would tell his uncle in the morning, first thing.

"We must get ready then," John stated after Jacob informed him of his decision.

"My Pa will most likely not be happy."

"Sometimes a man must do what is right, no matter what. Don't worry overly much about it. You've made a choice. Your Pa will just have to live with it." John busied himself before the fire, re-heating the remains of their previous evening's supper.

"We must round up our traps and clean up the skins. They'll sell for a higher price if we do. We'll spend a few days here, so that we can complete the drying process for what we have on hand."

They busied themselves through the day, gathering their traps and building more drying frames. They stretched taut the skins they had on the frames, scraping away the bits of flesh that still clung to them. They set the frames before small fires they built to help them dry.

"I have a good man in Mobile who will give us a fair price for the furs. He works at Campbell's store. We'll use the money to get for supplies for our trip north. We will also need horses. It is too great a distance to travel by foot," John said as they sat before the fire.

"I have a question, Uncle. Why exactly are we here? Could we not have just stayed closer to Mobile? Would that not have been easier?"

There was a long silence.

"Perhaps it would have been easier. Our hunting would not have been as fruitful, however."

"Is that the only reason?"

Jacob could see a wide grin spread across John's face from across the fire. The weather had turned cold once again, and they both held their hands over the warmth of the blaze. The sun had long since set, its rays no longer combating the frigid air blowing in from the north.

"I'm beginning to think you don't like my company," John retorted.

"You know that's not true. But I've known you all my life. I have a sense there was another purpose for this trip. We've been out here a long time. Much longer than any of our other trips."

The smile slipped from John's face.

"Are you going to tell me?"

"I promised my sister that I would always protect and look after you, in the Creek tradition. But I have come to think of you as a son, Jacob. A son I never had. As such, it is my sacred duty to shield you from the storm that is gathering. The people around you – your family, your neighbors, the citizens of Mobile – are in a great shock over what happened at Fort Mims. They will not look kindly on anyone with Creek blood in their veins. Even those of us who have fought to preserve the peace will be suspect. My hope is that their fervor will fade in time, but I wanted to spare you the brunt of it."

Jacob thought about what his uncle had just told him. "But now you've changed your mind?" he asked.

"I suppose so. There is work to be done if we're to stop the killing. My services, and yours, are needed. My two Chickasaw friends brought word that there will be a gathering at Alvarez Station soon, of those who wish to end this upheaval once and for all. They will be heading north, to meet up with General Jackson. I believe we must crush the Red Sticks to finally achieve peace. The militia hereabouts are inadequate. The Red Sticks know it. The true threat for them is those forces that have arrived from the outside. That is why the majority have headed north."

"So what would you have done if I had chosen to go home or to fight with the militia?"

"I would have stayed with you. But I know you, Jacob. I knew if you thought about it you would arrive at the same conclusion I have."

The next morning, they began the business of packing for the trip back to Mobile. They separated their pelts – one pile for bear, one for fox, one for wildcat, and so on. All bundled in deer hide to protect them from the elements.

As Jacob gazed at the bundles, he was quite happy. They had mostly beaver pelts, which would bring them the most money. But then, he thought, how would they get them to town?

John seemed to read his thoughts. "Don't worry. I have a plan. We will build a couple of travois and drag them behind us. It will slow us down, but we'll get there, I promise!"

Late that afternoon they constructed their travois, using long straight poles they fashioned from some scruffy pine trees near the camp. They chopped them down, then used their hatchets to strip the branches. They found smaller limbs and connected them crosswise using rawhide, and then stretched deer hide between the poles.

That evening, for their last meal, they roasted a big, fat beaver over the fire. The sweet, tender meat satisfied their hunger. They rolled themselves up in their blankets and fell fast asleep.

The following morning, they placed their bundles of fur onto the travois. Jacob was now half a head taller than his uncle, and a good 20 or 30 pounds heavier. His travois carried the heaviest pelts – the bear and most of the beaver. The men positioned themselves between the poles, lifted them up and moved forward.

It was not easy going. They struggled mightily against the overgrowth on the trails they had followed at the beginning of their trip. The travois often got caught up in the tangle of vines and stumps that littered the path. They were frequently forced to take breaks, winded from the strain of their heavy loads.

After three days, they reached the Dog River. Beyond it lay civilization and the promise of a rich reward for their labors. There was not a soul in sight when they approached the bank. The river was calm enough when they reached it, but John said it would be foolish to cross at that point.

"It's too deep here, Jacob. The undercurrent might sweep us away. Let's move a bit north and see if there's a ferry or a ford."

So they lugged their heavy travois along the shoreline. The blisters that had formed on Jacob's hands were throbbing now, painful and raw, as they pulled and tugged their cargo over the debris heaved along the shore by the river. Fallen trees and immense root balls obstructed their path, impeding their progress. As they sweated and tugged, the afternoon dragged on.

John kept his eye on the current of the river. Finally in the late afternoon, he stopped. "I believe this will be a better crossing place. Let's leave our burdens here and test it."

Jacob thankfully dropped his travois. His hands had been bleeding for most of the day, and the thought of cool water bathing them was a comforting thought. He dutifully waded in, his uncle beside him. Midway, the river rose almost to his armpits but then subsided before they reached the other side.

As it was the end of November and the summer heat had long since departed the river's cold was a shock. By the time the men made it back to the shore where their bundles lay, they were almost frozen from the cold. They built a roaring fire alongside the bank and hunkered over it. As they warmed themselves, they were in good spirits.

"We'll balance our bundles on our heads and shoulders and make our way across. It will take several trips. First thing we'll do, however, is build a fire on the other side."

Jacob laughed. "I should hope so! We'll be useless otherwise!"

The next morning, they rose early. The temperature had warmed somewhat, and there was a heavy cloud cover, turning the winter landscape into shades of gray. Even the live oaks that lined the banks, having dropped most of their leaves for the season, had a silvery, ghostly hue.

After their first trip across, they dropped their bundles and dug a large pit, filled it with kindling and logs, and started a fire. They placed their bundles as close to it as they dared before heading back over the river.

They toiled at their task all morning. It was slow going, as the river clutched at their legs and the dead and dying debris on the bottom tripped them up. But by mid-afternoon, the job was complete. The last items they brought across were the travois.

Sleep came easily that night.

Chapter 7

Northward

Jacob and John were a strange sight as they made their way past the old Catholic graveyard, then down Conti Street to Royal Street. There were a few citizens of Mobile out and about, but they didn't pay particular attention to the two ragged men who pulled their strange conveyances behind them. It was winter, and it had been colder than normal for the last few weeks. Most of the good people of the city were behind closed doors, doing their best to stay warm.

At last, they laid down their travois in the muddy street before Campbell's store. John entered alone, while Jacob kept an eye on their belongings. There were enough shifty-eyed Spaniards and Indians about to give them pause as to what would happen if they left their prizes unsupervised.

After about an hour, John brought out his friend, Bernard Hutchinson, to inspect their skins. He was a short, balding man with a pair of spectacles balanced precariously on the end of his nose. He did his best to be all business as he rifled through the packs of skins, counting and inspecting each one, although Jacob caught the whiff of strong liquor on his breath. Jacob eyed his uncle and noticed a small lopsided grin on his face. The time inside the store had been well spent, Jacob guessed.

Eventually, Bernard straightened up and threw what he considered a hard look in John's direction.

"Pretty good haul, John. The beaver is worth the most, of course."

"What are you willing to offer us?"

"Well, that depends," Bernard frowned. "We are short on hard currency. I can give you more in trade. Business has been unusually slow for this time of year, what with those devilish Creeks rampaging around the countryside."

"We can take some in trade. We need supplies to head north. Balls and powder. Some extra blankets and some new shirts and breeches if you have them."

"That shouldn't be a problem."

"But our greatest need right now is horses."

Bernard sighed. "That could be an issue. What with the war going on and all, horses are hard to come by."

John thought for a moment. "How about across the bay? Over in the Villages?"

Bernard scratched his bald pate. "Well now, you might have some luck there. I hadn't thought of it."

"Can you issue us some chits for trade if we find any over there?"

"Yes, that I can do." Bernard turned to Jacob. "Here, boy, help load these bundles into the store. Put them in the back room if you can find a spot."

Jacob did as he was told. While he shuffled back and forth, John picked out what they needed from the merchandise displayed neatly on shelves in the store, and then received a piece of paper from Bernard. Jacob had no idea what the paper said as he had never been taught to read, but his uncle seemed satisfied with what had been written.

"It's been a pleasure doing business with you, Bernard."

"Thanks for coming in, John."

They shook hands with Bernard and left. They immediately found a spot between the buildings that fronted Royal Street and stripped themselves of the ragged remains of their shirts and donned their new ones. The leggings they wore were still serviceable, so they stowed their new breeches in their packs.

"You need to go talk to your Pa and tell him our plans," John said, as they reentered the street. "He deserves to know."

Jacob nodded.

"While you do that, I'll see if I can find someone to hitch a ride with across the bay. If you don't see me on the piers when you return, you can assume I was able to find passage across. Wait for my return."

Jacob walked down Dauphin Street, turned right onto Conception and then made his way to the front door of Sophia's uncle's house. It was a sturdy affair, two stories tall, with a whitewashed exterior. The front garden was small but well tended. He strode to the front door and knocked loudly. It was answered promptly by a rather large black woman, dressed neatly enough in a calico dress, apron and cap. She looked askance at Jacob in his new shirt, worn leggings, moccasins and full beard.

"Is Mr. Whitworth at home?" he asked politely.

A burly man shortly appeared in the doorway. He was near elderly but well dressed, with a sour expression and a pair of spectacles balanced on his large, bulbous nose.

"What can I help you with?"

"I'm sorry, sir, if you don't recognize me. I'm Jacob Worley."

Mr. Whitworth looked startled. "Jacob? I didn't recognize you. Perhaps it's the beard."

"Yes, sir. I'm here to inquire about my father. Is he here?"

Mr. Whitworth drew himself up to his full height, which was considerable. "Where have you been, boy?" he asked imperiously.

"My uncle and I have been hunting, sir. Is my father here?"

"No, he is not." Mr. Whitworth stood firmly in the doorway, with no indication of letting Jacob enter.

Jacob hesitated for a moment. "Where has he gone, sir?"

"So now you show an interest in the whereabouts of your parents? They waited weeks to hear word of you. I must say, they lingered longer here than necessary," he huffed.

Jacob shuffled his feet uncomfortably.

"If you must know, they left here two weeks ago, heading home."

Jacob nodded. "Thank you, sir. If you hear from them, could you let them know I came by?"

"Most certainly."

"I will be on my way, sir."

With that, the door was shut firmly. Jacob paused for a moment on the porch, then made his way back to Royal Street. He wasn't sure what to make of the news, but felt a sense of relief at not having to share his plans with his father. It was obvious to him that he had been abandoned, probably by the design of his stepmother. She must have been in a hurry to find out what had become of their farm. He didn't think his father would have left him without the prodding of his wife.

He shook off his speculations and went back to Royal Street. He eyed the three piers that jutted out of the tangle of marsh that fronted the town. As he neared, the smell of dead fish and decay assaulted his nose, and he winced. It would take a lifetime to get used to such smells. He was more accustomed to the scent of turned earth and fresh breezes slowly sifting through the pines that bordered his father's property. He looked around at the few Mobilians that shuffled along the muddy street, seemingly unaware of the stench that surrounded them. He supposed one got used to his own surroundings. He thought it would take him a great deal of time for him to tolerate city living.

He saw no sign of his uncle. He must have already caught a ride across the bay. He plopped himself down on the bank, on a firm spot near the marsh, and observed a few hardy souls with fishing lines cast into the muddy waters of Mobile Bay. Occasionally one would pull out a catch and deposit it in a nearby pail after knocking it in the head. Some would get a free supper that evening.

As he sat patiently waiting, he observed several types of boats plying the waters. He spotted a couple of large canoes, from their topknots most probably manned by Choctaws or Chickasaws, making their way toward the pier to the north. There was a small schooner and a couple of other modest, sailed vessels crisscrossing the shallow waters, also heading to the piers. He watched as the canoes tied up, and the occupants unloaded large bundles of hides and skins.

The air grew cooler as the afternoon progressed. The fishermen had given up as the sun lowered. They pulled in their lines and hefted their buckets as they scrambled up through the marsh and headed to their homes. Jacob searched the eastern horizon and wondered what had become of his uncle.

Before the sun set completely, he saw a shallow-bottomed boat heading his way. It had two sails and made its way smartly to the middle pier. He saw his uncle holding the bridles of a couple of horses, both fine roans, who shifted their feet nervously and threw back their heads in alarm as the boat tied up. He made his way swiftly down the muddy bank onto the pier.

His uncle greeted him. "Ho, Jacob, they aren't much and the saddles are a little worn, but I think they will serve our purpose!" he cheerfully exclaimed.

As Jacob helped unload the horses, John turned to his two companions. "Thank you, fine gentlemen, for the lift!"

"You owe us a favor now, John!"

"Yes, I do. I will do my best to pay you back accordingly, Felix."

John and Jacob walked the horses over to Campbell's store where they had left their packs for safekeeping, and affixed their belongings on the animals' backs. Just as John had said, their new means of transportation were not in the best condition, being rather thin and skittish, but they would have to do.

They headed north, the length of Royal Street as the sun began to set and then along a well-worn road. There was little traffic at that time of the evening, and after a few miles they decided to pull aside and rest for the night.

They were up before sunrise the next morning and by mid-morning they had reached Alvarez Station with its scattering of small houses and huts. Both John and Jacob were familiar with the place, as it was where John had been raised.

It was not hard to find what they were looking for. On the northern side of town they found a small gathering of men, idly hunched over campfires. They were greeted with enthusiasm as they rode up. Miko and Sabe were there, as well as half a dozen other men. Jacob recognized two others – Solomon and Henry Johnson, brothers, who he had seen at various Creek ceremonies throughout his childhood. They were both older than he, but like all the others gathered round, were very familiar with his Uncle John.

"John! Happy to have you join us!" Solomon exclaimed.

"Glad to be here! I was hoping we would not be too late."

As they dismounted and squatted down with the others, it was obvious to Jacob that John felt right at home. He knew all the men present and quickly introduced Jacob.

"My nephew, fellows. He's decided to ride with us."

There were nods all around, and Jacob was easily accepted into the group. Within two days, they were joined by enough others to round their number up to twelve.

These were not just any ordinary recruits, but men hardened by life in the wilderness. All were proficient in the use of their muskets, bows and arrows, hatchets and knives. They were rough around the edges, to be sure, but firmly convinced that their mission was a just one.

At night, as they gathered around their fires, they spoke of all they had lost. Solomon and Henry had family members who died at Fort Mims. Others had lost their lands and possessions to the rampaging Red Sticks. There was not a white man among them, least not a pure one. To some extent, all had Indian blood coursing through their veins – either Creek or Chickasaw or Choctaw. All had their minds set on restoring order to the wilderness they called home.

After a couple of days, the group decided it was time to move out. Understanding the basics of war, they voted Jacob's uncle John to be their chief, as he knew each and every one of them, and was the most adept at communicating in their mixture of languages. He could even write and read on paper. He soon issued his first orders.

"All right, men. We will head north from here. I propose we avoid Fort Stoddert altogether. All of us know members of the militia there, and if we approach it we will have to fend off requests to join them. I know their cause is as important as ours, protecting our kin's homes. However, I aim to meet up with the strongest fighting force in these parts, and that happens to be the army from Tennessee under General Jackson. That is also where the bulk of the enemy is. This war needs to stop, and the best way to do that is to take the fighting to them. If any of you have any objections, I am happy to entertain them."

Silence ensued.

"We are off then!"

Chapter 8

Finding Their Way

After the harrowing trip from Fort Pierce, Moses and Sally had put their time in Mobile to good use. They had taken advantage of the unusual freedoms afforded them, fostered by the confusion of the times and the disruption of the family by their sudden appearance at the household of Sophia's aunt and uncle. There were whispered conversations with the household's slaves, and with those they encountered on the street while serving their masters. Tidbits of information were gathered, and a plan began to form in Sally's head.

She might not be an attractive woman, but she had a quick mind. Moses could look past her physical flaws and see the spark of her intelligence in her dark brown eyes. It inspired him, and got his heart to racing to think they had a chance to gain their freedom. Without her, he doubted he would have ever contemplated such a move.

Rumors ran fast and thick about the bands of free blacks that dwelled in the back country, living their lives as free men. They were hidden deep in the forests north of Mobile, not far from Thomas Worley's farm. There were others in the Spanish territory, near Pensacola. Roving communities, peopled by those who had managed to free the bonds of slavery and live as they chose. Among them, they heard, were a few Indians who had been rejected by their own tribes and clans for one reason or another, and had a hand in keeping the groups alive, with their knowledge of the woods and the survival techniques handed down by their ancestors.

Once they returned to the farm with Thomas and Sophia, Moses and Sally began to plot and plan, huddled at night in the miserable shed they were penned into each evening.

The shed was small and cramped, only about eight-by-eight feet square. The interior had a small bed frame and a worn straw mattress crammed into a corner, a stump that served as a chair, and a chamber pot. No other furnishings were afforded them. Thomas Worley had constructed the hut with four small slits between the wood sidings, one on each wall. These were about shoulder high and did little to keep them comfortable in the boiling heat of summer or the freezing temperatures during the winter months. But one thing the confines of that wretched shed could not do was keep their minds from working.

Sally was not only smart, she was a good listener. Sophia's constant nagging and complaining was to her advantage. Sally often heard her moans and protestations about the situation in which the family found itself. She heard about the small bands of Red Stick warriors still in the area, and the militia's attempts to round them up. She heard the same stories from the occasional neighbor who would stop by, although she believed they stopped only by way of courtesy and not because they enjoyed Sophia's company. She heard about the movements of the militia and the devastation of the small Creek communities nearby, the scattering of the women and children for lack of protection, as their husbands, fathers and brothers warred against each other.

"Don't you see it, Moses? It is time, I tell you," Sally would exclaim, her face animated and her eyes brightly shining. "The countryside is in an uproar. There would be no one to track us down other than Master Thomas. The militia is busy keeping watch out for the Red Sticks."

And so they began the gathering of supplies. A handful of ground corn, flour or dried beans, dropped into a pocket of Sally's apron almost every day and then hidden under their bed in the cramped hut that housed them each evening. A worn blanket was used to hide their cache, knotted in such a way to keep the foods separated, each in their own compartment.

For his part, Moses was tasked with finding something to pry open one of the slits in their dwelling. It would not be easy, as Thomas supervised almost every move he made each day. He had found a dead, knotted tree branch on the edge of the farm, near the pine woods to the north. It was the right size – about two feet long, and seemed sturdy enough. He felt if he could just get the first board under the slit on one side of their hut to give way, he and Sally could finish the rest of the job with their hands. It was a full week before he had the opportunity to grab it and shove it into the waistband of his breeches. He could feel it dangling down, along the side of his bad leg, and prayed fervently the master would not notice. He didn't, and Moses was happy to see the look of jubilation on Sally's face when he presented it to her that evening.

It was mid-December by then. The weather had been stormy, with strong gusts streaming up from the south, laden with pelting rains. The two waited patiently for the rains to cooperate. They waited, their hearts full of anxiety and anticipation. Once the sky had cleared, they knew it was time. Moses used the hard stick he found to pry loose the first timber under the slit furthest from the Worley's home. He and Sally used their hands to tear away two more boards underneath it and then jammed themselves through the opening. Sally carried the worn blanket with their supplies. Moses took the opportunity to make his way quietly to the Worleys' chicken coop and grab up the first hen he could get hold of. They were off, for a new life on their own.

Jacob and his companions crossed the Tombigbee River by ferry, manned by a congenial old fellow who didn't question them about their destination. It was best not to inquire, as the answer might be uncomfortable for him. Business is business, was the old man's philosophy. Although these particular customers were armed to the teeth, they seemed harmless. A few of them were dressed in their native garb, but most were clothed in breeches and shirts and coats, like white men. Most of them looked like white men. Besides, they paid him in hard money, which was difficult to come by. They crossed well south of Fort Stoddert, so were not heading north to join the militia, that was assured. But who was he to question anyone willing to pay his fees without complaining? Not me, he thought to himself.

The party made a course to the northeast, traveling through heavy pine forests and large swathes of swaying grass, withered brown and gray by winter's cold blasts that occasionally came swooping down from the north. Uncle John led the way, a few hundred feet in advance.

From time to time they came upon half-deserted Creek villages, where women and children and the old and infirm waited patiently for their men to return. Hunger was rampant among them. They had harvested what they could the preceding fall, but it had been a small yield. Spring and summer had seen the villages in an uproar, with preparations for war in the air, continuous religious ceremonies to anoint their warriors and encourage their gods to protect them in battle. What need was there for squash, corn and beans when one's very existence was at stake? Besides, they had been told by their prophets that their men would be protected and that the white men's bullets were no match for the spells and incantations they had been taught to recite. Sadly, they had learned this was not the case. Now, the strong young men who had usually inhabited their towns were off fighting, some with the Red Sticks and some with the Mississippi militia. They were left bereft, without the means to provide for themselves.

John had instructed the men to only use their bows and arrows to provide sustenance, as to not draw attention to their party with the firing of their muskets. As they were all well practiced in the use of the bow, whenever they came upon such a town they took it upon themselves to spend a day or two hunting for the starving townspeople. Their efforts were always appreciated. What's more, their politics were never discussed.

They had been traveling about ten days and had settled down for the night when they were greeted by a shout from a horseman fast approaching their campsite. They all grabbed their muskets, not knowing if he was a friend or foe. The rider slowed and came closer and was soon recognized.

"Ho, Benjamin Morris! What brings you to these parts?" Solomon shouted.

"Is that you, Solomon? I'm on my way back home," was the reply.

"Any news?"

"Plenty!"

He dismounted and drew close to a campfire.

"Where have you been? Why are you riding at night?"

"Been out scouting for General Jackson. Decided it warn't for me, so I'm heading back south."

They all knew Benjamin Morris. He had a place some ten miles from Jacob's home. As he held his hands over the fire, Jacob remembered the rumors and gossip shared regularly about him. He was not a particularly good neighbor, known to be on the lazy side. He seemed to always be in need of borrowing from those around him, and slow to return what he borrowed. He was married to a full-blooded Creek, Susanna, and had a handful of children by her. The talk was that he mistreated her and the children, and was therefore not well regarded among the other settlers.

"You're traveling mighty fast, Benjamin. Why are you in such a hurry, especially at night?" John inquired.

"Well, I don't suppose they know I've left," he replied.

There was dead silence.

"Look here, fellas, it warn't my fault," he whined. "They don't got any food, and those fellas from Tennessee are deserting right and left! A bunch have already left and headed back home. I don't see why I can't do the same!"

Looking at his disheveled appearance, Jacob thought he might be telling the truth. He looked thin, and there were dark smudge lines underneath his eyes. His worn buckskins had holes and tears, exposing naked flesh on his arms and legs.

"Heard tell General Claiborne has built a fort north of home, and that he's got the militia with him. They think he's aimin' to hit those Red Sticks, prob'ly at the Holy Ground. That means, fellas, we ain't got nobody around to look after our folks, you know."

"So you've taken it upon yourself to do the job," John replied.

"Well someone's got to do it, ain't they?" Benjamin replied, a note of irritation in his voice.

"Any news there is trouble back home?" Solomon asked.

"Not exactly. But it only figures, don't it? I mean, with no militia . . ."

"Do you have word as to who is in charge of the Red Sticks? Last we heard it was Billy Weatherford."

"Red Eagle. Leastways, that's what the Tennesseans call him. He's been in charge since Fort Mims, you know. They think he's holed up there at the Holy Ground, along with Josiah Francis."

"Josiah Francis," John repeated quietly.

Jacob knew about Josiah. He was considered a prophet among the Creeks, and a powerful medicine man. He had met him once, before the death of his mother. His Uncle had told him he was one of the main agitators and instigators, responsible for their current situation, having been swayed mightily by the orations of Tecumseh. It was also believed he was a driving force behind the attack on Fort Mims.

"Good for General Claiborne. I wish him God speed," John pronounced.

The next morning, after sharing some meat with Benjamin, the group saw him off, much relieved his plans were not part of theirs. They then sat down to council.

"Well, the news we've received isn't good," John stated.

There were general nods around the circle.

"So it's only fair that we decide together what our next steps will be. I am open to anyone's opinion on what that should be."

There was a silence, each man weighing his own thoughts.

"If we head east, we should most assuredly run into General Claiborne and his men. I'm sure our assistance would be most welcome," Solomon volunteered.

There were nods and grunts around the circle.

"If what Benjamin said is the truth, if we join Jackson we would go hungry," Jacob said.

More nods and grunts.

"But nephew, we must look at the source of our information. I don't know about the rest of you, but I've never been one to believe all I've heard from Benjamin in the past. He could be simply weaseling himself out of a situation he found too difficult," John replied.

Miko cleared his throat. "Maybe so, maybe not."

"I'm all for continuing on with our original plans, fellas. I can't see all the Red Sticks confining themselves to the town at the Holy Ground. We all know about the place – we've heard the stories. There are far more Red Sticks outside the town than in it, I would wager. I'm sure they're planning to attack Jackson. He's already defeated them a couple of times, at Fort Leslie and Tallushatchee, I heard. We know them. They are our people. They will want to seek revenge against him. We can place bets on that," Henry said.

"So we have a choice, men. Which shall it be? Shall we continue on or turn back?" John asked.

"I vote for continuing on," Henry said.

"I as well," Solomon agreed. "I think the greatest threat to peace lies with those who are aligned against Jackson."

"Any oppose?" John asked.

Two hands went up.

"Your objections?"

"It's winter. My folks need me back home. I figure I'll get back quicker if we ride east," Nicholas Slater said. His best friend, Robert Fernandez, whose hand was also raised, nodded in agreement.

"We won't hold you here. If you two have decided that would be the best course for you, you are free to go," John said.

They looked at each other, then Nicholas said, "I suppose it's settled then. We'll ride east."

Late that morning, the two groups departed after breaking camp, heading off in different directions. What their destinies were, none could know.

CHAPTER 9

THE TENNESSEANS

As Jacob's group tracked northeast they ran across more mostly deserted villages, each with the same look of neglect and wretchedness. Withered weeds had grown up among the huts, the ball fields deserted and abandoned, the people left hungry and destitute. They did what they could for the mainly old or feeble inhabitants, which wasn't much. It was fully winter now, and the hunting had grown more difficult.

They did, however, receive news of the whereabouts of Jackson and his troops. A young Creek boy, not yet old enough to wield weapons of war, explained that they had recently constructed a new fort on a bluff overlooking the Coosa River. He pointed in the direction in which it could be found. After receiving the news, the men gathered to discuss the new information.

John spoke. "We're getting close, boys. We will soon have to worry about scouts and pickets."

The men that encircled him nodded.

"Our best course is to stay together. No more scouts of our own. Less chance of them getting shot."

"But what if we stumble upon a party of Red Sticks?" Jacob asked.

"We'll just have to take that chance. Keep your muskets primed and ready."

They moved steadily forward, cautiously eyeing what lay before them. Jacob was nervous. He checked and re-checked his musket, making sure it was primed. He glanced with apprehension at his companions. Could they all be trusted? Considering the circumstances, he certainly hoped so. They hadn't traveled more than half a day when a voice rang out from a tree line in front of them.

"Ho! Stop!"

A shot was fired over their heads.

"Put down those weapons!"

They all obeyed, dropping their muskets to the ground.

"Raise your hands, boys. Let them see we mean them no harm," John instructed.

Two horses with riders approached. They each held long rifles pointed in their direction. As they drew near, Jacob noted that one of them was dressed in buckskin from head to toe, the other one, thin and taller, wore homespun. The shorter of the two addressed them.

"Where you fellers from? And where you headin'?"

John spoke for the group. "We've come in search of Andrew Jackson's army. We mean to join up."

The speaker eyed him with suspicion. "Is that so?" He looked pointedly at the group, especially those looking more than half Creek. "You didn't answer my question. Where you from?"

"We come from down south. Around Mobile," John answered.

The speaker seemed to perk up at that answer. "Mobile, you say?'

"Yes, sir."

"How long you been gone?"

"Almost three weeks. It's not been an easy journey."

The questioner seemed to relax in his saddle. "Someone prob'ly'll want to talk to you. Preacher, let's gather up these muskets and take them in."

"Sure thing, Sam." The two dismounted and gathered up the firearms that had been dropped to the ground. They bundled them together, each taking half, and carried them in one arm while still maintaining the position of their rifles, trained menacingly at Jacob and his companions.

The man called Preacher led the way, while Sam took up the rear of the train. They made their way past the trees that had hidden them so successfully and headed straight north. There was little conversation among them. John and Jacob rode side by side. Jacob looked anxiously at his uncle from time to time, but John remained stoic and straight-faced. When he caught a glance from Jacob he would simply nod, indicating all would be well.

They soon arrived at the Coosa River, flowing swift and sure between banks cluttered with the wintry, barren arms of oak and birch, interspersed with the vibrant green of magnolias and littered with the dead limbs of old timber. Continuing north, they soon spied a bluff with an imposing fort comprised of walls of upright logs, driven deep into the earth. Each corner of the fort had a blockhouse situated high above the walls, giving the four corners an impressive view of the surrounding land. It had been named Fort Strother.

As they drew near, Jacob noted the campfires that surrounded the fort, with groups of men either lounging around them or puttering with one thing or another before the fires. Those men glanced curiously at the group but then resumed whatever they had been doing.

"Hey you, hold these here horses fer us. We got business with the Genrul," Samuel growled at a group of loungers at the entrance to the fort. A few rose and dutifully grabbed the reins of their steeds.

Swaggering ahead, Sam led them into the interior of the fort. It was neat and tidy enough, with a few low-roofed buildings against the walls doubling as parapets and several rows of neatly tied tents. They approached a larger building in the center of the compound. Attached to its front was a broad, wide stoop.

"What do you want, Sam?" a man in a smart, blue coat asked as they advanced.

"We need ta talk to the Genrul. We got these men he might be intrested in," Sam spoke with bravado.

"How so?"

"They claim to have come from Mobile."

The sentry nodded and withdrew into the building. He soon returned, followed by another officer. He was tall and wiry, with a narrow face, a high forehead and a long nose. His red hair was turning gray, which only seemed to emphasize his deep blue, piercing eyes. He was clothed in a blue uniform coat and gray trousers, and held his back tall and straight, like a ramrod.

"What have we here?" he asked.

John spoke up. "Are you General Jackson?"

"Yes, I am."

"We've come to join you, sir."

Jackson eyed him closely. "What's this I hear, you've come from Mobile?"

"We have, sir. We left a few weeks ago."

"Why?" Jackson asked abruptly.

"We decided we had a greater chance of defeating our enemies if we fought with you, sir."

"Do you know something I don't know?"

"Back home, the Red Sticks are scattered because of their losses at Fort Mims. They killed a lot of us, but our people mauled them bad. The militia is rounding up the ones left, but I believe most have moved onto a greater target, which would be you and your men."

Jackson nodded. "Perhaps. I just got word that General Claiborne attacked them at the Holy Ground and killed quite a few. Most of the warriors escaped, though. I've been informed they're under the leadership of William Weatherford."

"You mean Billy. We all know Billy," John replied.

"You know him personally?" Jackson asked sharply.

"Yes. Most of us here do. My nephew Jacob here grew up not far from his father's plantation."

"We need to talk further," Jackson declared. "Sam, you and the Preacher find a spot for these men to camp until I can make permanent arrangements." He turned to John. "Come back here after you get settled." With that, he turned and reentered the building.

Sam led them out of the compound. They gathered their horses from a tether rope and followed him to a spot a pretty fair distance from the fort on the western side.

"I guess you fellas can camp here, next to us. Those dirty rotten skunks have done left, so there's room," Sam began muttering under his breath.

"Now Sam, that's enough," Preacher spoke, quietly but forcefully.

"Fine," he replied grumpily. "Camp here till the Genrul tells you otherwise. You can put yer horses in the corral with the rest."

"Some of you will need to report to General Jackson. I suggest you select the best ones to do that among yourselves," Preacher stated.

Saddles and the rest of their equipment was unloaded. John picked Solomon and Jacob to accompany him back to the fort. The three made their way and reported to the sentry manning the front door. They were ushered inside.

They found Jackson seated at a table, pen in hand. He looked up when they entered.

Jacob felt a flutter in his stomach when Jackson's eyes took his measure. He wasn't sure what it was about the man that caused him to react that way. Perhaps it was the firmly set lips or the piercing gaze. He knew instantly, though, he did not want to be on the wrong side of this man.

He wondered also why John had picked him for the meeting. He wasn't sure he would have anything to add. He barely knew William Weatherford. But for whatever reason, he was there.

"So you know William Weatherford," Jackson stated.

"Yes, sir," Solomon replied. "We know his father as well. He's got a big place not far from Fort Mims."

"What sort of man is he?"

"He's quite handsome. And strong. He looks like any ordinary white man, to be honest. He was raised as a white man. He's not quick to temper. Until recently he lived his life as a farmer and plantation owner."

John interjected, "Until Tecumseh showed up, anyway."

"If he lived as a white man, then why the change? Why has he now turned against the way he was raised? What sort of power did Tecumseh have over him?"

"In our culture, the women's bloodline is most important. Billy's mother was a descendant of the Wind Clan. Her father was a trader named McPherson. Her mother was half-Creek. So even though Billy is only part Creek, his mother's blood makes him a full member of the tribe. He would have been raised in our traditions. A powerful orator, one who is able to sway an audience, mixed in with that, is what I believe turned him," John stated patiently.

Jackson nodded. "He has most assuredly been a serious problem. We've been told he led the attack on Fort Mims. Can you verify that?"

"Yes."

"Do you have any further information on that attack?"

"Me and my nephew here were posted at Fort Pierce, within hearing distance of the attack. Thanks to the quick thinking of Lieutenant

Montgomery, we managed to escape to Mobile. But we heard the gunfire, and I was part of the scout to survey what had occurred the evening of the attack."

"And what did you see?" Jackson asked curiously.

"If hell could be described, it would be what I witnessed there. I saw the burned buildings and blockhouses and heaps of bodies, both inside and outside the fort. I saw the remaining Red Sticks still scalping the dead and pilfering what they could find. They lost many during the attack. The settlers and half-breeds inside the fort put up a hard fight, but were overwhelmed by superior numbers. They didn't kill the slaves, or not many. There were still Red Stick sentries posted all through the woods. Thanks to the darkness of the hour, I was able to slip through. I had painted myself as a Red Stick so they assumed I was one of them," John said calmly, but firmly.

"I lost my cousin and his family in the attack. Never recovered the bodies," Solomon said through gritted teeth. "What those devils did was pure evil, General, and that's a fact."

"I myself lost three cousins," John added. "Their crime was their desire to live in peace with their neighbors. Fort Mims was an unnecessary escalation, sir. Those who carried it out deserve to be punished. We all have chosen to participate in giving them their due. We have come to freely offer our services to you with no reservations."

Jackson nodded and then changed the subject.

"Tecumseh is dead. Now what to do with you and your men. All Indians, I expect? You came on horseback, correct?"

"That is correct."

"General Coffee is in charge of the cavalry." He grabbed a slip of paper. "I am assigning you to his command." He scribbled a note and handed it to John. "Your service to your country is well noted. We are in a tough position here." His face grew red. "I've had the devil of a time getting supplies, and I continue to be plagued by my fellow Tennesseans who desert at the drop of a hat. You are strictly volunteers. I will not hold you if you desire to leave."

Solomon smiled wryly. "We just got here, sir. We don't aim on leaving until we see this thing through."

"Good. Now, let me resume my correspondence."

With that, the three returned to their comrades, who had started a fire and had made themselves comfortable, with their saddles and supplies neatly stacked, their horses placed in the nearby corral.

As darkness fell, Jacob could sense a feeling of unease emanating from the group of soldiers next to them, comprised of Sam, Preacher and three others. Sam kept throwing glances their way and was quite obviously expressing his opinion about their presence among them.

"I don't think Sam appreciates us," he said to his Uncle John.

"Little wonder. Can't say as I blame him. They know little about us, only that we've shown up unannounced and claim to be on his side. I think we can remedy that somewhat. They've had difficulty getting supplies, the General said. We have a haunch of deer meat here. I suggest we go and share our bounty with them. Perhaps that will ease the tension."

They approached their neighbors' campfire with their peace offering. Sam looked at them with little reaction other than a slight nod of his head. Jacob noted on inspection that Sam might be short and slight but was still powerfully built. He had sandy colored hair and a large, broad nose with close set eyes and bushy eyebrows. He, like the others, was clean shaven, although Jacob could easily imagine him with a long flowing beard. He wore regular breeches coupled with a stained and worn buckskin shirt, dyed brown.

Preacher, who sat next to him by the fire, was more welcoming. He smiled as they approached and was the first to offer his thanks as they shared the cuts of meat. He was a handsome man, with regular features and shockingly blue eyes. Unlike the others, he wore no buckskin, but a pair of breeches and a well-worn homespun shirt with a tricorn hat jammed on his head.

Their three messmates seemed welcoming enough, and pleased by the offering Jacob and John had brought. One of them spitted the meat and placed it over the fire.

Preacher spoke. "Thank you, gentlemen, for this fine piece of meat. Supplies have been short here for some time, and your generosity is appreciated. It has been awhile since we've had the taste of fresh venison. Back home, it's a staple we can hardly live without."

John took a seat among the circle. Jacob followed his lead.

"Where's back home?" John asked.

"We hail from the eastern part of Tennessee. From the Blue Ridge Mountains."

"We're not used to mountains down where we hail from. But we have a fondness for venison ourselves," John spoke easily.

Sam poked viciously at the fire, sending the flames skyward and sparks flying.

"Ain't you all Injuns?" he asked jeeringly.

"In a manner of speaking, yes," John replied.

"What does that mean?" Sam said.

"Well, my mother was half Creek. Jacob here is my nephew. His mother was also half Creek, which means he is more white than Indian, as am I."

"Don't know very many Injuns I can trust," Sam shot back.

John replied, "I don't know your story, but ours is simple. Our way of life is being destroyed by our kin. People duped into believing they can return to the old ways, before the white man arrived. A foolish idea, by all accounts. We've been tested and tormented by those who claim that only war can bring back those ways. We are here to show them otherwise. To prove them wrong. Although we may have started from different places, our goals are the same. We are brothers in arms, whether you like it or not."

"Well said, John," Preacher interjected. "We have the same goals, even if we have arrived here from completely different circumstances. I, for one, welcome your assistance. It will take us working together if we are to teach these Red Sticks a lesson."

Chapter 10

On the Move

Tensions eased somewhat between the two parties after John's peace offering. Over the next few days, a lively banter between them began. The two groups would catcall and halloo at each other, jesting at each other's doings and dress.

Jacob noticed the many empty spots scattered among the soldiers camped outside the fort. On one lazy afternoon, after their horses had been tended to and food had been procured, he wandered over to the Tennesseans to inquire.

"I can't help but notice that there seems to have been more men here at one time." He pointed where the remains of old campfires littered the grounds around them.

Sam's response was a growl.

"Yes, there were at one time many more of us," Preacher replied.

"What happened to them?"

"Well, if you must know, they took tail and run!" Sam interjected.

"Ran where?"

"All the way back to Tennessee, with their tails between their legs!" Sam replied, heatedly.

"Sam is particularly sensitive about that subject," Preacher said.

"Sensitive? Sensitive? Preacher, you got it wrong. I just don't like cowards. Not one bit!"

"Their terms of enlistment were up. They decided to go home," Preacher explained.

"After the Genrul begged them to stay. Don't forget that part."

"He didn't beg them, Sam. He tried to reason with them, but when that didn't work he had to get tough."

Preacher turned to Jacob. "The situation here grew a little tenuous. The General had a difficult time finding supplies for us, so many of our fellow soldiers grew impatient. As soon as their enlistments were up they decided to return home. Some of them who left were volunteers, so I don't suppose they felt the need to stay since they weren't getting paid."

"Bunch of lily-livered cowards, that's what they was!" Sam exclaimed. "See here, we come south to do a job, didn't we? These Injuns need to be taught a lesson. Somebody's got to put a stop to 'em. Goin' round, scalpin' and murderin' innocent folks. Turnin' these parts into a killin' field." Sam let fly a string of curses under his breath. "You know it ain't right when the Genrul has to threaten his own men with a cannon jist ta get them ta do the right thing!" He spat on the ground sucked in a breath.

"The Genrul, he understands. Ain't no one else in these parts can do it like he can," Sam continued. "Most folks haven't figured him out like we do. He's like a dog with a bone, he is. He ain't givin' up, even if he only has a handful of us to back him up."

"And I'm afraid we are down to a handful," the Preacher said. "General Coffee is off now, north of here, trying to get the men who deserted to return. I'm not sure he'll have much luck. Sam and I and a few others stayed put, knowing it would not be wise to leave the fort unattended. Although we're assigned to Coffee, as I expect you are, we are strictly volunteers."

"I know yur supposed to be an Injun, but you and your uncle seem to be more like reg'lar white folks to me." Sam shot a glance over at Miko and Sabe as they huddled over the fire at Jacob's mess. "We don't care much for Injuns, back where we come from. Our Pa's had their fill of 'em during the last war. Them damn Cherokee looted and scalped aplenty back in those days. We had Shawnee too. Did their best to keep us from fightin' the British. Warn't no use, though. They gave those lousy lobsterbacks a whoopin' at Kings Mountain. The Preacher's Pa and mine were there."

"That's all in the past, Sam," Preacher said quietly. "You know there are some Cherokee here with us now."

"The only thing the Genrul hates worse than Injuns is the British. You know that's a fact, Preacher."

Jacob interjected quietly, "My grandfather died at King's Mountain. He was on the other side."

"Is that so?" Preacher said quizzically. "My father's name is Caleb Anders. He was a mighty fine sharpshooter that day. Sam's father is James Cox, who also made a name for himself there."

"Well, seein' as it was only your grandpa who fought aginst us, I suppose it don't matter no more," Sam said.

Jacob hurriedly changed the subject. "Why do they call you Preacher?"

My Christian name is Nathaniel. My parents sent me to Blount College in my youth to go to seminary. I didn't last, however. I came home and have since taken over my father's farm. I suppose my fellow soldiers have assigned me that name as a result."

Sam laughed. "It ain't just that. He spends plenty a' time tellin' us what we should be doin' and not doin'."

Within a week of their arrival, Jacob's group heard that General

Coffee had returned. Red-faced, he had to report to his commander that his attempts to win back the deserting troops had been fruitless. He returned with only a handful of men, and rumors flew through the camp of Jackson's ire and despondency at the lack of men willing to continue what he had started. There were reports of him pacing back and forth in front of his headquarters, smoking relentlessly on a pipe clenched tightly between his teeth, gesticulating furiously at his underlings who tagged along behind him.

And then, on a cold day in the middle of January 1814, a shout arose from the men stationed near the front of the fort. Jacob and his companions raced around to the front of the stockade and saw a quite a sight – several hundred men were marching toward the front gate, in ragged formation, the barrels of their muskets glinting in the muted light of a cold winter sun. Some carried their muskets easily over their shoulders and marched quickly and smartly. Others seemed to slink along, gaping at the crowd that had gathered to watch them while throwing glances of admiration at the structure before them.

"I imagine Jackson is one happy soldier today," John told Jacob.

"All the letters he's been sending Governor Blount in Tennessee have finally paid off," Preacher surmised. "He's been begging him for weeks for reinforcements to replace those who were more worried about their private concerns than fighting for their country."

Jackson wasted no time taking advantage of his good fortune. Within days he had packed up and prepared to move the army south, leaving a small contingent of soldiers to man the fort in his absence. Before leaving the confines of the stockade he had commanded to be built, he addressed the men assembled for the march from the saddle of his horse.

"Men, I know many of you have never faced the fire of an enemy force. I want to give you some assurances to ease your minds. Please remember – the Red Sticks do not have the firepower we possess. Many still rely on their bows and arrows to fight. As for your own comportment, I ask that you make every shot you fire count. Do not be dissuaded by the yells and noise you will be subjected to. When instructed to charge, move forward and ignore the temptation to let their howling keep you from doing your duty. Obey the commands of your officers. We have an opportunity to strike a blow against these hellish devils. See that each and every one of you take advantage of it. But be warned – if we find ourselves retreating, our enemies are well equipped with axes and war clubs. They will not hesitate to use them against any that fall behind."

They moved southeast, with pickets thrown out in front and behind. Jackson sat tall in his saddle at the front of the column. Jacob and his friends, under the command of General Coffee, took up the rear, shepherding the foot soldiers in front of them.

Within a couple of days they arrived at Fort Leslie, signs of the battle fought there by Jackson and his men the year before still visible. Upon arrival, fortune smiled upon Jackson once again. There was a contingent of friendly Indians waiting for him. Among them were many Creek warriors, as well as a scattering from other tribes. They joined in the march.

Jacob rode along with his companions easily enough, at least outwardly. But he shielded a sense of dread that he did not feel comfortable sharing with anyone, not even his Uncle John. It sat deep in the pit of his stomach. He thought back to that day at Fort Pierce, when Fort Mims was under siege, when he stuck the muzzle of his musket through a gunport, wondering if he had it in him to fire at a human being rather than a hunted animal. He hoped that when the time came he would perform well, if for no other reason than to prove to his uncle and his companions that he was a man. And yet, he knew in his heart this was dirty business, even if it was necessary. He silently cursed those who had brought this calamity upon him.

Jackson's spies had brought him news of a large Red Stick fortification known as Tohopeka along the Tallapoosa River. He had his men camp about three miles away, near a small creek, and dispatched his scouts as darkness fell.

Jacob and John had rolled themselves in their blankets as close to the fire as possible – it was a bitter cold evening – and waited for what news the scouts would bring.

"Are you ready, nephew, for what might happen tomorrow?" John inquired.

"I hope so," Jacob replied nervously.

"Don't be concerned. If we stay together, we will weather this just fine. We'll follow the orders given us and use our weapons wisely, just as Jackson told us to do. Just be mindful that we cannot fall into the hands of the enemy. Our fate would be disastrous. They would discover who we are soon enough, and use us to send a message to others in our tribe."

Jacob gulped at the prospect. He knew full well what the Red Sticks were capable of.

It was midnight before word was passed around about Jackson's next move. They were to reinforce their positions where they were. The Red Sticks were well aware of their presence, according to the scouts. War dances were in progress. They could expect an attack in the morning.

Jackson immediately began to array his forces. He had his men form a sort of hollow square, with the infantry forming the outer rim and the men on horseback, including the small cannon they had dragged along and all their baggage, grouped inside it.

It had been a long night, and Jacob found himself nodding off despite the growing fear of what he was about to face. Just before dawn, as he and his companions were attempting to kindle fires after their nerve-wracking wait in the darkness, shouts rang out. The pickets came tearing into camp. The sounds of advancing Red Sticks, whooping and screaming, indicated they were hot on their trail.

John reached over and grabbed Jacob's shoulder. "Steady, son."

Jacob nodded in reply. The time was at hand. As fear gripped him in the stomach, he mounted his horse and steadied his musket across the saddle.

The Red Sticks attacked first on the left, but were repelled by the steady fire of the new recruits who had just joined Jackson. Their withering fire caused the enemy to retreat, with Tennesseans in hot pursuit. In the darkness, shredded by the light of the morning fires that had just been lit, Jacob could see the sprawling, bloody bodies of a dozen warriors. In the first haze of battle, his mind all aflutter, he wondered how many of these men that lay before him, dead, had been responsible for the spark that had ignited this war – the massacre at Fort Mims. Maybe all of them, he decided.

Before he could continue his reverie, orders were shouted that all on horseback were to follow General Coffee. He could see the General by the glancing light of the newly rising sun, his large frame sitting comfortably in the saddle of his horse. His square-jawed face showed determination as he raised his hand and led them out of the square, leaving their comrades on foot behind.

He led them on a course over the hill that sheltered Jackson's position and headed toward the fortification that had been built by the Red Sticks just a few miles away. As a precaution, he sent out scouts to assess the situation ahead of the column and they soon returned with bad news.

"General, we are unable to see a way to get at them."

"How so?" Coffee asked.

"They've built a wall, sir. Reinforced it with logs and mud. It's too high for us to jump, and it's manned with plenty of warriors. They seem eager for a fight," one of the scouts replied.

"Take a message back to Jackson," Coffee told one of his aides. "Let him know that we cannot take the town without the whole army alongside."

The aide spurred his horse to a gallop and returned the way they came. Coffee addressed the men gathered around him. "We must turn back for now. There's nothing else we can do here."

They all spurred their horses and rode back to the camp, again taking up positions in the center of the square. Not long after, a group of Red Sticks viciously hurled themselves against the right side of the formation. A few warriors reached the square, and a screaming melee with clubs, knives and tomahawks took place before the surviving Red Sticks fell back. Now Jackson shouted for Coffee to counterattack with half his men.

Jacob and John rode forward with the advance, and with a trembling arm, Jacob raised his musket and fired. He could not tell if he hit anyone, and cursed himself for not aiming properly. Before them was a teeming mass of bodies, faces painted for war, with spiked clubs raised and muskets leveled in their direction. Amid the shouts and screams he calmed himself and reloaded, not an easy task while sitting on the back of a horse. He glanced over at his uncle and saw he was grim-faced as he raised his musket and fired.

Behind them, Jacob could hear the clamor of another attack on the main force. He determined not to look back and instead keep his focus on what was before him. He pulled rein to reload and then spurred forward and fired again.

It soon became automatic – aim, fire, reload. He could feel the hot metal of the return fire whizzing past his head but did his best to pay it no mind. Arrows flew by on either side, sometimes piercing a man's leg or a horse's flank. Jacob concentrated on the task at hand, which was to punish those who had wreaked so much havoc on his neighbors and kinsmen.

Coffee's advance soon faltered. Instead of collapsing before the horsemen, the numbers of enemy seemed to grow, despite the bodies that lay still or squirming all around. Jacob saw them, bloodied and torn, their limbs at odd angles. He could see in the early light the lifeless eyes of the killed, staring skyward. He glanced around and spotted his uncle, and they locked eyes for a moment. The steady gaze of the man who had been so much a father to him gave him an unusual sense of calm, despite the chaos all around.

Then a fresh group of riders joined them and reinvigorated the fight. Jackson had sent reinforcements, for which all those at grips with the enemy were most grateful.

Inexorably, the battle shifted. Where once they had been stalled, the fresh infusion of new troops catapulted them forward. Coffee called out "Charge!" and with their last burst of energy, the men spurred their horses and the Red Sticks before them began to run.

They gave in to the chase. Jacob and John rode side by side as they pursued the enemy. Hatchets were loosened from belts and liberally used on the fleeing enemy. The Indians scattered, heading left and right for the nearest tree lines, but dozens more were killed in the pursuit.

After about a mile, Coffee called a halt. As they stopped, waves of fatigue and weariness washed over Jacob, as he realized he had not had a bite of food or even a sip of water since the evening before. The sun was in full flight across the western sky as they headed back to the rest of the army. There they found their jubilant fellow soldiers. The battle had been won.

CHAPTER 11

RETURN TO FORT STROTHER

Orders were dispersed that they were to stay in the encampment for the night. Jacob did not mind helping to bury the dead. To prevent the Red Sticks from returning and digging up the graves of the poor soldiers who had lost their lives in the engagement, they burned fires, bright and hot, over the graves.

There were also wounded to be tended to, including General Coffee, who had taken a shot in his thigh. The night was tense, as all were aware an attack could happen at any moment. Despite being tired from the battle and his exertions in helping to bury his comrades, Jacob slept fitfully that night. Images of the horror he had witnessed filtered into his dreams. He finally rose before dawn and joined his uncle at a campfire. There was very little food to go around, and Jacob's stomach grumbled at the lack of it.

"Do we know yet what Jackson's plans are?" Jacob asked.

"We're in a pretty difficult spot," John replied. "It's obvious we don't have the men we need to overwhelm their fortifications. Word is we are to return to Fort Strother and regroup."

"A retreat?'

"I wouldn't necessarily call it that. Let's just say a wise man knows when to withdraw and collect what he needs to gain victory."

"I saw the bodies of many Red Sticks."

"Yes. They lost quite a few warriors. But word is they have more men than we do. I think it's wise to withdraw and then return when we are better prepared."

They left mid-morning, hampered by their lone lumbering cannon and the wounded, carried on litters constructed by stretching blankets between two poles and then attached to horses, front and rear. It was a slow-moving column, much slower than it had been when they advanced. The men were tired and hungry, and with their bloodlust gone, anxious to return to their place of safety.

And then, just as the column was crossing a creek and as the cannon they were hauling entered the water, the Red Sticks struck again. Their howls and screams split the air, and they were upon them within moments.

Jacob struggled to gain his composure in the melee that ensued. He could hear the high-pitched voice of Jackson from the far bank, screaming his orders to the remaining troops. "Hold the line! Maintain your positions!"

Jackson reacted to the ambush by ordering his advance guard to turn around and counterattack the Red Sticks on both sides. But they didn't have time. Jacob watched as the rear guard gave way to the onslaught, rushing into the creek, their eyes wide with fright, their weapons forgotten as they flapped and floundered in the cold water.

There was firing all around, but the crisis was in the rear. Fewer soldiers were now making it to the creek, and instead, a mob of shrieking Red Sticks came down to the water, waving their blood-red clubs. At that moment, the artillerymen, who had pulled their gun up the far bank, were able to get a shot off at the swarming cloud of Red Sticks, their gaping faces howling in defiance at the men still struggling in the water.

Jacob emerged from the creek and saw that the soldiers had recovered their surprise, now calmly loading and firing. The Red Sticks could only attack by slowly wading across the knee-deep creek, and the water ran red as the enemy was beaten back.

After burying their dead, it took the column four days to make its way back to the fort. Despite the bitter cold, low rations and the struggles of exhausted men transporting the wounded, more numerous after the second fight, spirits were high. Most of the men had never seen battle before, and they felt confident they had comported themselves well. Jackson himself praised their courage and fortitude. He also carried himself with more assurance. Astride his horse, his back seemed even straighter than before.

News of their recent engagements raced to the outside world, and beginning in February their numbers swelled. Recruits poured in by the hundreds, and then by the thousands. At the end of the first week of February, the little army was joined by the 39th Regiment of United States Infantry.

Jacob and his group had returned to the spot where they had previously bivouacked, on the western side of the fort next to the camp of Preacher and Sam. All were in good spirits, and news and gossip were shared liberally between the two groups. Sam was now more accepting of their presence, and even attempted to carry on conversations with Miko and Sabe, whose English had not improved since their arrival. At times laughter would break out as he tried to decipher their mixture of Spanish, French and Chickasaw.

"I ain't good at figurin' out what yer sayin'," Sam would exclaim. "But I figure it must be alright, seein' as how you did your part against the red skunks."

Miko and Sabe would nod their heads vigorously, even when it was clear they had no idea what was being said to them.

Jacob was also more at ease now. He was happy that he had held his own on the battlefield and had not shirked off in fright like some of the other new soldiers. His uncle assured him he had acquitted himself well, and that was all he needed to hear.

One evening, Preacher had offered to write a letter home to his Pa for him. After a moment of thought, Jacob refused the offer. For one thing, his Pa could not read and would have to enlist a neighbor to decipher it for him. He knew his Pa would not be pleased to find out what he had been up to and would prefer he had returned home to work on the farm. Sometimes things were better left unsaid, he reasoned. He explained this to his uncle, who remained silent about the matter.

Rations were still in short supply, despite Jackson's efforts to get food to his men. Some of the new recruits were assigned to building roads through the wilderness in order to alleviate the shortages. Others were assigned to building boats to fully utilize the numerous rivers and creeks that crisscrossed through the country of the Creeks.

Once the regiment of regulars arrived in camp, Jackson began to mold his troops into a real fighting force. Discipline was instituted, with strict guidelines as to how his men were to conduct themselves. There was no more lounging before the fires during the day. Men were taught how to march and shoot and obey the orders issued by their superiors. Those who still mutinied and demanded to go home were subjected to extreme punishments, up to and including death.

Those in the cavalry, like Jacob, were trained in the same manner. They were also responsible for the care of their horses. There was very little grumbling among the troops that had already faced the Red Sticks in the last campaign. They had proven themselves and felt satisfied they could do so again if called upon.

The new recruits, however, were a different matter. Rumors flew among them and many complained about the new rules being enforced. This drove a wedge between the old fighters and the new men. Fights would break out, and all involved were dealt with harshly by their superiors.

There were also rumors about the fortifications the Red Sticks had built as were reported by Jackson's spies and scouts. Those who had viewed them were repeatedly asked about what they had seen, often by men whose voices cracked in fear. What had Jackson gotten them into, many wondered aloud.

Jacob and John found themselves in a crowd gathered around one such scout on an evening, whose name was Emmanuel. He was hunched down, with a stick in his hand, which he used to draw a crude map in the dirt.

"See, it's like this." He used the stick to draw a line from north to south, and then a big loop. "This here's the Tallapoosa River. There's a big bend in the river, as you can see." Those gathered around him nodded.

"Them Indians done built them a barricade right straight across the neck here." He used the stick to draw a line. "Behind that there line is a big village. Prob'ly the biggest village I ever seen."

"What is the barricade made of?" someone asked.

"Looks to be timber and dirt. We couldn't get too close, for fear of getting our heads shot off."

Silence fell.

"Does it look like the walls of a fort?"

"Land sakes, no. It's much thicker than any fort wall I ever seen. The timber is laid crossways, not up and down like a fort. And it's tall, too. I figure close to eight feet. No way a horse could jump it, that's fer sure."

The next evening, after the days' drills were finished and they were gathered around their campfire, Jacob used the opportunity to question John about what they had heard.

"Uncle, have you ever heard of our people building fortifications like that?"

John shrugged. "No, I haven't. But someone has been smart enough to understand the importance of protection behind thick, strong walls."

"Do you think it's Weatherford?"

"Of course it's him. He most certainly learned a lesson from Fort Mims. A wall made only of logs can be breached, especially if you leave the front gate open, like what happened there. One thing's for sure – Billy is not a fool, unfortunately."

"What do you think we'll do?"

"I have no idea. But then, I'm not a military man. I'll leave the plans up to Jackson and Coffee. They seemed to have everything in hand during our last expedition."

"But we left the battlefield."

"A smart move, in my opinion. Better to withdraw and gather your strength in order to fight another day."

News of the war against the British had filtered down to the troops, none of it particularly good. The death of Tecumseh, the Shawnee leader who had been instrumental in turning the Red Sticks against even their own family members, had been great news. Since then, the far distant conflict seemed to have little impact on the hardy group of volunteers and regulars struggling to survive in the brutal environs of Creek country. They faced the task at hand with acceptance if not enthusiasm, driven by the patriotic fervor and passion of one man – Andrew Jackson.

If anyone in that small army, huddled desperately together in and near the fort constructed with their own hands in the vast wilderness that surrounded them, questioned the motivations of their determined leader, their fellow soldiers readily shared his story. At the tender age of thirteen he had been a Patriot soldier, alongside his brothers, in the backcountry of the Carolinas. He had been captured and beaten by a British officer. His deep-seated hatred of the British began then, only to intensify when he became an orphan upon the death of his mother, who had taken it upon herself to nurse the sick and wounded patriots in Charleston and died from cholera for her efforts.

To defeat the British is what drove him. He would not rest until he could taste their defeat. If that meant destroying their allies in this unforgiving wilderness, then that is what he would do.

"Lord help anyone who stands between Jackson and a redcoat," Sam would say. "They just be askin' to git shot fer their trouble."

Thomas Worley did not know what he was going to do.

The slaves he had paid good money for had run off. He cursed their very souls.

He did a lot of swearing when he discovered they had disappeared. He had even gone so far as to saddle a horse and ride south to Fort Stoddert and demand the militia help him in retrieving his lost property. He was sternly rebuked by a lieutenant.

"Do you think we have time to hunt down lost slaves? We're in a war here. We have Creek warriors to round up. Be gone!"

"But what am I to do?" Thomas pleaded.

"That is your concern, not ours. Perhaps they are dead. Perhaps they have joined up with other runaways, or found a place of refuge in a Creek village somewhere. We have no time for this!"

Thomas mounted his horse and returned home. On the journey, as he viciously kicked the sides of his horse, he contemplated how he had wound up in this situation. He decided the majority of the blame rested on the shoulders of his wayward son.

"Where is that blasted Jacob?" he thought to himself. "If he had been here, he could have helped me keep an eye on them! Instead, he's off somewhere with that no-account uncle of his," he fumed.

Things had not been well at home since Sally and Moses left. Sophia had let the house go. He was hard pressed to even get a decent meal out of her. His three young sons were running wild with little supervision. They were constantly underfoot, keeping him from performing the chores necessary to keep up the fields and livestock. And to top it off, he had to tolerate the constant whining of his wife about the unfairness of him expecting her to run the household without help. It had gotten to the point he avoided the house as much as he could, preferring the company of the animals in the barn rather than face the wrath of his own wife. He shook his head at the injustice of it all.

"If only Jacob had returned, like any good son, I wouldn't be in this predicament. Now I will be forced to buy more slaves. More money and more of my time gone. If he ever turns up back here, he will get a piece of my mind. I have held my tongue all these years and allowed him to fulfill his obligations to his mother's people. I see now I have been too lax. I will not make that mistake again.

CHAPTER 12

HORSESHOE BEND

Jackson's ever-growing army was soon joined by about five hundred Cherokee warriors at the beginning of March. Some of the Tennesseans were none too happy at their sudden appearance – memories of the years of vicious fighting between the two groups had not faded sufficiently for some.

"I don't like it. Not one little bit," Sam complained. "Nothin' against you fellers, but I don't trust Indians, 'specially Cherokees," he opined to Jacob and John. "They's the ones them lousy redcoats used to go against our people. Many a settler back during the last war lost their scalps to those red devils."

Preacher interjected, "But times have changed, old friend. They're willing to help. We need to let bygones be bygones."

"Maybe so. But I still don't like it. And I don't trust 'em, that's fer sure."

The men all knew by instinct what Jackson's plans were. He was not one to run from a fight. It was against his nature. To have left that immense Creek village in the bend of the Tallapoosa River, with a fine, sturdy wall guarding it, must have been frustrating for him. Horseshoe Bend, as they called it, would soon see his return.

"I sorta feel sorry fer them folks. Andy ain't a man you want to get on the wrong side of," Sam said.

"But you don't really feel sorry for them, Sam," John replied with a smile.

Sam grinned back. "No, I guess not. But we'll be in fer a hell of a fight. Might make it a little easier if Andy hadn't taken away the whiskey. A good stiff drink always has a way to help a feller git his courage up."

On March 14, before the army marched out of Fort Strother, Jackson addressed his men. He sat upon his horse, neatly dressed in a blue coat and fawn-colored breeches, his black boots glistening in the morning sun. His high-pitched voice rang out.

"Some of us have already met the enemy. Others of you have not. But my message to you here today is the same as it was the last time we took this journey. Use your ammunition wisely. Make each shot count. I call upon you to stand firm and do not retreat. Anyone who gets caught fleeing the battlefield will be shot." Not a sound could be heard among the troops. "We will meet a determined enemy. But I have the greatest confidence we will overcome them."

The infantry moved out first, while Jackson sent the 39th Regiment, in their faded and worn blue coats, down the river with supplies to begin building a stockade to house the troops before the planned attack. He left several hundred men to maintain Fort Strother, ever careful of his rear.

Jacob and John and the group of men they had come with, including Solomon and Henry Johnson and Miko and Sabe, moved with General Coffee's cavalry. Sam and Preacher were there, too, as were other Tennesseans who had stuck with the little army, despite the lack of food and the strict discipline that Jackson had instituted. By the time they reached the meeting point, some thirty miles down the river, the walls of a new fort had begun to rise above the floor of the forest. They could see Jackson on his horse, riding among the men busy chopping down the large pine trees common in that area, encouraging them to move quickly. He had dubbed the new structure Fort Williams, and it would be the starting point of the final push southeast to Horseshoe Bend, some sixty miles away.

Jacob did his best to remain calm as they waited beside the rushing waters of the Coosa River. He looked to his uncle for guidance. John's demeanor showed no sign of distress.

"Are you not worried, Uncle?"

"Perhaps a little. But there is no point being troubled by what hasn't happened yet. All I know is, this war needs to end. Too many innocents have suffered because of the willful disregard shown by a few men that cannot abide living in peace with others. If we can do our part to put a stop to it, then I am satisfied."

They arose well before sunrise on the morning of March 24th. By 5 a.m., the army was on the move.

They crossed a wide swath of wilderness, guided by their scouts and spies. The terrain was treacherous, dotted with hills and valleys and the seemingly endless, dark forests of pine and hardwood. Jacob, astride his horse, felt pity for the foot soldiers as they floundered through the deep underbrush that clung and dragged at their legs. Horses struggled to pull their two cannons through, as well as the carts to carry their ammunition, without the benefit of even a footpath.

They fell to the ground, exhausted, at the end of each arduous day. They had been given rations for eight days but did not have the luxury of fires with which to heat them. Jackson did not want to give away his position or the size of his force. The men ate their cold rations, thankful enough to have something to fill their growling bellies. They would pull their blankets tightly around their bodies in the blustery, cold winds that buffeted them, and slept fitfully, if at all. They would arise again before dawn the next day and be on the move once again.

After three days of marching, Jackson ordered a halt to set up camp. The next morning, he commanded General Coffee to gather his cavalry and all the Indian volunteers to swing wide to the west, and then south to position themselves on the opposite side of the Tallapoosa River from the village the Red Sticks had created, named Tohopeka, nestled in a crook of the river. Jackson and the rest of his troops would make a frontal assault.

Jacob felt the now familiar quivering of fear in his belly as he and his comrades from home dashed off with Coffee and his troops to guard the rear of what would be the battlefield, with the clear understanding they were to prevent any Red Sticks from escaping. They were a fierce lot – a mixture of hardened Tennesseans and painted Cherokee warriors, with a healthy number of Lower Creeks and Choctaws in their midst.

John had prepared himself for battle with the war paint used by his ancestors. He had stripped his shirt off, despite the cold, and his face looked threatening, painted half black and half red.

"Why have you painted yourself, Uncle? Aren't you afraid of being mistaken for the enemy?" Jacob questioned, as they crossed the waters of the Tallapoosa, well west of the bend in the river.

"It is our tradition, Jacob. Whatever my fate today, I choose to present myself as what I am," John replied calmly.

Jacob glanced at him quizzically. Did his uncle have a foreshadowing of what was to come? Was this wild ride through the unrelenting wilderness, dodging the underbrush, brambles and the jagged remains of the dead trees that lay scattered all around them, a path to their destruction?

Once they arrived at their position, Coffee planted a large group of cavalry, astride their horses, on a small rise along the riverbank. Most of the Cherokee and Creek warriors, along with a few Tennesseans, dismounted and lined themselves along the bank itself. They were instructed to shoot any who tried to flee across the river.

Jacob stood on the ridge alongside his uncle. He gazed across the wide, shallow river and noted the numerous canoes that lined the opposite shore. He could see a series of huts and hovels behind them, and then a small rise, on which stood the rest of the village.

He glanced nervously around. There was not much discussion among the men who stood beside him. The looks of his comrades were of steady resolve. He wondered if any of them felt the same flutter of unease that he was experiencing.

The Cherokee warriors among them were decked out in their finest. Many wore embellished sashes, festooned with ornaments and decorated with beaded designs tied around their waists. Some had elaborate turbans atop their heads. It was their tradition to wear their finest apparel into battle. Yet despite their finery, all in his sight had a sobering look about them, as any man would who was about to face his enemy.

They hadn't been there long before they heard the booming of Jackson's two cannon. They could hear the sharp, piercing sounds of musket fire interspersed with the thumps. Jackson's assault on the fortification, sturdy and strong, had begun.

Jacob kept his eyes trained on the opposite bank as the battle commenced. He could see women and children scurrying and scuttling among the huts of the village. A few warriors were there also, although Jacob had no idea why men would be hiding behind the skirts of their women.

The muskets beside him began to fire across the river. A shout went out to remind them to kill anyone who tried to use the river as a means of escape. Jacob did as he was told and pointed his musket at the few Red Sticks who attempted to make their way to the numerous canoes tied along the bank. He fired, although he knew he had little chance of hitting anything at that distance.

Growing restless at the sound of gunfire at the front of the fort and the peppering spray of return fire in their direction, a large number of Cherokee warriors entered the shallow waters of the river and began to make their way across, their hatchets raised above their heads.

Spontaneously, John grabbed Jacob's arm and shouted, "Let's go!"

They left their muskets behind, their knives and hatchets tucked firmly in their belts. Jacob followed him into the cold, running water. It rose to his waist, and then to his chest. The Cherokees that had entered the river before them began to cut loose the canoes tied along the bank that the enemy had stashed to help with their escape. Dozens were sent afloat down the river.

Jacob fumbled with his knife as he tried to follow their lead. His uncle was there beside him, busily cutting through the rawhide strings that secured the canoes to the bushes and small trees that lined the shore.

Once the canoes had been set free, the Cherokees rose from the water and lit the array of small huts close to the bank on fire. They danced before the inferno they created, letting out the horrific sounds of their war whoops. They wielded their hatchets and knives against the scattering of braves they chanced upon.

Jacob spotted groups of women and children huddled together in fear. For a moment, a deep sense of sorrow overcame him. He thought about his mother, and the times he spent in her village. These women and children represented a part of him he could not deny. The look of terror that crossed their faces tore at his heart. What had brought this madness to them? As the acrid smoke of the burning huts swirled around him, he wondered what his mother would think of him now.

He did his best to stay close to his uncle, but within a few minutes they were separated. He found himself alone in the smoke and flames, amid gruesome scenes of death and dying. He saw blood-spattered bodies, tossed about every which way, with gushing wounds inflicted by the hatchets and knives of his fellow soldiers. He spotted Miko and Sabe gustily swinging their hatchets at opposing warriors. The Johnson brothers were to his left, Solomon and Henry.

More huts were set afire, and the heat from them grew intense. Jacob was confronted by warriors swinging their clubs – their painted faces, half black and half red, leering at him through the smoke. He found himself using his hatchet quickly and forcefully, as his uncle had instructed him. He found little resistance, for the most part. His greater size and longer arms were an advantage. He took no pleasure in defending himself from the onslaught. This killing, this chopping and stabbing . . .

More Red Stick braves began to rush at them from the wall of timber and mud that stretched across the neck of land at the front of the village. Soon Jacob spotted soldiers, his fellow soldiers, who had breached the tremendous fortification that had been built to impede them. He could still hear the occasional thumping of the cannon, but before long it stopped.

Chaos reigned all around him. Smoke continued to whirl, burning his throat. Time seemed to stand still as the killing continued. Mounds of bodies began to pile up, the bloody and ruthless result of the hand-to-hand combat now taking place. He could hear the sound of muskets behind him, coming from the other side of the river, as those who were trying to make their escape were gunned down in the clear cold waters of the Tallapoosa.

The hours drifted by. Three, four, five. The proud warriors of the Red Sticks refused to surrender. They shielded themselves in the numerous huts and structures that comprised their village until they were burned out. Some of them hid themselves in small gullies and ditches, only to be routed out and killed by Jackson's men.

In the midst of the melee, Jacob began to look for his uncle but to no avail.

At some point, he noticed his left arm had been slashed. He could not remember how it happened, and only noticed it because the knife he was holding in his left hand became slippery from the blood that flowed down his arm. His other hand, which held his hatchet, was spattered with the blood of the men he had cut down. He shuddered.

As the afternoon waned, the fighting slowed. The firing at the river grew in intensity, as more braves attempted to flee the slaughter. There were only small pockets of resisters in the village by that time, and they were dispatched with some difficulty. The Red Sticks were willing to die, to a man.

When night fell, torches were lit to assess the damage. By that time Jacob was desperate to find his uncle. He queried his friends, but no one had seen him. Jacob retraced his steps, a torch in his hand, and searched through the bodies, grotesquely piled in clumps, not far from the river. He finally found his Uncle John, dead. He had been shot through the head.

Chapter 13

The Aftermath

Jacob tugged his uncle's body out from the pile of dead in which it had been entangled. He pulled it as far away from the carnage as he could. There were still burning fires, and the light they gave off, along with the glow of the torches held by Jackson's men, detailed the ghastly scene before him. There were sounds of the dying, men who had somehow survived the brutality of the attack. A moaning, wailing sound from their throats filled the air.

He wept bitter tears. His uncle, who had fostered him and taught him so much was gone. How could this be? How could this man, so full of energy and life, a leader among men, be cut down in such a manner?

The musket ball that had killed him had entered near his left ear. Jacob swabbed at it with his shirt sleeve. What was he to do now that his uncle was dead?

The hours of darkness crept by. Jacob stayed by his uncle's body, guarding it from anyone who would disturb it. He saw some of his fellow soldiers wandering through the carnage, and before long it dawned on him their task was to kill any of the Red Sticks that survived. Before morning, there was nothing but deathly silence all across the battlefield.

He saw others furtively leaning over the bodies of the dead and stripping them of anything of value they could find. Those that approached him soon steered clear when he raised his hatchet menacingly in their direction. He spent time in prayer over John's body. He prayed to the god Ibofanaga, who was responsible for the souls of the dead and made the way safe for them in the afterlife. He prayed Ibofanaga would find his uncle's life to be one of virtue and would guide him successfully over the bridge to the hereafter.

When dawn broke, Jacob was still there guarding John when Preacher found him. He hunched down next to him and put his arm around his shoulder. Jacob shuddered at his touch and glared up at him.

"Someone has killed my uncle."

Preacher looked at him. The tracks of Jacob's tears coursed down through the blackened soot that stained his face. He nodded.

"No one is to touch his body. I will not allow it to be defiled," he spat angrily.

"Can I help you, Jacob?" Preacher asked kindly.

"I must protect him. If someone scalps him, his soul will be forced to wander the earth and be denied entrance to the afterlife."

"I will be happy to stay and help you," Preacher sat down.

They sat in silence. No words passed between them. After an hour, Sam appeared.

"I been lookin' fer you, Preacher." He stopped when he saw Jacob, cradling the body of John.

"See here, I'm sorry Jacob. Your uncle was a good man."

"I must see to his burial," Jacob replied. "We left our muskets on the other side of the river. I must get my uncle's musket. He will be buried with it."

"I'll fetch it fer ya, Jacob," Sam said.

The grisly task of counting the dead had begun. Jackson had sent out a number of men with the grim business of cutting off the noses of all the Red Stick warriors that had been killed in the battle.

Jacob and Preacher watched as they went about their task, some with gusto, some with a grimace of disgust on their faces.

When they approached Jacob, Preacher waved them off.

"This man is one of ours."

"But look. His face is painted jist like the rest of these here skunks," one of the men responded.

Preacher replied firmly. "This man was a member of good standing under General Coffee's command. Leave him be."

Sam soon returned with Jacob and John's muskets.

"I was feared someone would a' took 'em, but I found 'em," he said.

"But I got bad news fer you, Jacob. We ain't buryin' our dead. The genrul's afeared their bodies will be dug up and scalped. He wants us to sink 'em into the river instead."

Jacob nodded. He lashed his uncle's musket to his side with strips taken from his own shirt. With the help of Preacher and Sam, the body was lifted and carried to the Tallapoosa. Sam searched the bank of the river until he found a stone of sufficient size. He used his knife to cut some new, young tendrils from the sweet gum and hickory trees that lined the river and knotted them together. They tied the heavy stone around the body, waded into the middle of the river and dropped it. Jacob watched it sink, and fresh tears coursed their way down his face.

"Lord, please accept the soul of our friend John. He died for what he believed in, willingly sacrificing himself for the benefit of others. I humbly ask you greet him and welcome him into your arms. I pray you will bring comfort to those whose lives he touched. Amen," Preacher intoned as the body sank to the bottom.

Jackson was well pleased with the results of the battle. His men's count of noses – a rather ghastly but necessary way to truthfully gauge the results of their hard-fought victory – totaled more than five hundred. Some bodies had drifted down the river. General Coffee estimated that number to be about three hundred. He reckoned at least a couple dozen had managed to escape. The women, children and the elderly had mostly scattered into the woods. He had left strict instructions that none should be harmed, but the heat of the battle had been so intense that some bodies of women had been discovered.

What was more concerning to him was that he had been informed that a few of his men had been caught taking scalps, and some had gone to the extreme of cutting strips of skin from the dead warriors to make reins for their horses. He had ordered a halt to these activities as soon as he became aware of them. He understood, however, that such atrocities were bound to happen in the circumstances in which they found themselves.

He had been disappointed that the cannon he had dragged through the woods at a great cost of time and effort had been of little use against the fortification of logs and mud the Red Sticks had built. Its construction had been directed by someone with knowledge of engineering. To see those cannon balls bouncing off it had left him frustrated. The enemy had taunted and mocked his soldiers, shielded as they were by the sturdiness of their redoubt. If it had not been for the distraction of the actions of General Coffee's men from the rear, the battle might have turned out differently. Once the Red Sticks had understood their back was defenseless and had turned their attention toward it, his men had attacked from the front, climbing over the massive fortification. Attacked effectively from both front and rear, the Red Sticks did not have a chance.

How many Red Stick warriors were left in the region? He had no idea. For now, he must tend to his men. Their victory had been complete. He was more than satisfied overall with the conduct of his troops. He was now in charge of a real army, one that was capable of doing the job to which they had been assigned – eradicating the threat of the Red Sticks on the American frontier. Soon enough, he could turn his attention to the real threat to the new, struggling country: the British.

The army gathered back together and marched back to Fort Williams. Jackson sent out small groups to seek out and destroy any enemy encampments they could find along the way.

Jacob discovered, on the way back to the fort, through the haze of his grief, that most of the men who had traveled north with him from Alvarez Station had disappeared. The only ones left were Solomon and Henry Johnson. Where they had gone he had no idea. He assumed they had left for home after the battle. Perhaps some had been killed. They were not among the wounded, according to Solomon. So instead of setting up their own camp on the return to Fort Williams, the three of them attached themselves to the campfire of Preacher and Sam. One of their number had been killed in the battle. Two others were among the wounded.

Upon their return to the fort, Jackson had his troops parade before him. He then addressed them, praising their courage and determination. The men cheered lustily at his words. Jackson told them they had broken the Creek Nation, and they wholeheartedly believed him.

The army rested. Day to day activities resumed for most of them. Jackson sent off smaller groups to ferret out any remaining Red Stick villages in the area. Once found, they were destroyed by fire. Any braves that were discovered were dispatched.

What was left among the Creek towns was a growing number of starving women and children. The winter had been a hard one. Their men had been busy plotting and planning against their enemies and had not seen to the needs of their families, in the bloodlust that had consumed them. The crops normally gathered in the fall and stored for winter by the women had been left neglected in the fields. They had been on the move to avoid their enemies. Now, they were suffering the consequences.

Jacob muddled through those days as best he could. The shock of losing his uncle had not yet worn off. At night, he had visions and dreams. In one, he saw his mother, her black hair flowing down her back, dressed in her finest, dancing in the town square of her little village during the Green Corn Ceremony. She turned and smiled at him as the ceremonial fire in the middle of the square burned brightly, signifying the rekindling of village life, where all transgressions of the past year had been forgiven and a new year dawned with a clean slate for all. Then suddenly, the death face of his uncle would appear, its mouth open as if to speak, and then blood gushing from it instead. He would awake with a shudder, sweating profusely.

Sitting around their campfire at night, Jacob did his best to keep up with the conversations and banter between his comrades. The talk always turned to the fate of any remaining Red Sticks. How many more were there? Where could they be headed? Could they expect another attack?

"Them scouts a' ours ain't seen no sign of 'em," Sam opined one evening. "And they're good scouts. If'n there were any left round here, they would a' tracked 'em."

"What do you think, Solomon? They are your people, after all," Preacher said.

"I don't have any idea at this point. As for being my people, that's only partially true. My people are the ones that stayed home and tended to their business. Many of them have taken up arms against the Red Sticks, you know. And some of them have paid a dear price for it." He rose and poked at the fire. "Not all Creeks are bad people. You must dispel with the notion that we are all the same. That just isn't correct. Look at us here – myself, my brother and Jacob. Do we look like the raging maniacs that we faced just a few days ago? I certainly hope we don't!"

Preacher replied in a soothing voice, "You are correct, Solomon. We should know better, after our people dealt with the Cherokee for so many years. Some were out for blood, some for peace. Yet here we are, with hundreds of them now supporting us. I fear the battle would have turned out differently without them being willing to cross that river and attack at the bend."

"That's how it is with the Creeks. Our loyalties depend upon the leaders we choose to follow. Take for instance, you white people. Are the goals and aspirations of the people in Tennessee the same as those in New York? Or Boston? Or England, for that matter? I should hope not," Solomon continued with passion. "I would imagine there are many of you who have no desire for this conflict with England. They would prefer peace over war."

"But it ain't the same," Sam chimed in.

"Why isn't it?" Solomon replied.

"I don't know fer sure. It just ain't."

"Is it because of the blood coursing through our veins? Have we not proven ourselves over the last few months to you, Sam? Look at Jacob. The loss of his uncle will have a profound effect on him for the rest of his life. We have come here willingly, to take up arms against people we once viewed as part of our family. What more proof do you need of our devotion to the cause?"

"Well I don't reckon I really thought about that. You fellers did a fine job, and that's the truth," Sam admitted grudgingly.

"These men have most certainly proven themselves. You can't deny that any longer, Sam. Perhaps it's time we take them as they are, and not judge them by what others of their kind have done," Preacher said.

Jacob could take it no longer and spoke up.

"Why must we continually choose between the heritage of our mothers and that of our fathers?"

There was silence.

"All three of us here were raised in a white man's household. Our attachment to the Creek nation comes from our mothers' family ties. We are not white and we are not Creek. We wander somewhere in between."

CHAPTER 14

THE MARCH CONTINUES

After a few days' rest, Jackson roused his army once again. His next target was the area known as Hickory Ground, at the spot where the Coosa and Tallapoosa Rivers meet. As they moved south, he was most anxious to join up with new troops that had been pledged to him. His superior, General Thomas Pinckney, had promised him militia companies from Georgia and North Carolina to bolster his own.

They slogged through the rains of early April. The weather slowed their progress, turning the ground on which they marched into a muddy morass that hampered their every move. Those on horseback had an easier time of it. The foot soldiers struggled as the mud splattered them up to their waists as they cursed and swore their way through each day.

All along the march, small groups of Creeks would approach the line of struggling soldiers. They were usually led by a lesser chief of the tribe. They would immediately be sent forward to Jackson himself.

Once they gained his attention, he would order that they be fed and then address them with a stern warning. "You must remove yourselves north, above Fort Williams. Take your women and children and move out immediately. I cannot guarantee your safety if you remain in this area."

With those instructions, Jackson was hoping he could cut the supply

121

line of resources regularly sent north by the Spanish and English in Pensacola. With his army between the two, he hoped his starvation campaign would help to defeat the enemy and thus spare the loss of more men on the battlefield.

He ordered General Coffee to take small groups of his cavalry and scour the countryside for any remaining Creek villages in the area. His command was to destroy any he found, but to spare any women and children he came upon.

Jacob found himself in one such group, along with Solomon and Henry, Preacher and Sam.

The rains continued. At times, it was so heavy it was difficult to follow the winding footpaths that made their way through the heavy underbrush and scrub pines.

At the end of the trails they would find the remains of a small village, mostly deserted, the huts that huddled around the large round meetinghouses, bereft and forlorn looking in the steady downpour that hampered them. At times they were met glumly by a few elderly or sick who had been left behind for the sake of convenience. It was harder for the inhabitants to flee while tending to them, so they were left to their own fate.

Despite the rains, the men were able to torch the buildings they discovered, and their progress could be gauged by the plumes of thick, black smoke that would rise up into the sodden air and that marked their path through the wilderness.

General Coffee seemed to be in good spirits whenever Jacob caught a glimpse of him. His round face and jovial expression, framed as it was by a large square jaw, could not be construed in any other way. Jacob resented the cheerful expression. To take delight in such destruction he found odd, considering the circumstances.

"Take no mind of him," Sam told him when he spied Jacob scowling at the leader of their expedition. "He's ain't a bad man. Coffee and Jackson go way back. They wuz business partners long before this here war started. He's most likely just happy to be doin' what Andy told him to do."

Jacob kept to himself. He was still in mourning and held a resentment for being selected for this particular sortie. He had seen enough spilled Creek blood to last a lifetime. Solomon, on the other hand, understood their purpose.

"Coffee will need us to communicate with any survivors we find," he told Jacob. "To get information from any of our people that we happen upon."

It was in one of the villages they came across that they made a grizzly discovery. That particular village had a rather large meeting house – much larger than usual. Curiously, some of the men entered it and looked upward. Hanging from arrows that had been placed on the ceiling were hundreds of scalps, mournfully hanging, like the ghastly trophies they were. Solomon was called to see if could decide their significance. It was he who looked closely enough at them to see that the hair color varied from scalp to scalp. He hurriedly left the building and scoured the compound for any survivors he might find. He came across an old woman, weak from hunger, lying on a mat in front of her decrepit hut.

"Hello, mother," he said in Creek.

"Who are you?" she replied weakly.

"I am Solomon. Son of Nila of the Alligator clan."

"And what is it you want, son of Nila? You have come here with the enemy," she replied.

"I would like to spare you, mother. I have some food for you." He reached into his pack and drew out a handful of parched corn.

She received it gladly and hurriedly stuffed her mouth. As she chewed, she eyed Solomon quizzically.

"What is it you want of me?'

"I see your council house has many scalps hanging. Some of them have the brown hair of the white man," he replied.

She looked at him in defiance. "We are a proud people, Solomon. Our braves gathered those and brought them home to show us their great courage when they faced the whites at their fort."

"Which fort?"

"The one south of here."

"It must have been a great fort to gather so many scalps."

"It was. Our men killed them all. They spared no one. This is the price that must be paid for invading our lands," she replied with a satisfied air.

"Was it the one they call Fort Mims?"

"Yes."

"Thank you, mother. We will share more of our food with you."

"I will die here, where I lays" she sighed weakly.

Solomon hurried away and sought out General Coffee.

"Sir, I have news."

"What kind of news?"

"Have you been told of the scalps hanging in the council house?'

"What about them?"

"I just had a talk with the old woman over there." He pointed to the shriveled body of the woman he had spoken with, lying before her hut. "She claims the scalps are those that were taken at Fort Mims."

"Is she sure?"

"Yes."

Coffee dismounted his horse and spoke to Benjamin Rawlings, his aide. "Do we have any other Creeks that can confirm it?" he asked.

"Sir, I speak Creek. I would be happy to talk with her."

Benjamin went over and engaged the woman in conversation. When he returned to the General, he verified Solomon's report.

"She seems positive, sir."

"Let's take them all down and examine them."

A half dozen men climbed the poles inside the council house and pried the arrows away from the ceiling. All the scalps were laid out on the dirt floor of the building. They were carefully inspected. All who did so concluded they must be from Fort Mims. The sheer number of them, and the telltale signs that they had been gathered at the same time, could lead them to no other conclusion.

General Coffee ordered a burial ceremony of sorts. A large pit was dug, and the scalps were carefully laid to rest. As some of the men heaped the damp earth over the remains, Preacher intoned a short prayer for the people whose lives had been taken that awful summer day.

When Jackson's army reached its destination – Hickory Ground, a well-known, large Creek village – he and his troops were surprised to find it deserted. All that was left were the buildings typically found in a Creek village – a large council house in the center with a series of huts and shelters placed around it. The wet, ashy campfires placed before the structures were long dead. The lonely ball field on the edge of the village had sprouted the weeds of the new spring, neglected and forlorn. Before his army could get their encampment set up, straggling groups of women and children, led by a handful of the once-proud warriors of their villages, made their way to Jackson's army to surrender.

Now it became the job of the army to feed this multitude of starving people. The number of them grew daily and soon it numbered hundreds. They came bearing the white flag of surrender. Within days, Jackson knew the Creek Nation had been defeated.

He didn't rest his army long at Hickory Ground. He moved his troops to what remained of Fort Toulouse, an old edifice erected decades ago by the French, just a few miles away, at the junction of the Coosa and

Tallapoosa rivers. Atop its ruins, his men built a new structure and dubbed it Fort Jackson, in honor of their commander.

As his men diligently cleared away the rubble of the old fort and proceeded to build the new stockade, Jackson was happy to accept the surrender of the numerous Red Stick war chiefs who appeared before him. He once again sternly ordered them and their people to move north of Fort Williams. He was not about to let the English get away with resupplying them.

But the capture of the man responsible for the massacre of Fort Mims still eluded him. Where was William Weatherford? Until he was captured, Jackson knew there was a chance the war could be rekindled.

There was much speculation around the campfires of the men busily constructing the fort. Jacob, Solomon and Henry were bombarded with questions about Weatherford and where they thought he might be.

"What are your thoughts, Solomon? You know the man, don't you?" Preacher asked.

"Yes, I know him. His plantation isn't far from my parents'. But as to where he might be, your guess is as good as mine."

"But surely you have an idea."

"Not really," Solomon responded.

"He could be anywhere," Jacob asserted.

"But you know him too, don't you?"

"I know of him. I could recognize him if I saw him. I have never had a conversation with him," Jacob replied, a tinge of anger in his voice.

"This here war would be over quick if'n we could git our hands on him. We all got business back home, ya know. We been gone months now," Sam interjected.

"Well, my thoughts are that he probably headed south, to Pensacola. I bet the fort there is chock full of Red Sticks," Henry opined.

Sam swore under his breath. "Them dirty, filthy redcoats and Spaniards."

"For all we know, he could be hidden on his own father's place, down on the Alabama River," Jacob said. "His father is quite wealthy and would have the means of shielding him."

"Surely the militia down there has kept an eye out for him."

"Maybe so. But who can say he hasn't headed north? He was a big follower of Tecumseh. Even though Tecumseh is dead, perhaps he's gone to seek shelter with the Shawnee," Solomon replied.

"Wherever he be, I hope we can get our hands on him soon. I got crops that need plantin'," Sam said.

The encampment was in a perpetual state of turmoil in the days that followed. Workmen were busy putting up the fort, sawing and hauling logs from the fertile forests that surrounded it, the first hints of spring showing in the new growth that sprouted from the trees that were chopped down. The draft animals and horses of the cavalry grazed peacefully on the new growth of nearby grazing fields.

There was a continuous stream of newcomers in the encampment – Creeks who had come to surrender, and the wagons and conveyances bringing supplies to the camp. The nearby Coosa and Tallapoosa were filled with the boats of suppliers. The crowds of people were thick at times. So thick, someone could slip in without anyone knowing.

Jacob noticed him while he was helping to haul water from the river to the fort. Great barrels had been filled, and he and a few others had loaded them on a wagon and were urging the hitched horses forward to the newly built, log-studded walls. The man was riding into the encampment on a thin, weary horse.

He was not an excessively large man. He was lean, with his head shaved on both sides and a long strip of brown hair growing down the back. There were feathers and trinkets woven into his hair, as was normal for a Creek warrior. He had a large, hawk-like nose and piercing eyes. He rode his horse with ease, looking straight ahead.

Jacob nudged Solomon, who toiled beside him.

"Isn't that Weatherford?" he asked.

Solomon looked up. "By golly, it is!"

Jacob and Solomon left their fellows to struggle with the hauling of water, and rushed over and followed Weatherford as he made his way into the fort. He dismounted when he approached the large, central tent in the middle of the compound. Jacob and Solomon could hear him as he spoke to the sentries posted at its entrance.

"I wish to speak to General Jackson. I am William Weatherford, the Truth Teller, chief of the Red Sticks," he said calmly.

The flap of the tent was flung open. Jackson appeared, buttoning up his uniform jacket. He sent a look of bewilderment at the man who stood before him.

"You are Weatherford?"

"Yes. I've come to surrender."

Jackson spoke not a word.

"Many of our warriors have been killed. My people are starving. Our women and children are dying for want of food. I've come to end their suffering." He spoke slowly, hesitantly, as he tried to convey his message in English. Even though he had been raised by a white man, he preferred the tongue of his Creek family.

Jackson opened the flap of his tent wide and indicated for Weatherford to join him inside.

Jacob and Solomon were soon joined by dozens of others, who gathered outside the tent. Word had spread quickly that Weatherford was there and in the process of surrendering to their unrelenting General. Some leaned in as close to the tent as they could, despite the warnings of the sentries. If they could just get a sense of what was being spoken inside . . .

After an hour or more, Weatherford left the confines of the tent. He mounted his horse and rode away. There were grumblings among the men as they saw him leave.

Jackson, still inside the tent, contemplated the meeting that had just taken place. He had been impressed with the bravery shown by his opponent. It took a great deal of courage for the Red Stick to put himself in the hands of his enemy. He had directed the many Creek chiefs who had already surrendered to bring him Weatherford, the architect of the Fort Mims massacre. His original plan had been to put him in chains once he had him in hand. But the eloquence of the Red Stick chief and the complete surrender he offered had thrown him off.

He directed Weatherford to relay a message from him to all the remaining chiefs who still desired war. If they did not surrender and meet all his demands, the war would continue. No mercy would be shown to any who resisted him. He would destroy what was left of their people. He would see to it that their women and children were left without any sustenance, and if caught, their warriors would be given no quarter.

And so, with a mixture of awe at the bravery displayed by the war chief and his utter distaste for the unnecessary war he had helped to wage against the white man, and even his fellow Creeks who had disagreed with the bloodshed, Jackson decided his best option was to send a message far and wide to all that wished to continue the struggle. He let Weatherford leave in peace. He would be of more use to him alive than dead.

CHAPTER 15

THE PEACE

Jacob was in a turmoil that evening, as he and his messmates lounged before the fire. Finding the scalps of the poor souls who had lost their lives at Fort Mims had been awful enough. Some of those scalps belonged to people he knew – even distant relatives. Watching what remained of them being buried had left an intense sadness deep down in his soul. So many slaughtered – and for what purpose? His Uncle John had been killed trying to bring justice for them. And yet, there was no justice. It angered him to see Weatherford ride freely away from the fort. This man had led the attack. He was responsible for the deaths of all those people.

He didn't contribute to the heated conversation among those who lounged beside him.

"See here," Sam said. "If'n he can bring more folks to surrender and end this, then I'm all for it."

"It wasn't your friends and family that died at Mims," Solomon replied quietly.

"Maybe not. But I lost a few friends from this here army, chasin' those devils through the woods."

"Your army was created because of what Weatherford did. If he hadn't started this killing spree, all your friends would still be alive."

"If'n it hadn't been him, it would a' been someone else. Big Warrior, or even Menawa. Ain't he the fella that we just beat at the Bend?"

"That's what they say. How he managed to escape . . ."

"This is all needless speculation," Preacher interjected. "Jackson has made his decision. We all must learn to live with it."

Within a few days of Weatherford's surrender, General Thomas Pinckney appeared. He was an old soldier and statesman, having fought in the Revolution and had even been a diplomat and a member of Congress. He was cheered upon his arrival. Technically speaking, he was Jackson's superior, being in charge of the federal military of the southern district. Of course, the army that fought under Jackson didn't necessarily view him as such, although they held him in high esteem. The battles that encompassed the rest of the struggling nation were far distant and of little concern to the men fighting the Red Sticks.

News of the war up north had trickled down, through letters from home and an occasional newspaper that arrived, tattered and well worn. But most of the men stuck in the wilderness of the Mississippi Territory paid it little heed. Their war was occurring right then, in front of them. Survival against the Red Sticks is what they were most concerned about.

There was a large banquet prepared, at which the newly arrived General from Washington praised the efforts of the little army, and toasted the well-fought Battle of Horseshoe Bend. The men happily accepted the compliments. Despite the odds – with the shortages of men and supplies, the cunning ingenuity of the enemy, and the dense forests that surrounded them – they had eked out a victory that was already being celebrated throughout the rest of the country.

Pinckney announced that the army would be relieved of its duty. The peace between the volunteer army and the Red Sticks would be negotiated by others. They were free to go home.

Whoops erupted at the news. Yet Jackson maintained his authority. Three days later, he marched his army back to Fort Williams in preparation for their return to their homes in Tennessee.

Jacob, Solomon and Henry remained with the army for the time being. They listened to Jackson's farewell speech at Fort Williams, in which he extolled the virtues of the little army spread before him. He spoke of his great pride in their stamina and determination. That despite the deprivations and hardships, they had followed him and had sacrificed much for their hard-fought victory.

"The bravery you have displayed will long be cherished in the memory of your general, and will not be forgotten by the country to which you have so materially benefited."

After saying goodbye to the friends they had made from Tennessee, the three young men who had traveled a far distance to join them saddled their horses and headed south. Jacob, Solomon and Henry were unsure what to expect when they reached their homes. But they each carried with them new scars and experiences that would shape their futures in ways they perhaps did not understand. They had traveled north as mere youths. They returned as men.

The three returned using the same route they had used when they headed north. There were differences, however.

The small Creek villages they came upon were bereft of any living soul. It was as if a great hand had reached down and scooped the living up and deposited them somewhere else. The accouterments of life lay where they had been last used – blankets, farm tools, baskets of all sorts and sizes. Wood gathered to feed campfires lay in neat piles before the huts. They found hatchets and the materials needed to make bows and arrows. All left precipitously, as if the humans who used them had disappeared into thin air.

Mongrel dogs wandered within the confines of the towns, and at their approach the starving animals, barely alive, attempted to attack them. Out of pity for their sorry condition, the three used their hatchets to dispatch them. There was no sense that anyone would ever return to tend to them.

It was spring, the normal time for the Creek women to begin planting the corn, beans and squash that the tribe would depend on during the coming year. There would be no planting, no tending to gardens that year, at least not in that part of the Creek Nation.

Unwilling to fire their muskets for fear of the attention it might draw, Jacob, Solomon and Henry depended on the wild fruits and plants they could find among the forest and fields for their sustenance. A few days away from Jackson's camp, they found a beaver dam. They fashioned a couple of traps out of the soft, new shoots along the banks of the creek where it was located, then hid themselves nearby, downwind so as not to be detected by the delicate noses of their prey. They waited patiently into the night, and when they heard the rustling sounds of the curious beasts on the top of the dam, they rushed forward and dispatched two of the fat, furry creatures. It was enough meat to see them all the way home.

At night, around their campfire, they would discuss what could possibly lay ahead for them.

"Ma and Pa will be glad to see us home," Solomon said.

"They surely will. It's spring planting time. Pa said before we left he was hoping to add a room to the cabin. Maybe even build a new one. I'm sure Anna will be happy to see you on our return," Henry replied slyly.

"Who's Anna?" Jacob asked.

"Anna Perkins. You know her, Jacob. She lives a few miles from us, down closer to the river."

"Yes, I know her."

"Well, Solomon's been courting her."

"Isn't she a might young?"

"She's fifteen," Solomon declared defensively. "Not too young to know her own mind."

"Are you planning on marrying her?"

Henry laughed. "I suppose he is!"

"Maybe."

"Where will you live?"

"Pa's got a big place, you know. Almost three hundred acres. He can't keep up with it, even with our slaves. He said he reckoned I could have the back one hundred if I'd be willing to clear it. It's still got the pine forest that was there when he bought the land twenty years ago."

"What about you, Jacob? What are your plans?"

"I don't know."

"Well, I'm sure your folks will be glad to see you."

Jacob thought otherwise.

"They don't know where I've been. I suppose they will be happy to see an extra pair of hands," he replied, a tinge of bitterness in his voice.

The three parted ways when they reached the Alabama River. Solomon and Henry headed south while Jacob searched for a ferryman to take him across the wide, deep waters. He finally found old Mr. Winters, who had plied the river, taking passengers and supplies across for many years.

"Is that you, Jacob Worley?" He asked when he spied the young man, wrinkling his bushy eyebrows together and peering with intent at the man on the horse.

"It is, Mr. Winters."

"You've grown some since the last time I seen you."

"I suppose I have."

"Where you been?"

"I've been off fighting." Jacob changed the subject. "I see you've been able to resume your services."

"Yes. Things have calmed down since we heard about Jackson. Still not safe, but a man has to make a living. Here, grab that rope and help me. You're big and strong. No reason you can't do your share."

Silently, the two pulled themselves across, using the sturdy rope tied between the two shores. Once they reached the other side, Jacob thanked the old man and paid him with one of the beaver skins he and his companions had collected. He turned his horse and headed home.

As he approached his father's cabin, he saw that parts of the fence had fallen around the east field. He noted the weeds had taken it over, normally neatly plowed and seeded by this time of year. He entered the unswept yard before the house and dismounted.

Before he could get to the front door, it flung open. His stepmother stepped out, and he saw his three younger brothers peeping from around the door frame.

She was in a huff. Her face was puffy and red, and he observed she was even fatter than he remembered. She bore no resemblance to the young, healthy woman his father had brought home eight years ago.

She glared at him.

"Where have you been?"

"I've been off fighting with General Jackson."

Her voice raised. "Off killing your own kind? I don't believe you!"

Jacob made no reply.

"You and your dirty filthy relatives have destroyed what so many have spent years to build!" By now, she was screaming. Flecks of spit flew from her mouth; her face grew even brighter red.

Jacob looked around. "Is my Pa here?"

At that moment he spotted him, exiting the barn. The commotion caused by his wife must have caught his attention. He lumbered slowly over to where the confrontation was taking place.

"Here's your wayward son, Thomas. He claims he's been off fighting with Jackson." Sophia spat the words out, a look of disdain on her face. "I don't believe him! Do you?"

Thomas said nothing.

"More likely you've been off with Weatherford. Your kind always sticks together," she said.

"That's not true," Jacob replied, as calmly as he could.

She continued. "You should have been here, helping your father. If you had been, we wouldn't have lost our slaves."

"Sally and Moses?"

"Yes," she sneered. "Sally and Moses."

"They ran off a few months ago," Thomas said.

"I don't understand what that has to do with me. I wasn't even here," Jacob replied.

"You don't understand? If you had been here to help guard them, they would have stayed put," Sophia's voice rose once again.

Thomas said nothing. Jacob looked at him, as he stood with his arms folded and his gaze focused on the doorway of the cabin, while his three younger sons looked on, bug-eyed at the scene playing out in front of them.

"Do you have anything to say to me, Pa?" Jacob asked.

His father simply shrugged. He was caught in an awkward situation, he thought to himself. His anger at Jacob was real enough, but Sophia seemed to have matters well in hand. No point in adding his own frustration into the conversation.

"I don't want a dirty, filthy redskin living around my boys. You are nothing but trouble, Jacob. That's all you've been since the day I married your father. You have never carried your weight around here. Then you leave without a word, and your Pa and I have struggled mightily while you've been gone. Now we will have to replace the slaves you helped to escape."

"I had nothing to do with that."

"Oh yes you did!" she screamed at him. "How do you expect your father to carry all the burdens of running a farm without your assistance?" She was crying now. "I have no one to help with the house, or the cooking or the gardening, or to help tend to your brothers. Now your Pa will have to replace the slaves, at great cost."

"Am I to take it I am no longer welcome here?"

"Yes, you take it!" Sophia shouted.

"Fine. If that is what you want." He looked at his father. "Pa?'

"I must have peace in my household," Thomas muttered.

"There are a few things of mine in the barn. I will fetch them," Jacob said.

He gathered the reins of his horse and walked to the far corner of the barn where he had left a few of his belongings. There was a sturdy bow and a half dozen arrows in a quiver that his uncle had helped him make. He had hidden away a whetstone and an extra hatchet and knife under a small pile of old, moldy straw. He was surprised to see they were still there, but happy to have them. It was always wise for a man to have extra tools, he reasoned.

There were no tears. He had known all along that his stepmother held him in contempt. Not for anything he had done, but for the blood that ran through his veins. He was not particularly shocked that his father had gone along with his banishment. He, too, had never understood the predicament Jacob had to face every single day of his life. Was he white? Was he Creek? Where exactly did he fit in? He had sensed his father's disapproval ever since his mother's death, and all the time he had spent with his Uncle John. It had now, finally, been expressed through the vicious words of Sophia.

Once he had gathered his belongings, he led his horse out of the barn and mounted. His parents stood watching, his father with his head lowered, his stepmother with her arms crossed angrily across her large bosom.

"Go live with your uncle," Sophia spat out angrily.

"That would be impossible. He lies dead at the bottom of the Tallapoosa River."

And with that, Jacob rode off.

CHAPTER 16

THE RETURN

Jacob headed south. There was no particular reason for it. It was as if his horse decided on his own the direction they would take. Jacob held the reins loosely and allowed the animal to go where he would.

To say his rejection by his family did not hurt would be a lie. The stinging words of his stepmother and the silent response of his father to her cruel and unjustified insults would live with him for a very long time.

Within a day or so, he found himself at the confluence of the Alabama and Tombigbee rivers, where they joined together and formed the Mobile River. He gazed across the Tombigbee at Fort Stoddert, sitting as it did like a fat, lazy watchdog, as if it were taking a break from the humid, fetid air of summer under the cool relief offered under the spreading branches of a live oak tree.

Except there were no trees. And there was no activity, at least not any Jacob could see. As he drew closer, he noted there were not even any guards posted at the yawning entrance to the fort.

He crossed the river with some difficulty. There were no ferries or boats in sight. It looked like the whole area had been deserted.

He rode into the fort. There were a few soldiers lazing about, scratching themselves and looking disinterested in his approach. He stopped and asked if there was anyone in charge. The soldiers shrugged and pointed toward one of the blockhouses.

"See here," Jacob said. "Where is everyone?"

"They've gone. Just a few of us left."

He looked around and noted the ramshackle appearance of the fort. Weeds were growing on what used to be the parade ground. The men he spotted were unkempt, their uniforms in disarray.

Without another word, Jacob turned his horse around and left.

He continued south. It was just as well, he thought to himself. Interacting with others held no interest for him. He had not really wanted to happen upon someone he knew. It was better to be on his own.

But a decision had to be made. Where, exactly, was he heading? If he continued in the direction he was going, he would be in Mobile before long. Did he really want to go there? Did the sleepy city by the bay have anything to offer him?

He decided not. He stopped and set up camp and pondered his options. As he hung his tarp over the branches of a spreading oak, it suddenly came to him.

He remembered the idyllic time he and his uncle had spent last fall, hunting and trapping and answering to no one. Although those days were just a few short months ago, it now seemed like a lifetime. If he headed southwest, he would be there, in the same place, in just a few short days.

He checked his supplies. He had all he needed to set up camp anywhere he chose. He had a good supply of powder and shot, an extra hatchet and knives, a cooking kettle and the knowledge needed to supply his daily needs.

He arose the following morning with his plan set. Perhaps he had no home at the moment. But he had memories, and they would sustain him, he felt sure.

The heat of summer had already arrived, although it was only May. But Jacob, a man of the Mississippi Territory, was used to it. He knew how to hunt, and how to forage for his needs in the piney forests and lowland grasses, the bogs and creeks and ponds, alive with the sounds of all sorts of creatures that inhabited the land around him. He could survive on his own. His uncle had seen to that.

Soon enough, he found himself in familiar territory. He found signs of the encampments he and his uncle had set up before the last winter. He found the beaver dams and the groves of live oak, their low hanging branches touching the ground and providing a spreading cover when the quick summer rains fell. The ponds and bogs welcomed him as if he was an old friend. They readily gave up the bounty that lay hidden in their muddy, brown waters.

He moved frequently. He used his musket sparingly and tried to rely as much as he could on his other weapons so as not to alert anyone who might be close by of his presence.

The hunting was not good, it being too hot for most creatures to be about in the daytime, but he did manage to fell a few deer and an occasional bear. He used his bow and arrows for the deer, but to drop a bear he was forced to use his musket.

He would get up before dawn each day, as the hunting was better in the early morning. As the sun fell into the western sky, throwing out its orange and red hues, he would again take up his weapons and pursue what beasts he could.

He spent his days fashioning the snares and traps to use on the smaller game – the foxes and raccoons and beaver. He also used the time to stretch the skins of what he caught in frames and placed them before a fire to dry out. He made jerked meat the same way. He spitted the meat, after cutting it into thin strips, and dried it before the glowing embers of his fire.

The deer hides he soaked in water. Then, he would scrape off the hair and the fat that clung to the inside of the skin. He attached them to frames, and continually pulled and stretched them to make them more pliable.

In the evening, he often found himself caught up in the memories of his past. He thought of his mother and her untimely death. Of the close bond he had with his uncle, and the experiences they shared together in the very woods he now lived in. He tried not to hark back to the discord with his stepmother and father, and the loss of his home because of it.

At night, his dreams were filled with the horrors he had witnessed on the battlefield. The dismembered bodies, the blood, the savagery. Images of his swinging his hatchet at some faceless enemy would awaken him, sweat pouring from him at the horror he had been part of. He would arise and sit before what was left of his evening fire until he was sure he could sleep once more.

At times, he pondered the universe as he gazed skyward after darkness fell, the stars and moon glowing softly in the night air. He would breathe deep and slow, and wonder. He had been taught about many gods. The one worshiped by Christians, and the many gods worshiped by the Creek. It seemed to him that the Creeks had been misled by the prophets and seers of their people. They had predicted a complete victory over the white man. Some even insisted the guns of the whites could not kill them.

They had been proven wrong. He himself had witnessed the destruction of the Red Sticks at Horseshoe Bend. Surely, if the gods they venerated had been powerful, they would have prevented the ruin of the very people who held them in such high regard.

Other times, he thought about his own future. He decided he was a little jealous of his friend Solomon. His plans were set. He had a home and plans to marry. Jacob thought about Betsy Manford, a young, pretty thing that lived not far from his Pa's place. She had light hair and blue eyes and a nice figure. Not too plump and not too thin. He had always liked her but didn't know if he liked her well enough to marry her. Besides, he had nothing to offer a woman. He had no place, no profession.

Summer dragged on. The pile of skins he was stockpiling gradually grew. He kept busy, despite the brutal heat. He stayed in camp during midday, working on the furs and hides he had accumulated. He knew he would get a better price for them if they were cleaned thoroughly.

He attempted to repair his moccasins, though he was not satisfied with the result. Plying the needle he had fashioned out of a sliver of wood was awkward. He did what he could, and decided one of the purchases he would make when he made it back to civilization would be a pair of sturdy boots.

He also decided he needed to trade in the musket his father had bought him for a long rifle. The men from Tennessee had them, and they were far superior to what he was using. If a life of hunting was what he faced, he knew he would need the best weapon for distance shooting. His musket was not very accurate. He had to draw too close to his prey for it to be effective.

It was the second week of August when he decided he had gathered enough furs and hides to warrant a trip into Mobile. He had spent three months in the wilderness, and in all that time he had not laid eyes on another human being.

In preparation for his return to civilization, he attempted to scrape the beard he had grown. It was not easy as he had no mirror. The razor felt unwieldy in his hand, and he nicked himself several times, but the job was finally done. He bundled together the hides and skins he had gathered, tying them tightly together so that they would fit snugly on the back of his horse. He grabbed the reins of his steed, mounted, and headed east.

Jackson had been greeted in Nashville with great fanfare. He was feted and celebrated by his citizens and officials alike. Newspapers across the country trumpeted his victory at Horseshoe Bend, sorely needed good news during a time when the war against Britain was not going well. In response to his defeat of the Creek Nation, he was promoted and given command of the whole southeast, including the Mississippi Territory.

Yet, he was not satisfied that the victory had been complete. He was well aware there were a number of Creek warriors that had eluded him and had made their escape to Pensacola. Supplied by the British through their friends, the Spanish, who had control of that city, he foresaw that they would continue to wreak havoc among the settlers and frontiersmen in the territories.

Negotiations for peace were continuing at Fort Jackson in his absence. With his promotion in hand, he decided there was no one better to arrange that peace than he. After all, it was the blood of his soldiers that had been spilled. He and they, together, had gotten revenge for the massacre at Fort Mims. They were responsible for bringing the Creek Nation to its knees.

The call went out quickly. The troops gathered together once again, with new recruits anxious to share in the glory of which they had heard. Jackson would lead them south, back to the fort named after him, and see to it that the Creeks would no longer be the cause of heartache and pain. He had a plan, one that would not be well received. He would strip them of their southern lands and place a wedge between them and the devious, scheming British, who would continue to supply them with weapons of war until they themselves were defeated and driven from the continent.

There was a different air about Mobile when Jacob found his weary way there, after having some difficulty crossing the Dog River with his overladen horse. Perhaps it was the quick-stepping Americans he noted in greater numbers along the streets. The sleepy, drowsy town he had last seen appeared to be more alert and alive, despite the stifling August heat, than he remembered.

It was just a few weeks shy of the anniversary of his first visit to

Mobile, after the terror-filled flight from Fort Pierce, engineered by the resourceful Lieutenant Montgomery. He remembered crossing the choppy waters of Mobile Bay with his family. Much had changed since then. What safety and security he had enjoyed then was gone. His uncle was dead, he had withstood the trials and tribulations of the battlefield, and his parents had forsaken him. He was a man on his own now, not the youth he had been.

He immediately proceeded to Campbell's store, where he and his Uncle John had last traded their skins. When he entered, he noticed Bernard Hutchinson, his bald head managing to shine despite the dim light of the room, in an earnest conversation with another patron.

The man he was talking to was elegantly dressed, with a green coat embroidered with gold thread that fit snugly across his broad shoulders. He spoke with a slight Spanish accent, and used his hands, as well as words, to express his meaning.

"But Bernard, I fear this new treaty with have a grave impact on our trade with the Indians! Stripping them of so much land – how will they supply us with what our port depends on if they no longer control the hunting grounds?" he asked animatedly.

"I would not concern myself too much with that, Mr. Hidalgo," Bernard replied briskly. "We will have to depend more on what the plantations and farms produce. I think we will be just fine." He handed over a small packet to his customer. "Be sure to give my regards to your wife."

At that, Mr. Hidalgo glanced over his shoulder and spotted Jacob, looking him up and down. Jacob sheepishly wondered what he must look like, having not seen another human all summer. "Have a pleasant day, Bernard," the Spaniard said, and bowed and made his way to the door.

Bernard looked at Jacob. "I'm sorry to hear about your uncle. He was a good man and treated all with respect and fairness. He will be sorely missed."

"Thank you," Jacob replied.

"What can I do for you, young man?"

"I have some furs to trade," Jacob replied.

"Well, bring them in and let's see what you've got."

Jacob went outside and unloaded his horse, who whinnied in gratitude that the heavy burden had been lifted off his back. It took him a few minutes to get his bundles inside the store.

Bernard proceeded to dig through the piles. He had a slip of paper, on which he tallied the totals for each type of fur or hide. He eyed each one through his spectacles before he marked it down.

"Despite the time of year, you have done quite well," Bernard observed.

Jacob nodded in reply.

"What are you aiming to trade these for?"

"I was hoping you would have a long rifle. I would be willing to trade my musket in for it, along with any credit you could give me."

"Let's see your musket."

Jacob handed it over and Bernard eyed it, then hefted it on his shoulder and stared down the barrel.

"Looks to be in pretty good shape. I remember selling this to your father."

"It's seen some action. I carried it when I fought with General Jackson last winter and spring."

"I do have a couple of long rifles and you're welcome to look at them." Bernard went to a cabinet, unlocked it, and drew out two weapons.

"Best you get them now, before Jackson and his men arrive."

"What do you mean?" Jacob replied, stunned.

"Word is they're on the way here. I don't know how he managed it, but he got the Creeks to give up most of their southern holdings and now he's heading our way. We've been told he is preparing to confront the British."

"Here in Mobile?"

"All along the coast."

After a moment, Jacob replied, "Can I get a trade for this rifle?" He held up the one he had picked.

"I suppose so."

"I will also need some balls and powder. Oh, and a pair of sturdy boots."

"That will be fine. I think we can manage that."

After he left the store, Jacob mounted his horse, his new rifle in hand. He was unsure of the news he had just heard from Bernard. Could it be true?

He rode past the walls of Fort Charlotte and headed west once again. He decided to camp just outside of town, and searched for a dry patch among the bogs and marshes that dotted the area. He would need to think about his next step. Should he return to the wilderness or stick close to town and see whether Bernard had been correct? As he sat before his campfire that evening and chewed a piece of the dried meat he had saved in his pack, he decided to stay put, at least for a few days. If Jackson showed up in Mobile, he would have a big decision to make – rejoin his comrades or continue on with the lonely existence he had figured would be his lot.

Chapter 17

Decisions Made

Three days later, Jacob reentered the town, seeking information. As he walked his horse down to Royal Street, he noticed a certain amount of pep in the steps of the citizens he encountered. It was if they were expecting and waiting for some sort of big event. He heard the name "Jackson" spoken, jumbled up in sentences of French and Spanish. Some of the voices were angry, some were matter of fact. He looked for any faces he could recognize but found none.

He tied his horse to a post and wandered down the swampy area directly in front of Royal Street to the middle pier. The water in the bay was rough, crashing against the sturdy poles that held it in place. He gazed across the water and noticed a few boats, pitching and rocking through the waves as they made their way toward the docks. He glanced south and saw ominous storm clouds in the distance, their gray forms towering heavenward. He glanced north and saw a long canoe, straining and battling against the waves as it made its way to the pier on which he stood. There were four men in it, desperately battling the water that threatened to overturn them. As the canoe drew closer, he recognized one of the men who strained at an oar. It was Solomon, his black hair and dark skin noticeable among the packs and bundles that surrounded him. He called out to him and Solomon smiled and yelled back as the canoe drew near.

In between the men were bundles of furs and sacks of grain. The harvesting of corn in the fields to the north had begun. Solomon sprang out of the canoe as he and the others did their best to tie up to the pier.

"What are you doing here?" Jacob asked.

"I decided to come down with this load of goods sent by my Pa." He turned to the last man to alight from the canoe. "James, will you see to it these goods are given to our account? Campbell's store."

"Where's Henry?"

"He's at home."

"Where are you staying?"

Solomon, with a sobering look, replied, "I haven't decided yet. I came at the last minute."

"I have a campsite west of town. You're welcome to stay there with me."

The two of them climbed up to Royal Street. Jacob untied his horse and they walked through and past the town with few words spoken between them.

As Jacob rekindled the fire before his tent, he looked at his friend and decided it was best to stay quiet and not ask any questions. Solomon looked tired. He was not his normal, talkative self, so it was not hard for Jacob to realize something was bothering him.

"Anna refused my proposal," Solomon stated with a dead, flat tone to his voice.

"I'm sorry to hear that."

"While I was gone, fighting, she found another."

"Who?"

"Some fellow she met. He was part of the militia. Came from St. Stephens."

Both were silent for some time. Solomon poked at the fire before them, his head lowered.

"You heard about the treaty, of course," Solomon said.

"Not much. Just that the Creeks handed a large part of their lands over to the government."

"Folks at home are pretty upset."

"How so?"

"Jackson took millions of acres, Jacob, and gave them to the government. All the Creeks are now confined to the northern region of their territory. Hundreds of families have been uprooted. Their homes are gone, their lives in tatters."

"What about those of us who helped Jackson win against the Red Sticks? Surely we have been spared."

"We were given no consideration. In fact, he blamed us for allowing Tecumseh to come down here and stir things up. Big Warrior represented us before Jackson and pointed out our contributions, but it did no good. His mind was made up. Of course, we all know that hundreds of Red Stick warriors escaped and are now operating out of Pensacola. Jackson is determined to keep them separated from the rest of the Creek Nation. He means to use the land taken as a buffer between them and the upper tribe. If he can keep them separated, he believes there will be peace."

The deep, dark rain clouds that Jacob had spotted to the south of Mobile began to roll in late that evening. The winds picked up, thrashing their way through the camp where the two huddled, trying to sleep despite it. By morning, torrential downpours were upon them. The spread of canvas Jacob had used to form a tent was of little protection, as the winds howled and tore through it. No attempt was made to start a fire. It would have been impossible.

By late afternoon the sky had cleared, and the two men got to work resetting the camp. Most of the wood Jacob had gathered had been soaked through, but they managed to find a few pieces buried deep in the pile that were still dry, and they set it ablaze. As they hunkered down before the small fire, they discussed their plans.

"I'm not sure what to do. I thought I would try to find some work at the docks. I have no desire to return home anytime soon. Too painful, with Anna gone," Solomon said mournfully.

"You could always be my hunting partner," Jacob suggested.

"You're a much better hunter than I. My mother had no brothers, so I didn't get the guidance you did, Jacob. I spent little time with her people. My father has always been a farmer and had no real interest in hunting. Besides, it would be too lonely of a life."

"I could teach you."

"Thanks for the offer. I will consider it," he replied. "I've also been thinking of joining back up with Jackson." Solomon paused. "I think in some ways he's right. The British have caused enough trouble. Their meddling in our affairs needs to stop. If it weren't for them, the war among our people would have died out. If the British hadn't supplied the Red Sticks with muskets and encouraged them to war, things would be different. The only way we can stop them is to send them back across the ocean."

"Jackson is a hard man."

"He is. But he always treated us fairly when we were fighting under him. He did his best to see to our needs and had trust in us."

"They say he will be here any day."

"You could join back up, too. I see you've got a long rifle now. And a horse."

"I hadn't really thought about it. I'm not sure that would be a good choice for me."

"Well, at least think about it. We could do some good."

The next day, the two entered town, only to find it swarming with militia. They had floated down the Alabama River with Andrew Jackson, and they seemed happy to be on solid ground once again.

The two hurried along the street, through the throngs of volunteers and militiamen milling around. They looked to see if they recognized anyone, but did not.

Once they reached Fort Charlotte, they peered inside and saw men busily setting up tents on the parade grounds. Surely, Jacob thought, there wasn't enough space there for the hundreds of men milling around the town.

"Let's go to Campbell's store and see what Bernard has to tell us," Jacob said. He knew of no one else to ask.

Just as they reached the front of the store, a familiar figure called out to them.

"Hey boys!" It was Sam. He was standing in the street, his rifle tucked into the crook of his arm. Jacob noted wryly that he wore the same stained buckskin shirt from the previous spring.

Before they could speak, Sam continued. "Surprised to see me, ain't ya?"

"A little. What are you doing here?"

"Well, I decided wherever Jackson goes, I'll just tag along. Figgered he could use my help."

"Is Preacher here?"

"Yup. He's around here somewheres."

"I thought you all had business to tend to at home."

"Well, I got my crops planted. Harvestin' will be tough without me, but it'll get done. My wife'll see to it as best she kin."

"I'm a little concerned about all the confusion. What's happening?" Solomon asked.

"Don't worry 'bout it. Andy's got things under control."

"It doesn't appear that way."

"Well, he planned on usin' the barracks at that sorry excuse for a fort." He paused and pointed a finger south toward Fort Charlotte. "But they ain't fit fer it."

"So what's he going to do?"

"He's settin' up tents for the officers. Rest of us, he's tryin' to get the fine folks of Mobile to put us up." He grimaced wildly, indicating he didn't think much of the fine folks of whom he spoke. "They ain't too happy about it," he concluded.

"I have a small camp just on the outskirts of town. You and Preacher could camp with us," Jacob said, grudgingly.

Sam eyed him warily. "You sure?"

"I supposed it could support a few more people."

Sam looked around. "Let me find Preacher. You fellas wait here." He disappeared into the throng of men that had congregated along Royal Street. He reappeared a few moments later with Preacher.

"Glad to see you boys!" Preacher said with a smile.

The four tramped through the muddy streets, past Fort Charlotte and through the outskirts of town to Jacob's camp. The two newcomers unloaded their packs. They attached their lengths of canvas to Jacob's, and he had to admit it was now a fine shelter.

"So, what are your plans?" Preacher asked, once they settled down before the fire.

"I think I might want to join back up," Solomon said.

"Well, you would be most welcome," Preacher said. "Anyone who knows these parts would be an asset."

"I don't know them as well as Jacob."

"Jacob?" Preacher asked. "What about you?"

"I don't know. Being a soldier is tough business, and Andrew Jackson is a tough man."

"He is, no doubt," Preacher nodded.

"But you fellas gotta realize these is tough times," Sam piped in. "Them filthy redcoats have done enough to us already. They aim on destroyin' us," his voice raised. "We ain't gonna let 'em take us back! Too much blood's been shed to get rid of them the first time. Our Pa's done us a favor by kickin' em out the first time! We can't let it all slip away!"

"But you have to understand, Sam, that fight didn't happen down here. The people in these parts had no part of that fight," Solomon said.

"Well, maybe not. But you're a part of it now. These lands belong to us. What happened in the past here has little bearing on the situation at hand," Preacher said. "The British are not your friends. If it hadn't been for them, the bloodshed we have all witnessed would most likely not happened. It was them who gave the Red Sticks the means to fight. They did the same during the Revolution. They sent the Cherokee against our folks then as well. They must be stopped. We must control our own destiny, without the interference of the British. Even now, there are hundreds of Red Stick warriors sheltered in Pensacola, just waiting for a chance to continue their fight. They are being aided and abetted by the British. We must do our part to finish them off."

"We heard about the treaty at Fort Jackson."

Preacher winced. "Yes, to some, that would seem unfortunate. I will admit that Jackson could have been more considerate of the Creeks who fought alongside him at Horseshoe Bend. But there is no getting around it – these lands are meant to be settled. There is no holding back, gentlemen. Our people need land, and they will get it."

Preacher reached across and squeezed Jacob on the shoulder. "At least, give it some thought. We could use you."

That night, Jacob lay contemplating the stars. After the previous day's storm the sky had cleared, as it often did following a gale. He thought about his prospects and his future.

He knew there was no going home. His father and stepmother had made that perfectly clear. And now the war he had left had suddenly reappeared. Jackson's plans were well known now. There would be no peace along the Gulf Coast until he rid it of the British and faced off with the Spanish. There was no place for him to hide. No place that could shelter him from the coming storm.

He thought about his Uncle John, and how much he missed his sage advice. What would he advise? A picture of his uncle's dead body disappearing under the waters of the Tallapoosa River flashed into his mind. What, exactly, had he died for? What would he expect of him?

He decided right then. His uncle would want Jacob to finish what they had started. Sometimes peace could only come by means of war. There were still Red Sticks, ready and willing to continue the fight, protected by the British. Until their flame was extinguished, there could be no peace. Jacob determined he would do his part to end the conflict that had deprived him of the one person he had held most dear.

The people of Mobile did not like Andrew Jackson. Not one bit.

The French had originally built the town in 1702 farther up the Mobile River on Twenty-seven Mile Bluff, but it had been flooded out. The resourceful colonists had simply moved to the present site in 1711, where they constructed a fort, then known as Fort Louis. Later, they rebuilt it of brick, instead of the original mud and logs, and renamed it Fort Conde.

There they happily established a trade with the Indians that surrounded them – the Chickasaw, the Choctaw, the Creeks, and various other, smaller tribes. For fifty years, the French maintained their dominance of the area until the Seven Years' War, when the British cleared them out of the territory. In 1763, the people of Mobile quietly succumbed to the new order of things, including the name change of their beloved fort to Charlotte.

English rule had not been so irksome. They had tolerated their Roman Catholic faith and allowed them to carry on as before. When the American Revolution took place, it had little effect on Mobile, other than being a refuge for a small flood of Loyalists after the war ended.

Of course, that happened right after the Spanish had taken it into their heads to snatch Mobile from the British in 1780. The British soldiers in the fort had endured a brief siege of only two weeks. The British gave way, and then Mobilians were under the rule of the Spanish. For thirty-three years they remained under the control of Spain until General Wilkerson forced his way onto the scene and demanded the Spanish leave. According to the Louisiana Purchase, they were now considered to be part of the United States.

It was all so very tiresome. During the humid, cool winters and the horrendously hot, steamy summers, the people of Mobile had endured much. Unlike most places in America, they were a truly cosmopolitan city, with the French, Spanish and English doing their best to get along. They were never in a hurry – the weather didn't allow for that – and were quite satisfied with the status quo. Their lives had a symmetry to them – a routine.

And then Jackson burst in. He was in a rush. He was demanding. He was not one to mince words. He had a plan, and he meant to see it through, whether the people of Mobile liked it or not.

He had brought with him thousands of soldiers that flooded their town and put a strain on their resources. Food and fodder was in short supply, and the townspeople resented having to share what they had. Jackson was also insistent that they help house these ruffians, these men who spoke neither French nor Spanish. Uncouth, the lot of them.

When they gathered at church to celebrate the Mass or met each other in the stores and other establishments in the city, they quietly discussed the stressful situation among themselves. They had tolerated the English and the loyalists from the American Revolution that had filtered their way into their midst in the past. When General Wilkerson had come and taken over Fort Charlotte for the United States just last year, he and his men had been quite decent about it. General Flourney, who had replaced Wilkerson, had the good sense to stay in New Orleans and had left them alone. But these new Americans – these hard charging, rude and vulgar men that had invaded their quiet place – were a different matter entirely. They would suffer their presence but were in no hurry to make it easy for them. The newcomers would have to bend to the will of the people of Mobile, they told themselves. It would take more than General Jackson to change their town.

CHAPTER 18

JACKSON PREPARES

Andrew Jackson never much liked the Spanish. After the Louisiana Purchase in 1803, he resented the way they clung to the continent. The Purchase was between the French and the Americans. Spain's holding in Florida was not part of the bargain, unfortunately. This was an American continent, in his view. He believed they should pack up and go home, back to the confines of Europe.

After he arrived in Mobile, he sent a flurry of letters to his superiors in Washington, imploring them to allow him to attack Pensacola and end Spanish control of the city. Not only were they sheltering the remnants of the Red Stick Creeks, but they were allowing the British to use the fine harbor there, which could provide a jumping off point to attack the newly acquired American lands along the Gulf Coast.

His superiors, including Secretary of War John Armstrong and President James Madison, were all in a tither, afraid Jackson would ignite a war against Spain, which would be catastrophic for the new nation. They were in a fight for their lives against the British. They could not afford to antagonize Spain.

But Jackson was betting Spain was in no position to conduct a war. They were no longer the dominant force of previous years. The Spanish homeland had been wracked by war since Napoleon's invasion and had survived only through an embrace of the British. They were meantime beset with numerous revolts all across their colonies in the Western Hemisphere. Waging war against the United States would not be in their best interests.

Jackson's goal all along, even before the Creek War, was to protect the American city of New Orleans. Whoever controlled New Orleans, controlled the mighty Mississippi River, which emptied the heartland of the United States and was a vital route for trade. If it hadn't been for the Creeks' inter-tribal war that had escalated into an attack on American interests, he would have already been there, preparing for the British attack both he and his superiors believed was coming.

His plans had been delayed by circumstances beyond his control, but he had not given up. He would see to it that New Orleans remained in the hands of the United States. If that included denying the British access to Pensacola as a staging ground, then he would take matters into his own hands, if need be.

For now, he must go about the business of denying the British any sort of base of operations from which to attack the city of New Orleans. Mobile and Pensacola were both small ports and small cities, but they had the potential to give the British what they wanted. He would do his best to see that didn't happen.

Jacob and Solomon both signed up for a six-month enlistment. Jacob wasn't sure it was the right thing for him to do, but his comrades had persuaded him. Sergeant Wilson, a grizzled old coot who sat behind a makeshift table at the entrance to Fort Charlotte, had them make their marks on the scraps of paper that outlined the terms. Preacher was with them, and he assured them of what they were signing. Jacob was relieved. His inability to read was usually of no consequence, but that day was an important one. He had never been asked to sign anything in his young life.

After they signed, Preacher leaned over the table and spoke. "Sergeant, is Lieutenant Blaylock hereabouts?"

The sergeant looked at him suspiciously, as he shifted the wad of tobacco in his mouth from one cheek to the other. "What you wanna see him for?"

"I have some information he might find useful," Preacher said smoothly.

"He's back there," the sergeant replied, using his thumb to point to the makeshift tents on the fort's parade ground.

"Let's go, boys," Preacher said.

The two young men followed Preacher as he nonchalantly meandered through the tents, looking this way and that, for the man he sought. Most of the men they spied were busy cleaning their equipment or sitting around talking. They paid little attention to the three as they wandered about.

Preacher spied the lieutenant. He was tall and thin, with tufts of reddish hair that stuck out of his forage cap every which way. His dark blue coat was rumpled, and the white trousers he wore were too short for his long legs. Jacob noted an impressive number of stains and wondered if perhaps they were what was holding his trousers together.

"Lieutenant Blaylock!" Preacher called to him.

The man looked blankly at him and made no reply.

"Sir, I have a couple of boys here you might be interested in."

The lieutenant looked Solomon and Jacob up and down and made no reply.

Preacher continued, "These fellows are from these parts. They might be useful to you for scouting duty."

"Is that so?"

"Yes, sir."

"Where are you boys from?" the lieutenant asked.

Solomon spoke up. "North of the Mobile River, along the Tombigbee."

"Are you Creeks?" he asked suspiciously.

"We both have Creek blood. Both our mothers were Creeks."

"Do you have horses?"

"I have one," Jacob said.

"How long did you sign up for?"

"They both signed for six months, Lieutenant," Preacher said.

The lieutenant nodded his head. Jacob noted his forage cap jostled slightly at the movement, indicating it didn't fit him any better than his trousers.

"I suppose I can use you. Where are you staying?"

"We have a camp to the west, just past the edge of town."

"Fine. Be sure to check in every day. I will be here, for now. I will let you know when I have need of you."

After picking up some provisions from the quartermaster – a few pounds of salt pork and a small sack of grain – they left the fort, and as they entered the town they noticed an uptick of activity down Royal Street, mostly around the building Jackson was using for his headquarters. There were several horses tied out front, and men were flitting in and out. There was no other activity in sight. They didn't set eyes on a single civilian as they made their way west to their campsite.

Sam was there where they had left him. Preacher handed him the provisions they had picked up. He unwrapped the salt pork from the burlap sack and gave it a sniff.

"Don't know how they think we's supposed to fight when they feed us this!" He threw it down next to the fire in exasperation. "It's done spoiled in this damnable heat."

Jacob laughed. "Have you ever eaten alligator?"

"Can't say I have," Sam replied. "Is it any better than that?" He pointed with disgust at the salt pork.

"Most definitely," Solomon replied.

"You two wait here. We'll be back soon," Jacob said.

He and Solomon retrieved their bows and arrows. They followed a footpath heading straight west. They soon came upon a series of bogs and small ponds. They crouched beside a small stream that connected them and silently took stock of what lay around them.

They soon spotted their prey. Among some fallen timbers, they noticed three or four alligators sunning themselves in the noonday heat. Quietly they approached and Solomon whispered to Jacob.

Let's take the one nearest us. It's only about four feet long. I'll take the first shot and then you can finish him off."

Jacob nodded.

They crept up as silently as they could. Solomon rose suddenly and shot the animal in the side of the head. His quick movement frightened the other animals, and they slid quickly into the water. The wounded alligator flopped into the water and began thrashing its tail. Blood from his wound trailed into the muddy water. Jacob rushed forward and shot it in the back of its head with an arrow, killing it. Its carcass rose slowly to the surface.

Jacob grabbed it by its thick, muscular tail, threw it over his shoulder and they quickly retraced their steps back to their camp. They flung the animal down before the fire.

Sam looked at it in disgust. "How do ya eat them things? Me, I might have another think 'bout that salt pork."

Solomon had drawn out his long knife and was busy cutting off the tail. He worked quickly and deftly.

"The best meat is in the tail," he explained. "We'll spit it over the fire and let it cook for awhile." He had removed the thick skin of the beast and cut the meat into chunks. Jacob got the spit and strung the meat along it and then placed it over the fire.

"Must be an Injun thing," Sam said as he watched them work.

"True. We do like our alligator. But they are plentiful around here, and everyone enjoys it when they can get it," Solomon answered. "Sometimes we eat it like this, over a fire. But sometimes folks will make a stew or a soup with it. Very fine eating."

"Well, I'm most certainly happy to try it," Preacher said.

As they watched their dinner cook, the four struck up a conversation about what they had to look forward to.

"Andy's been fumin' about New Orleans ever since we got into this dang war," Sam said.

"He most certainly has," Preacher replied. "But don't forget Pensacola. They've been a thorn in our side for decades. Even back during the Revolution, the British used it as a base to send supplies to the Cherokee, who terrorized our own folks at home."

"That's the truth," Sam nodded.

"What do you think our next move will be?" Solomon asked.

"I don't know for sure," said Preacher. "But I do know this – we will wind up in New Orleans, one way or another. You can bet on it. The General will not let the place continue to go undefended. But as to what will transpire before we get there – your guess is as good as mine."

Once the meat on the fire had finished cooking, Jacob used his knife to cut off chunks and placed them on slabs of bark and handed them around. There were a few moments of silence as they hungrily gnawed on it.

"Hey, this ain't half bad!" Sam exclaimed as he chewed noisily. "And it's a sight better than that old salt pork! A fella could get used to it mighty quick!"

"Tomorrow I'll make you a stew with it," Jacob said.

Sam nodded vigorously. "Sounds good to me!"

Pierre Durand sat dejected on an empty keg he found on the marshy ground between the city of Mobile and the three piers that jutted out into the muddy waters of the bay. He watched balefully as a large group of men, more than 150 from the 2nd U.S. Infantry, tried to wedge themselves onto a group of barges and flatboats anchored along the piers. There was much shouting and confusion as they went about it. It was late August, and the heat was withering. The men sweated and cursed and jostled each other as they tried to find a place to seat themselves among the boats.

At this rate, he thought, it will be several hours before I can catch a lift across the bay. It was bad enough he was being sent away, but to bide his time among the stinking grasses and muck along the shore while these soldiers dithered about was almost more than he could bear.

His drinking spree over the last few weeks had been the final straw for his father. He had written an acquaintance, Raphael Allard, who owned a large plantation along the eastern shore of Mobile Bay, to see if he had a use for his wayward son. He could no longer tolerate his drunken behavior. It had affected his ability to concentrate and had culminated in several mistakes in the ledgers he was supposed to keep for the family's business. Allard had replied that he did have a need for a bookkeeper so his father was sending Pierre off, in the hope that he would straighten his life out. At least, there wouldn't be as many taverns or bawdy houses across the bay to tempt him.

Louis and Eloise Durand had done their best, in their minds, to raise their children properly – three sons and two daughters, with Pierre being the oldest. They had seen to their education, sending them to classes at the Church of the Immaculate Conception, to learn their scriptures and the teachings of the church. Further education at home had come from both parents. All of their offspring had been given lessons in reading, mathematics and languages. They had done their best to keep them away from bad influences, and to honor those that had come before them.

The Durands were very proud of their French ancestry. Both lines of the family had been among the first French settlers in Mobile. So proud, in fact, that they discouraged their children from having much to do with the Spanish and the English that had settled there when Mobile had changed hands. These new people were upstarts, in their opinion. Better to stick among their own kind.

At times this had been difficult, particularly at church. Thankfully, the Mass was read in Latin, so the Spanish priests who had taken over the church had not had too much influence. Of course, they had to rely on those very same priests to educate their offspring in the ways of their faith, but that couldn't be avoided. They went to Mass and to the feasts and memorials, but spent their time while there with other French citizens.

Louis Durand was in the Indian trade. He had built a fine business through the years, a culmination of hard work and long hours. In Mobile, he was one of its more prosperous citizens, as could be seen by the storefront he maintained on Royal Street and the possession of one of the largest homes in the city.

Pierre had always known that his parents expected much of him. For most of his life he had been cooperative. He had been born with a gift for languages and had picked them up quickly. He could read and write in both French and Spanish and had a tolerable ability to navigate English as well. This, along with a knack for mathematics, had been a great benefit to his father. As the eldest of his children, Louis was planning on making Pierre a partner one day, and then, when he died, the sole proprietor of the Durand Company.

But then there had been Rosa.

Pierre had met Rosa Alonso when they were still children. She was two years younger than he, so he took little interest in her at first. He and his friends viewed the younger girls in town as nothing more than annoyances. They hopped and skipped and chattered endlessly whenever they were about. The boys had more important things on their minds, like who could run the fastest or jump the highest.

But then she matured. At fourteen she was already turning the heads of Pierre and his friends. She had a way about her that would interest any man. Growing full-figured with dark hair and deep brown eyes, and a golden skin tone common among the Spanish, she could set his heart racing by simply being near her.

He couldn't tell whether she had any interest in him, as she was usually escorted by her older brothers when in public. Occasionally, she would throw him a quick side glance accompanied by a sweet, simple smile. He could feel himself blush at her gaze. He would softly curse under his breath, sure that the heat of his face from the blush would show and give away his feelings.

He began to keep track of her routines. What times and what days she would venture out, and which times she would be by herself – very rare – and which times she would be escorted by her male relatives. After a few weeks he decided he would take a risk and speak to her while she was hurrying between her home and that of her grandparents.

He decided a bold approach would be the best.

"Good morning, Rosa," he spoke cheerfully as he neared her.

She looked at him, slightly startled. "A fine day, Pierre."

"I was wondering if I could walk with you to your grandparents' house."

"How do you know where I'm going?" she asked, laughing.

"I don't know," he smiled. "I just assumed."

And so it began.

There were other young men craving her attention, he knew. They called at her home regularly. But Pierre was determined. He knocked at the front door of her parents' home a few days after their encounter and asked if he could call on their daughter. Mr. and Mrs. Alonso had no objections.

Pierre was very happy. He and Rosa laughed and talked and enjoyed each other's company despite the chaperoning of her mother whenever he appeared. The small, stuffy parlor of the Alonso home saw him frequently over the next few weeks. He was allowed to accompany her now, when he was not at work at his father's business, along with her brothers, when she took to the dusty streets of Mobile.

He had not talked to his parents about his interest in Rosa, but word soon got out. It was a small town, after all, and wagging tongues were as common there as anywhere else. After only a few weeks, his father confronted him when he arrived at work one morning.

"What is this I hear about you courting Rosa Alonso?" his father asked sharply, as he peered over his spectacles, a deep frown creasing his face.

Pierre responded, "Yes, I have asked permission from her father to call on her."

"Don't you think you should have discussed this with your parents first?"

"I'm not sure why that would be necessary."

"Come now, Pierre, you know how your mother and I feel about the subject. You should be showing your favor to someone of your own stature. The Alonsos might be fine people, but they do not have what we have."

"You mean they aren't French," Pierre quickly retorted.

"No, they are not. And besides that, Mr. Alonso is nothing but a simple carpenter. I'm surprised he is able to maintain the home they reside in."

"He's a good carpenter, father. He has three laborers who work under him."

"Pierre," Louis Durand responded sternly. "I don't want to argue with you about this matter. There are several young French ladies you could be spending your time with." His voice softened. "What about the daughter of Jean and Marie Dubois? Young Marie would make a suitable match for you. Her father is in the same business as we are, and is almost as successful. She would be more acceptable to your mother and me."

"I think it should be up to me to decide whom I choose to court," Pierre replied stubbornly.

For all of his young life, he had done his best to follow the rules his parents had set forth for him and his siblings. But on this one matter, he would not budge. Rosa was worth the defiance, he decided. She was beautiful and witty, smart and engaging. She was all he could hope for.

As the months went by, Pierre did his best not to displease his parents in any other matter while he pursued Rosa. He attended Mass and scrupulously followed his father's instructions at work. Still, there were heated arguments in his home over the courtship, and at one point his father tried to command him to stop seeing her. But Pierre wouldn't listen. He was in love, and there was nothing his parents could do about it.

And then, just like that, it was over.

The swamp fever came to town and took his Rosa. It happened quickly and suddenly, and Pierre was heartbroken. At eighteen, he lost the love of his life. The injustice of it almost drove him mad. He took solace in the only way he could find – the bottle. He could forget the one person who had given meaning to his life only by drowning himself in drink.

His drinking led to more arguments at home. When not at work, he spent his time at the local taverns and would stumble his way home in the small hours of the morning. He would bang on the back door until Claudia, their cook who slept on the floor of the kitchen, would let him in.

His parents were aghast at his behavior. They had little sympathy for his situation, and since they had never approved of his relationship with Rosa, they could not understand his pain. They only saw their son, who had always been so obedient, falling into a deep, dark pit. If only he would listen to their advice and accept the harsh reality that Rosa was gone and that he must move on. But no amount of persuasion could get him to change. The drinking was affecting his work, and his exasperated father did not know what to do. And so he decided his only alternative was to send him away. Perhaps a change of scenery would set things right.

Pierre was relieved once the soldiers on the pier had been loaded. He watched as the barges and skiffs that contained them headed south on the calm, muddy waters of the bay. He looked to the east and saw a small sail heading his way. He had a few coins. Perhaps he could persuade its captain to give him a lift. As for what lay ahead of him, he did not know.

CHAPTER 19

FORT BOWYER

Fort Bowyer was a small, low-walled fortification that had been hastily thrown up at the mouth of Mobile Bay, on the eastern side, when the United States had taken control of the area from the Spanish in 1813. Made of logs reinforced with sand, it wasn't much to look at, but it did contain fourteen impressive cannon arrayed along its crescent shape. For some reason, it had been abandoned earlier in the summer, but with word now out that the British had forced themselves onto the Spanish city of Pensacola, Jackson grew worried. His spies had reported that the British flag now flew over that city, equal in height to a competing flagpole with the ensign of Spain.

Jackson felt as if he were in a spider's web, the clinging strands an impediment to any forward movement. Which way would the British go? Were they prepared to attack Mobile and use it as a base to terrorize the new American territory just to the north in the Mississippi territory or Georgia, or use the large and deep harbor of Pensacola for the same purpose? He knew also that either port would be acceptable as a staging base for the capture of New Orleans, a city that the British were desperate to control, as it sat among the swamps created by the flowing waters of the Mississippi River.

He wrote letters; lots of them. He informed his superiors in Washington of the impending disaster he saw coming, and of the threat of British ships now anchored in Pensacola Bay. He wrote to the Spanish Governor of Pensacola – stern letters informing him that he knew of his treachery. Spain itself was neutral in the conflict. Why was he giving succor to the British? Why was he giving shelter to what was left of the Red Stick warriors who had trickled south after their defeat at Horseshoe Bend? He was also deep in correspondence with the citizens of New Orleans. Were they prepared for the storm that was approaching? Were the residents of that city aware of their perilous situation? If so, what preparations were they making to strengthen their city from the disaster that loomed over them?

The first thing he knew to do was protect his present position. He sent a strong contingent thirty miles south across the waters of Mobile Bay to repair Fort Bowyer and reinforce it. For that important work, he sent a force of regulars, not militia or volunteers. Among them were artillerists who understood the workings of the cannon already in place, and he felt confident the rest could be trained to use them effectively.

And then he waited.

Jacob and Solomon were making their daily trip into Mobile to check in with Lieutenant Blaylock when they noticed the hurried scramble of men moving to the piers. They looked past the marshlands and saw them loading themselves into flatboats and barges. Curious, they asked the Lieutenant what was going on.

"We're sending them down to Fort Bowyer. It's been left vacant. The General's afraid it will be attacked."

"By who?" Solomon asked.

The lieutenant gave him a withering look. "By the British, of course." His facial expression softened as he continued, "If they make it into Mobile Bay, we could be in serious trouble."

"Do you need any help?" Jacob offered. He was not used to having so much time on his hands. The waiting and watching for a time to be of use was taxing. Better to stay busy, he thought.

"Not today." The lieutenant eyed them both. "You're both big, strong lads. Perhaps you can be of some use when we send supplies."

It was now September, though the heat of summer had not waned. Jacob was used to it, but he felt a certain amount of sympathy for his comrades who had traveled south to join Jackson. Sam, in particular, was vocal about his discomfort.

"Is there any time a person kin get some relief from this heat?" he would complain. "It's even hot at night! This ain't no way for a man to live!"

Jacob and Solomon would laugh.

"You'll get used to it."

"Harrumph," he'd reply as he mopped his brow. "Even the rain ain't no help. It's like being showered by water heated over the fire!"

"Cooler temperatures will be here soon. And then, you'll complain of the cold and damp!" Solomon said.

"There's no place like home, right Sam?" Preacher would say.

A few days later, while Jacob and Solomon were checking in at the fort, the lieutenant hailed them from his tent.

"Boys, we're taking some supplies south later today. We will need your services."

"Yes, sir."

"I'll swing by the camp and let Preacher and Sam know we'll be gone for a bit," Solomon offered.

Later that morning, the two helped load a barge with foodstuffs – meal and salt pork – packed into heavy barrels. There were also kegs of fresh water that had been collected during the recent afternoon showers. They stowed themselves precariously on the side of the flatboat as it steered off into the bay.

Neither of them had been as far south as they were going. They watched the small city of Mobile disappear from view behind them just as they saw the hazy outlines of the eastern shore. It was cooler on the water. The soft breeze from the southwest wafted over them as the brown, silty water of the bay lapped at the sides of their small craft.

It was slow going, as the boat they were riding in was not made for speed, and the night sky was fast approaching when they spotted the stubby walls of Fort Bowyer ahead. It wasn't much to look at, Jacob thought. The walls were shorter than any fort he had ever seen, but he noticed the menacing cannon jutting out across the front of it and that gave him some comfort. He saw a crew of men working on the side of the fort facing them. They were packing sand around the vertical logs that comprised its walls. As the boat approached a shout was raised and the men ceased their labors.

Several gathered round to help with unloading the supplies. There was cheerful banter among them, despite their circumstances. Even though an attack was possible, the hardy men stationed there seemed to have little concern.

Jacob looked around at the fort. Its low-slung walls formed a semi-circle that faced out into the strait that formed the entrance to the bay. He noted the array of large cannon strategically placed along its sides. As darkness descended, it was decided the boat and crew should stay safely anchored beside the fort until the morning light.

There were more than 150 men camped inside, and they were in good spirits as they happily cooked the new supplies over their campfires.

Jacob and Solomon set up their own camp outside the walls. They hadn't brought much for shelter, but found a spot alongside the bastion on the land side of the fort to start their fire. Luckily, the skies were clear that evening, so they did not have to worry about rain. They hunkered down with their small packs and rifles and slept peacefully enough until the first light.

The following morning, as they were gathering their belongings, they were approached by a sergeant, who wore a tight-fitting blue jacket that had difficulty containing his rotund figure. The buttons of his coat strained as he raised his right arm and confronted them.

"Who exactly are you fellows?" he asked.

"We're scouts for General Jackson, sir," Solomon replied.

"Why are you here?"

"We came along with the supply boat. We helped load it and thought we could be of some use in unloading it."

"You ain't in uniform."

"We're volunteers, sir," Jacob said.

"The lieutenant would like to see you, I expect."

They followed the sergeant into the fort and into the presence of the lieutenant. His name was Montgomery but bore no resemblance to the man who had risked everything to save the lives of Jacob and his family more than a year ago at Fort Pierce. This one seemed rather impatient and arrogant, at least in Jacob's mind. He looked at them imperiously and demanded an explanation of their presence.

"As we told the sergeant, we're here as volunteers. We simply came to help unload the supplies," Solomon explained patiently.

"Well, I can't have you returning. Do either of you have any experience in warfare?" he asked haughtily.

"We both fought at Horseshoe Bend," Jacob answered.

"Have you any experience in scouting?"

"Yes, sir."

"Well, I have need of your services here. I'll send word back by the supply boat that I am requesting you stay. I have need of men to scout east of here, on the land side." He looked at the sergeant. "Take their names, then show them the trail nearest the shore." He turned to them.

"Take care you report back if you see any signs of the enemy. There are other scouts out, so be careful you don't mistake them for the British."

Jacob and Solomon followed the sergeant through the chaotic interior of the fort. Men were busily mixing sand and water and plastering it between the logs that made up the walls on the inside, while others sweated and cursed as they worked on the huge cannon, scrubbing them vigorously. There were men being drilled on the use of the big guns, with instructors demonstrating how to load and fire them. As they exited the fort, Solomon opined he was happy to be away from the confusion.

They trudged east, through large sand dunes and small groups of scrub pine. They saw the markings left by other scouts and did their best to follow them. To their right they could hear the crashing and rumbling of the waves against the shore, a sound unfamiliar to them, but somehow soothing, Jacob thought.

They spent their first night barely five miles from the fort. They didn't kindle a fire, as they were afraid it would be seen by others. They made their evening meal out of the jerked meat they had brought along, and found a place to sleep among the dunes, the white sand being soft and comforting.

They rose before the dawn and continued their eastward trek. The sun had barely risen when they spotted a group of men heading in their direction at a fast pace.

"Turn back! They've landed!" A lean man with a sharp, pointed nose shouted at them as they approached.

"What did you see?" Solomon asked.

"A large number of Indians and some Britishers just got dropped off by a big ship," he stated, waving his arms to the south.

"How far away are they?"

"Not far. We must make haste back to the fort," was the reply.

There were half a dozen or so men in the scouting party. The lean man led the way as they scrambled back over the dunes and forged their way west. Jacob and Solomon followed.

Solomon tried to get information from the group but got little response, other than an acknowledgment that the group of Indians appeared to be a mixture of Creek and Seminoles.

"Guess we'll just have to wait till we get back to Bowyer to find out anything of value," Solomon complained to Jacob.

"They have no obligation to share with us. They don't even know us," Jacob replied.

It took most of the day to reach safety. They all cursed at the sand dunes, some more than shoulder high, that impeded them. Climbing up and then down, from their peaks to their valleys, was exhausting. At one point, they drew closer to the sea and one man observed the tall, white sails in the distance. They were still a good way off the coast, but their intent was obvious. Once they were spotted, the small group of scouts redoubled their efforts to reach the fort.

Once they arrived, they found it in turmoil. All work on reinforcing the walls had ceased. The men were busy now, preparing for an assault from the sea. Balls and shot were being moved to the cannon, and small barrels of gunpowder were being rolled over to the big guns.

They found the Lieutenant in the midst of the turmoil. He was shouting orders when he spied the group enter the land side of the fort. He rushed over to receive his report.

"What did you find, Mason?" he asked the lean man with the hawk-like nose.

"A large group of men and Indians were dropped off a few miles to the east," he replied.

"How many do you reckon?"

"Not for sure, Lieutenant. We wanted to make tracks back here as quick as we could."

"You must have some idea," the lieutenant replied with an edge of anger in his voice. "Speak up, any of you. We must know what we're facing."

Another man from the group responded. He spoke quickly and excitedly, a look of terror clearly visible on his face.

"At least two hundred Indians, sir. And a hundred or so marines of the Royal Navy." He paused. "They were dragging three artillery pieces, sir."

The lieutenant looked at him piercingly. "Good man. At least one of you had the foresight to count."

He made his way to the center of the compound and spoke to Lieutenant Lawrence, the officer in charge. They watched as Lawrence stepped forward and blew a whistle. All the men stopped what they were doing to hear what he had to say.

"Gentlemen, as you know we have spotted four sails out in the Gulf. I've also received word that a significant land force has landed east of us." His voice grew louder and more determined. "But we are ready for them. I will assign those of you not engaged with the cannon to place yourselves on ramparts along the north and eastern side of the fort." He paused for effect. "I need not tell you that our situation is perilous. We are facing a force much greater than our own. But those we protect are depending on us, men. We cannot let them down! We must fight to the end!" The men gathered around him began to cheer. Lawrence finished, "We must not give up the fort!"

The rest of the day and evening were spent in nervous anticipation. Jacob and Solomon learned that Jackson had made an appearance at the fort while they were gone, to fuel the fire of patriotic fervor in the hearts of these toiling, sweating men, sent here by circumstance, with fervent words of encouragement.

Jacob kept his thoughts to himself that evening. Solomon was optimistic about their chances, detailing the strength of their fortifications and the enthusiasm of the men tasked with defending it. Jacob was not so sure. They were soon to be swarmed by hundreds of men bent on killing them. Some of those men might be acquaintances of his, if not distant family members. The Red Sticks were coming, and he longed to have his uncle with him, for his calming advice and counsel. The enemy they would soon face had killed the most important man in his life. He wondered if he was next, here at a fort built on sand and determination. Whatever his fate, he decided he would make his uncle proud, even if it was in death.

Scouts had been sent out during the night, and when the men rose the next morning they were told the enemy was camped less than a mile away. The back of the fort was less secure than the fan-shaped half circle that faced the sea. It had ramparts that eased into a point at the very back. This was where the men who would face the land attack were stationed. Jacob, with Solomon at his side, peered nervously through the slit he was assigned, carved between two logs of the wall. Others were stationed above him, as well as a number of smaller cannon, and they gazed apprehensively in the same direction as he. For a brief moment, Jacob thought about Fort Pierce, and the terror he experienced the day he was under the command of the other Lieutenant Montgomery, as they waited for the attack from the Red Sticks that never came. Much had happened since that time. He was older and wiser, he reasoned, but the fear had not changed.

It was noon before the enemy made himself known. The scraggly crew of Indian warriors and a handful of British marines set off three small cannon, aimed at the rear of the fort. How they had managed to drag the guns through the sand dunes was astonishing, Jacob thought, as he watched two of the balls shot in his direction fall short. And then, a horrendous explosion as one of the shots met its mark and shattered part of the fort's wall to his right.

Jacob and Solomon peered through their slits and saw the scrawny bodies of the collection of warriors scamper about, doing their best to hide among the dunes. They could see their painted faces and tattooed bodies cavorting and could faintly hear their war cries. They, along with all their comrades along the wall, took careful aim and fired.

"They're trying to dig trenches, boys!" their sergeant shouted. "Let's see that they don't succeed!"

Jacob and his comrades continued a steady fire. This was Jacob's first fight with his long rifle so he took careful aim, but targets were only fleeting. He could see puffs of white sand explode upward as the musket balls struck in front of the uneven battle line that faced them. Occasionally a cannon ball would be shot in their direction, but the sturdy walls of the fort were mostly impenetrable. The first volley that saw a direct hit had been a lucky shot. The small cannon placed above him on a sturdy ledge kept up a steady shelling, which kept the enemy before them busy dodging the grapeshot.

The ragged attack continued all day. It was insufferably hot inside the fort. The searing sun beat down on its defenders, and the light winds off the Gulf did little to alleviate the gun smoke. When the sun finally set, Jacob sighed with relief. He wolfed down his rations, grateful to have something to fill his gnawing belly.

The next day, the ragged fire from the dunes continued. Then in the late afternoon the large cannon facing seaward began to fire. When they first opened up, Jacob flinched at the roar. He had never heard the sound of such big guns, and the noise was deafening. He looked over his shoulder and could see the sweating crews of those guns. He could hear their cursing and shouts, and saw men ramming the powder and balls down the shafts of the cannon, and then watched them dodge the recoil that inevitably followed each shot. Billowing, acrid smoke filled his nostrils and mouth and stung his eyes.

The bombardment lasted until well after dark. Once night had descended, Jacob and his fellows that manned the land side of the fort were given a short reprieve. Food and water was passed around – the first that had entered Jacob's mouth that day. He gulped it down gratefully. With their backs to the wall, he and Solomon watched the fiery arcs of the cannon balls crossing the sky in front of them, headed out over the ocean. It was quite a sight to see, they decided. The continuous pounding of those guns that rocked the very ground upon which they sat made conversation almost impossible.

Jacob crouched over and moved to the middle of the fort. He then straightened and caught a glimpse of the sails of the four ships that had anchored before the fort, outlined by the flashes from their cannon and the return fire of his fellow soldiers. Solomon soon joined him.

They watched as the lead British ship seemed to quiver and then break from its moorings. It began to drift forward, straight in the direction of the fort. The cannon crews let out a loud cheer, loud enough to be heard above the roar of the guns around them.

As Jacob and Solomon watched the ship inexorably draw closer, moved forward by the currents of the bay, it suddenly came to a shuddering halt.

"It's run aground, men! Let's take her!"

At that point, every gun along the crescent of Fort Bowyer opened up on the ship. Jacob and Solomon drew closer and saw the shadowy outlines of men abandoning it, jumping over the sides. Rowed boats from another ship came up behind it for rescues. Within minutes, flames crept from somewhere in the bowels of the vessel and it was soon engulfed in a red, fiery blaze.

Ragged cheers from the exhausted men of the fort rang out. The gun crews, who until recently had been nothing but infantrymen with no experience in artillery, had managed to deal a defeat to a ship belonging to the finest navy on the face of the earth. The other ships that had ranged themselves before the fort were seen limping away. They abandoned their attempt to wrest Mobile out of the hands of the Americans. The bay had been too shallow for them to enter.

The Marines and Indians that had attempted to take the fort from the shaggy sand dunes that surrounded it had also abandoned their posts. Fort Bowyer had won a victory that would have a long-ranging effect on the war effort.

Close to midnight, a tremendous explosion erupted from the hold of the battered, burning, deserted vessel that lay before the fort in defeat. The powder magazine had finally ignited.

CHAPTER 20

REPERCUSSIONS

Pierre heard the explosion. It jolted him awake from his latest drunken stupor. He looked around and discovered he had not even made it into the small cottage that was now his home, but had drifted off while sitting on the stoop, a mostly empty bottle of rum beside him.

Mr. Allard had been welcoming enough when Pierre first arrived. He had set him up a small office in the main house, and provided him living quarters on the edge of the clearing around his large home. The cottage was small – not really much more than a shack – but it suited its purpose.

There was plenty of work to keep him occupied during the day. He kept up several ledgers, detailing the inflow and outflow of money and goods. He sometimes supervised the loading and unloading of carts used to transfer foodstuffs and the produce of the plantation – beef and hogs, corn and rice.

Mr. Allard was more prosperous than most. He had thirty slaves who lived in quarters right behind the main house, where the family could keep an eye on them. His main house was a two-story affair, with the family's living quarters on the top floor.

Pierre had been there only a few days before he realized he could get all the liquor he wanted under the bluff, down by the Bay, from the collection of small shanties and cottages called the Villages, that housed

181

people engaged in commerce with travelers who crossed over from Mobile. There, the liquor flowed freely, and he was more than happy to do business with them.

It was the nights that were the hardest. It was then that the images of his Rosa would flash through his mind. The stolen kisses while her mother bent over her needlework in the parlor when he was calling on her, the quick dimpled smile and side glances she would throw him when he least expected it, the way she looked in the dark blue dress that fit her figure just so. These were a torment to him, and the only thing that would banish them was what he found in a bottle.

As he groggily rose from his perch on the stoop and entered his living quarters, he wondered how long it would take before his employer realized the depth of his problem. He could have married Rosa and life would have been different. They would have set up housekeeping and raised a family. He would have worked happily for his father for the rest of his life. But now he had nothing to look forward to. What would happen when Mr. Allard discovered his penchant for liquor? What would become of him then?

Andrew Jackson, too, heard the explosion. It echoed down through the humid night air as he sat on the porch of his quarters on Royal Street, drawing on the pipe clenched between his teeth. He immediately rose and called for his aides. Due to the late hour, they were fast asleep, but his high-pitched bellow stirred them from their slumber.

He had no way of knowing what had exploded, only that it had come from the direction of Fort Bowyer. He had planned for any eventuality over the last few weeks, but the ominous sound unnerved him. If the British had slipped past Lieutenant Lawrence and his troops at Fort Bowyer there would be hell to pay. Fort Charlotte could not survive a frontal attack, despite the large cannon it housed. Its walls were in a state of decay, and the people of Mobile were ill-prepared for such an attack.

Anger boiled up inside him. He had warned his superiors of the precarious status of Mobile and its need for protection. The distance between him and his higher-ups in Washington had put a stranglehold on all his plans. It took weeks to get a response of any kind to the letters he sent continuously, no matter the urgency.

He had recently learned of the burning of Washington by the British. They had rampaged through the capital, destroying what the proud new nation had only recently built. It added to his frustration and anger. What would it take to blast the British empire off the continent and stop their meddling in America's affairs?

Well, he would just have to prepare for the worst. He shouted orders to his half-dressed aides as they tumbled out of the building. He would do what he must to protect those in his charge. He silently cursed the English and the Spanish who had enabled them. They would pay, he decided. He would see to it.

There was a scattering of dead bodies among the dunes east of Fort Bowyer. As September 16, 1814 dawned, the sergeant ordered Jacob and Solomon to join the detachment responsible for burying them.

It was grizzly work. There was not much left of those killed by the cannon. Arms and legs had been blown away, and some were missing their heads. Viewing the blood-spattered remains was enough to turn ones' stomach. Jacob had a difficult time keeping down the rations he had just eaten. As he glanced over at Solomon, he noticed a greenish tinge on his friend's face. His stomach wasn't the only one in rebellion.

Digging graves into the soft, white sand was more difficult than expected. For every shovelful of sand removed, it seemed as if two more fell back into the hole. The ten men assigned to the detail complained bitterly.

"What's the point, fellas? We ain't getting nowhere."

"Maybe we should just leave them for the animals."

"Hey, you men! Quit complaining! Get the job done!" the sergeant barked.

Jacob grasped the ankles of a dead warrior, shot through the belly. He used a piece of the man's leggings to strap his rifle to his body. He noted his tattoos but couldn't be certain which clan he was from. Perhaps the turtle clan, he thought, although it was difficult to tell, as his wounds had destroyed most of the markings on the middle of his body. As he lowered it into the shallow grave he had managed to dig, the sergeant ran up to him.

"See here, why are you burying that wretch with his musket? Don't you know we could use it?" he shouted.

"Sir, when a Creek warrior is buried, he must be buried with the things that had meaning for him in his life. This man was a warrior. He will have a difficult time in the afterlife without it."

"The afterlife? Why are we concerned about the afterlife of a stinking Indian?"

"It would be disrespectful to bury him without it," Jacob replied quietly.

"I don't care. Remove that musket. And also his hatchet. We have need of them," the sergeant ordered.

"But sir . . . "

"I will hear no more about it. This man attacked us. He tried to kill us and run us out a' here. We owe him nothing, soldier."

Jacob unhappily did as he was told.

"You must be an Indian yourself to know so much about their ways. You don't look like one."

"My mother was half Creek."

"You don't say," the sergeant replied. "I don't know as I like fighting with an Indian," he frowned.

Jacob looked at him defiantly. "The fellows at Horseshoe Bend were happy enough to fight with me and with Solomon here, even if we are nothing but Indians."

"Well, bury that body and be quick about it," the sergeant replied sternly. "There are plenty more here that need our attention."

They sweated all morning, getting the bodies in the ground. Jacob didn't know the exact number, but there had to be at least fifteen, closer to twenty of them, he thought.

When they returned to the fort, it was in a turmoil. Groups of men were cleaning the cannon, swabbing them down and reloading them. Others were working on repairing the damage to the fort, repacking sand between the logs where it had been dislodged. There were a number of wounded men that needed tending, and ten more bodies that needed burying, this time carefully. It was ordered their burial should take place right outside the fort, in a neat row. Jacob and Solomon wearily picked up their shovels again.

The men in the fort were tense. They had no way of knowing whether the British would return, despite the loss of their ship, the HMS *Hermes*. Its blackened wreck lay before the fort, a reminder of the bitter defensive battle they had fought the previous day. They sweated and cursed, cursed and sweated as they prepared for another attack.

Lieutenant Lawrence paced around the interior of the fort, doing what he could to encourage the men in his charge. The results of the battle the previous day had lifted his spirits, but he knew they were not in the clear yet. If the British returned, he must be prepared for them. He might not have the keen mind and tactical know-how of his commander, General Jackson, but he did at least know he could leave nothing to chance. He would do what was necessary to defend the fort, and the men there depended on him to make the right decisions.

There was an unease that enveloped the town of Mobile the day after the explosion. Rumors were rampant – the British had defeated the small force that defended them at Fort Bowyer and would soon be beating their way up the bay and attacking their fortifications. Others speculated there would be boatloads of Red Sticks sent their way to wreak havoc on the citizenry, just as they were known to do occasionally on the eastern shore of Mobile Bay. Tales of the raids and destruction caused by rampaging Indians on the farms and plantations across the water had been shared regularly, and the thought that this might be their own fate sent Mobilians scurrying about trying to secure their own means of escape, if necessary. Where exactly they could go was a question none wanted to answer.

Andrew Jackson himself was in a foul mood as he waited to hear the results of what clearly was an assault on the fort that guarded the entrance to Mobile Bay. Where were his reports? What was taking Lieutenant Lawrence so long in informing him of what happened? Perhaps his small force had been crushed and the British were now making their way to Fort Charlotte. His mind could not be at ease until he knew the outcome. He had done all he could to secure the town from an invasion by sea. The cannon that bristled from the walls of Fort Charlotte were primed and ready to engage any British ship that approached. He, like everyone else in Mobile, would have to wait for news. If there was one thing that galled Jackson, it was waiting; but wait he must.

It wasn't until the early morning of September 17 that word reached the town that they were safe, at least for the moment. Jacob and Solomon crammed themselves onto the small boat that carried word to Jackson of the British defeat. They hung on for dear life as the small craft with a single sail made its way up the bay, carrying a message to the General from Lieutenant Lawrence. It took several hours to travel the thirty miles up the bay, and they were hit with a thunderous rain shower halfway there. As the boat rocked and shuddered through the muddy waters, the two young men shared their happiness at being away from the fort.

"Fort life isn't for me," Solomon shouted at Jacob as he struggled to be heard over the sound of the waves beating against their small craft.

Jacob nodded and shouted back, "I don't much care for ship life either."

Once they had landed, they hurried through the streets and back to their encampment. They were happy to see that Sam and Preacher had kept their spot secure. They had taken care of Jacob's horse and maintained the fire and shelters. When they arrived, Sam was busy before the fire, stirring a stew that bubbled and boiled in the iron kettle.

Sam looked up as they approached.

"Where you boys been?"

"We've been at Fort Bowyer. You know that. We told you we were helping load supplies for the fort."

"Didn't think you would stay, though."

"We weren't given a choice. Once there, they saw fit to keep us. They needed the extra men."

"What happened? We all been worried everyone there got blowed up."

Solomon laughed. "Not likely. We beat them back. Even burned up one of the English ships!"

"You don't say! Preacher's in town. Once he gits back you can tell us all about it."

Preacher arrived a few minutes later, carrying a small packet of rations. He was happy to see them. Sam took a slab of salt pork out of the bundle Preacher brought and dropped it into the kettle. As the meal simmered over the fire, Jacob and Solomon shared their experience. The two older men smiled and nodded as the story unfolded.

"The General will be happy with the news, no doubt. He's been on a tear waiting for it," Preacher said.

"If'n there's one thing you don't want to do, it's to put Andy in a spot like that," Sam agreed. "Once he gets riled up, it's mighty hard to calm him back down. We've been laying low ourselves, waitin' for news." He gave the stew another stir.

"Hey, fellers, I got to thinkin'," Sam said, changing the subject. "You need to learn us how to catch them alligators. They shore as heck beat this lousy salt pork they keep feedin' us."

Jackson was much relieved at the news from Fort Bowyer. He sent off a dispatch to Lieutenant Lawrence, praising the good work of his men, and several letters north to Washington, in which he lauded the efforts of the brave soldiers who had defended the fort so well. Now it was time to plot the revenge he had in mind for the British who had commandeered the port of Pensacola, and the scheming Spanish who had allowed it. Their attack on his forces would not go unpunished.

It became obvious now that the British had planned to use Mobile as a base to do one of two things —strike out at the city of New Orleans or move north, perhaps to Natchez, and cut off the city from its all-important commercial traffic on the Mississippi River. Either way, the capture of Mobile would be a vital step in striking an earth-shattering blow to the United States.

He thanked God in his prayers that the waters in Mobile Bay had been too shallow for the large ships the British had intended to use in the capture of the city. Without that, the town would be in ruins now, as its defense would have been nearly impossible against the big guns of the British warships, despite the cannons housed in Fort Charlotte.

And yet, he was curious as to why they had made such a weak attempt to capture Fort Bowyer. If it had been him, he would have been able to take it, he was sure. A frontal assault from the sea was not a winning strategy. A stronger land force in the rear of the fort would have sufficed in overcoming the few men that defended it.

For now, he would stay put in Mobile. Desertions had become a problem, but word had come to him that his old friend General Coffee, at his direction, was marching southward with a thousand volunteers from Tennessee. Once they arrived, he believed his force would be strong enough to overcome the defenses of the city of Pensacola. What he had planned for the sniveling British and Spanish would be a just payback for their attempts to take from the United States what they had no right to – its freedom.

CHAPTER 21

ON THE ROAD

Jacob was glad to leave the soggy, unseasonably cold Mobile on that first day of November. He and his campmates had grown restless with the inactivity common to idle soldiers. There were only so many hands of cards to be played and stories swapped before tempers grew short.

He and Solomon, Sam and Preacher were members of the advanced guard of Jackson's forces. They and several dozen others fanned out ahead of Jackson's column, which numbered about two thousand men, along with cannon and baggage. As the column trudged northward it looked like the wriggling body of a slithering snake, but one that consumed everything in its path.

They marched through a heavy fog that rolled in from the bay on the first day. It was almost noon before it dissipated. The men marching on foot, stumbling through the marsh grasses and occasional bogs that marked their path, were happy to see it go.

The people of Mobile were not sad to see them leave. They yearned for the old days, when life was certain and the vagaries of rough strangers did not interrupt their peaceful existence. True, they were happy that an English assault had been prevented and the destruction that would have come had been averted, but they couldn't help but blame Jackson anyway. If he hadn't infested their town to start with, they felt sure the

English would have left them alone. They had already been under the rule of the British before the Spanish had taken over, and the yoke they had imposed at the time had been light. Would it have been so bad to have them as their masters once more?

Jacob and Solomon rode together, along a path they were both sure of. It had been worn down for centuries by their Creek ancestors and the struggling new settlers that had made their way to Mobile to barter and trade. However, far behind, the army that trailed them was forced to widen the trail considerably to account for the cannon and loads of supplies necessary to maintain an army.

They made camp the first night, after riding back and relaying the message that all was clear to the main body of troops behind them, and to receive orders for the following day.

"See here," Solomon said. "We're not far from home. I'm thinking we could swing by this evening and tell the folks howdy."

Jacob stirred the fire they had kindled. "You go ahead. I'm fine right here."

"You don't want to talk with your folks?"

"No."

"Why not, Jacob?"

"They made clear at our last meeting that my presence was unwelcome."

"Now why would they do that?"

"My stepmother will not forgive me for being the son of a Creek woman. My father let it be known he had no objection to the sentiment."

"So they've disowned you?" Solomon asked incredulously.

"You could say that. I'm on my own."

Solomon was quiet for a moment. "Well you would be welcome at my home. You could come along with me."

"Thank you for the invitation, but I think I'll just stay here. Besides, Preacher and Sam might show up, and they would be happy to have a fire going and supper started."

"That's fine, Jacob."

"Just be sure to be back before morning. Wouldn't want you to get in trouble for deserting," Jacob replied with a laugh.

It wasn't long before Sam and Preacher arrived. As they tied up their horses, they hailed Jacob heartily.

"I see you already got somethin' in the pot!" Sam exclaimed.

"It isn't much, just some salt pork and greens."

Preacher looked around. "Where's Solomon?"

"He'll be back by morning. He's ridden off to see his family while he has the chance."

"Don't your folks live close by here as well?"

"Not particularly close. It's a good ten or twelve miles from here."

"I see," Preacher replied. "I suppose it's none of my business as to why you haven't taken the same opportunity."

"That would be correct, Preacher. It isn't really any of your business," Jacob said sternly.

"There is something about having friends," he replied quietly. "They have ears to listen. It's one of the best things about friendship."

Jacob's tone darkened. "Not everyone's life is as easy as yours. You have parents and a wife and two children. You have a path forward. Some of us aren't that lucky."

Preacher replied thoughtfully. "What you say is true. The Lord has blessed me. But that doesn't mean he hasn't blessings for you too. They just haven't been revealed yet, Jacob. That's all."

"Life ain't easy for any of us. Look here, we gave up a lot to travel down here, Jacob. My wife and younguns have moved in with her folks while I'm off here, doin' my part to pertect this this country. We all make sacrifices, and they make life hard. You'll be all right on your own, Jacob. You got good sense, the way I sees it," Sam said.

"We'll see. For now, I'm ready to get some rest," he replied, without much conviction.

Jacob was stirred in the early morning hours when Solomon returned.

"Is all well with your family?" he whispered to him.

"Just fine. Now let me get a few minutes sleep. It's been a long night."

At full light they returned to the main body of the army to receive their orders for the day. It was a huge encampment, although well ordered. Tents were staked in neat rows, and they could see the men busy before their fires preparing their breakfast.

They met with Colonel Buckholt, who informed them they were to proceed to Fort Stoddert and then cross the Alabama River.

"Where are we heading, sir?" Solomon asked.

"We'll be meeting General Coffee and his troops close to Fort Pierce. Are you aware of it?"

"Yes, sir. Jacob here sheltered there during the massacre."

"Well, the Indians burned it down. We've built a new fort close by the old one. Once you reach there, stay and wait for us to catch up."

"Yes, sir."

They passed Fort Stoddert, forlorn now and bereft of soldiers. The ones who had been stationed there had all been moved to a new stockade called Fort Montgomery, just east of the Alabama River, not far from the ruins of Fort Mims.

"Isn't this where you sheltered during the troubles?" Jacob asked Solomon as they passed by Stoddert.

"Yes. We left home long before you did. We were here for more than a month, camped not far from its walls. It was a trying time, to be sure.

My father fretted and fumed at the inconvenience of it all, but it was a good thing, I suppose. And for some reason our place was spared the torch, though all our livestock was gone when we returned home."

They caught a ferry across the river and headed straight north. Riding hard, they reached the new walls of Fort Pierce by late afternoon. As they passed by the blackened ruins of the old fort, Jacob shuddered as he recollected his stay there, and the raw fear that had coursed through him during the night of the massacre, and the hard, difficult march south to Mobile.

The new fort was much sturdier than the old, and it was manned by a large enough force to maintain its safety. Upon inquiring at the gate, they were informed that General Coffee and his force had already arrived and were situated between them and what remained of Fort Mims, at Fort Montgomery.

They spotted a huge herd of horses before they made it into the main encampment. Coffee had brought his cavalry, and it was almost two thousand strong. Volunteers one and all, they displayed a dizzying array of what each soldier believed to be a uniform – mostly homespun with a sprinkling of buckskin. Some wore caps and tricorns, but most were bareheaded. Some of them huddled around the fires before their tents, while others were busy chopping wood to maintain them. Jacob could hear the sounds of axes against wood in the nearby scattering of pine and hardwoods. He spied a couple of makeshift blacksmith shops, with men hammering away, forging horseshoes and other metal instruments necessary to maintain a cavalry unit.

There were wrestling competitions and loud, boisterous card or chuck-a-luck games taking place in the center of the camp, on the trampled earth that formed a sort of parade ground. But their tents were in good order and aligned in neat rows. General Coffee would have it no other way.

The newly constructed Fort Montgomery was an impressive affair. It was star-shaped with a moat surrounding its log walls. The blockhouse in the middle of the compound was three stories high and along with a fixed parapet the fort had four cannon.

The group returned to Fort Pierce to await the arrival of the others. Soon enough, some of the other scouts showed up, and fires were started and shelters erected as they awaited the General. Preacher and Sam rode in and joined them.

"Seen anything to report?' Sam asked.

"No. All is quiet. We haven't seen any sign of anyone who would cause trouble. Of course, it would be foolish for the Red Sticks to nose around, what with Coffee's cavalry here."

"I think we'll find plenty of them when we reach Pensacola," Preacher said.

"Maybe so," Solomon replied. "But don't expect them to show themselves much. They know this territory, and they aren't fools. I doubt they will just pop up and wait for us to shoot them."

"Well, we got plenty a Choctaws with us. Maybe they'll be able to smoke 'em out," Sam replied.

"Once you see the lay of the land between here and there, you might reconsider that idea."

Once Jackson and his troops caught up with his scouts, one of the first things he did was ride over to the ruins of Fort Mims. Bleached bones from the massacre were still scattered around, both inside and outside of the burned stumps that were all that remained of the walls. The sight of the blackened litter of what was left of the blockhouses that had towered over the interior of the fort set his teeth on edge. He, like everyone else, had heard the stories of how the defenders had been shot as they tried to escape the inferno created when the Red Sticks had set those structures ablaze in the final push to overcome the fort's defenders.

This, after all, was the impetus for all that had transpired since. The call to arms once the news of the massacre had spread; his frenzied attempt to gather troops to head south to defend the settlers who had been so viciously attacked; the months of suffering his troops had endured because of a lack of food and supplies. Then there were the desertions of his own men, and his herculean attempts to keep them focused on their mission; the hard-fought battles and the men lost. Finally, the delay in his plans to defend the heartland by securing the port of New Orleans. It had all been because of what had transpired here.

As Jackson solemnly viewed the remains, he wondered if it had been worth it. He decided it was. No people deserved what had occurred there. There was no justification for it. William Weatherford and the Red Sticks had lit a fire they were not prepared to extinguish. Their ignorance of the power and might and the strength of the new nation was to their detriment. He had secured their defeat and had reaped the benefit of it by securing their lands in the name of the United States. The punishment would continue until there was no more resistance. When that would occur, he had no idea. But he would do all he could to see that such an incident would never happen again.

As usual, there was a constant supply of information brought in by Jackson's extensive network of spies. The clattering of hooves in the middle of the night was a sound very familiar to anyone under his command, as couriers raced in on lathered horses to relay the bits of news that had been gathered.

For weeks, he had been carrying on a correspondence with the Spanish governor of West Florida, Mateo González Manrique, in which he had demanded he expunge the British from the port of Pensacola, where several British ships were blatantly anchored. As a neutral power, he told the governor, Spain was obligated to stay out of the conflict. He also warned him there would be consequences for sheltering the remnants of the Red Stick warriors in his jurisdiction. The responses he received had been less than satisfactory. The governor had dithered and hedged in his replies. He would have to learn the hard way, Jackson decided, that he meant what he said.

The American army of four thousand men and a small contingent of artillery left the Alabama River and headed east first, around the thrusting, northern curve of Mobile Bay. As his men hacked their way through the virgin growth of tall pine and a dizzying array of shrubs and bushes, interspersed with rivulets, streams and bogs, he sat astride his horse, his back stiff and straight as a ramrod. It was just the posture that had helped give him the nickname "Old Hickory." The men understood that he was just as unwavering in his resolve as he looked, sitting atop his horse. Unbending and formidable, like the towering limbs of an old hickory tree.

The going was difficult for the men. The train of the army stretched for four miles, and reached nearly a mile wide. Forage for the horses was scarce, and the cavalrymen were forced to march on foot to spare their horses. The supply and ammunition wagons broke over the rough terrain, and stops were frequent as men hurriedly repaired them so they could again move forward.

Jacob and Solomon, Preacher and Sam, had been reassigned to General Coffee's cavalry. They were greeted by old friends and colleagues from the campaign that had resulted in the defeat of the Red Sticks at Horseshoe Bend. There were many new faces, too, mostly from men who had joined Coffee from West Tennessee.

They camped together at night and shared stories of their previous battles. Some of the men brought news from home, which was most welcome to the soldiers who had traveled south with Jackson months before.

Food supplies were short. There wasn't much to put into the kettles that hung above their fires, but there was little complaining. They would be in Pensacola soon enough, and they believed their bellies would be filled once they conquered the city.

"You should get a taste of them alligators," Sam shared with the new faces around their campfire.

"Aren't they nothin' but big lizards?"

"They're a sight more than that!" Sam replied. "They make real good eating, if you cook them just right."

"And what's the best way to do that?"

"Well, you chunk up the tail and roast it over the fire. Jacob and Solomon here taught us how to do it."

"I don't know, Sam. I think a good alligator stew mixed with greens is pretty good eating, too," Preacher opined.

"I ain't sayin' that ain't tasty, too. I just like it better over the fire."

"I suppose if I could catch me an alligator, I would eat it."

"There ain't nothin' to it. Best way, though, is with a bow and arrow. You have to sneak up on 'em real careful like. They scare easy."

"And if you find one you must kill it quickly. They slink away under the water quick as a wink if you aren't careful. Once that happens, the others around them are warned of your presence and will scatter," Preacher said.

"Why haven't we seen any?"

"The weather is cool. They're holed up for the winter. Besides, alligators are timid creatures. They have a very keen sense of hearing. With the stumbling and cursing and crashing this army makes, there wouldn't be an alligator within ten miles of us," Solomon said.

"There are ways to hunt them in the winter, though. You just have to know where to look. They hide themselves in the shallows and sink into the mud. They don't move much in the cold," Jacob interjected.

"If Jackson weren't in such a big hurry, we could get some good huntin' done around here."

"The element of surprise, gentlemen, cannot be overestimated," Preacher stated. "By striking quickly, we are more assured of a victory."

"Surely they know we're coming."

"Word is they don't. There are British ships in the harbor of Pensacola Bay, and a few hundred Spanish soldiers in the forts. According to my sources, they aren't making any preparations for our arrival."

"How do you know that?"

Sam chuckled. "Let's just say it pays to ride close to Coffee and his officers. No tellin' what kind of information you might pick up."

The march of Jackson's army took a southeast turn as it made the loop around Mobile Bay. Eventually it headed directly south, struggling its way through the dense terrain, hampered as always by the carts and conveyances that carried their supplies. Dog-tired long before they reached their goal, the men marched grimly onward, driven by their strong belief in the man who led them. Jackson had their loyalty, despite their trying circumstances.

As for Jacob, he understood their loyalty even though he didn't always share it. But the memory of his uncle's dead body slipping beneath the waters of the Tallapoosa River kept him moving forward. His own people had been responsible for it, and he believed the destruction of the Red Sticks who had caused so much death and unnecessary pain was now his mission. He jammed his hat tighter onto his head as he marched through the mud alongside his horse. He would do his part to see they paid a price for it. It was the least he could do for the memory of the man who had been such a large part of his life – the man who had willingly sacrificed himself for peace. A good man, who deserved so much more than he got.

Chapter 22

The Enemy

The people of Pensacola had had just about enough of Colonel Edward Nicholls.

He had arrived in their village during the hot, sultry month of August and had disrupted their peaceful town with his demands and high-handedness toward the Spanish governor and themselves, a people who much preferred the slow, steady pace of life they had known under the flag of Spain that flew from the staff of the fort inside their small city – Fort San Miguel.

But Nicholls had bullied their rather timid governor into allowing his own British flag to be flown alongside the ensign of Spain, and at the same height. Even the most dull-witted resident knew this was an insult, and what little enthusiasm there might have been for the arrogant Englishman soon waned after his arrival.

Pensacola, like Mobile, had changed hands several times over the decades – at first Spain held it, then France, then Great Britain, and then finally back to Spain in 1781. The people had grown weary of the constant battle for the possession of their small community, and by the fall of 1814 the rumors flew thick and fast that the Americans would soon march upon them. To many residents, this was not alarming. Perhaps, indeed, they would be happier and regain a peaceful existence if the Americans were to take possession.

Nicholls had been in charge of the disastrous attack on Fort Bowyer in September and had come limping back to their fine harbor, minus a ship. As his impudence and impertinence grew, many of the residents smiled at the memory of his defeat.

Nicholls' arrival had seen an upending to the routine of the city. He was incensed that the Spanish had not properly tended to the needs of the many Creek warriors who had fled the onslaught of Andrew Jackson during the Red Stick War and had sought refuge. He demanded that they be armed and properly fed, and the desultory response of the Spanish had angered him.

His plans for the city were simple – he would use its location as a gathering point for disaffected native tribes, including the Creeks and Seminoles, and the roving bands of runaway slaves throughout Spanish West Florida, and then send them against the Americans in southern Georgia. If he could gather a large enough force, they would be useful in the upcoming struggle for control of New Orleans as well. One of his first acts in the city was to commandeer most of the slaves held by the citizens of Pensacola. This would substantially increase the size of his misfit army.

Large numbers of warriors and blacks flocked to the small city, and the people were in a state of fear. True, their economy was dependent on the trade between themselves and the tribes, but they saw these refugee hordes as nothing less than an invasion, and the townsfolk looked with anger at the puffed-up Nicholls and his handful of Royal Marines.

They were equally angry at the lackluster response of their Governor Gonzales Manrique and his small contingent of troops. Weren't they supposed to be protected from the unruly and dangerous throngs of men who infested their town? What was the point of being under the Spanish flag if Spain was unwilling to safeguard their well-being?

There were a few Americans who had wandered into Pensacola to pursue their interests in the Indian trade. They had been accepted readily enough by the Spanish, as their presence was not viewed as a threat, but as mutually beneficial. They caused no problems and were respectful of the laws and regulations imposed by the Spanish crown. However, Colonel Nicholls held a different viewpoint. He made it clear that he thought the Americans were spies, and did his best to make their lives as uncomfortable as possible as soon as he arrived. He threatened them and put onerous limitations on their movements and their businesses.

Governor Manrique was in a tight spot, to be sure. West Florida stretched from the Perdido River west, all along the coast to the Apalachicola River. This was the area he was charged to defend from two warring sides, and maintaining peace for the citizens of Pensacola was getting more difficult by the day. He was new to the post, having only been appointed in 1813, and was a soldier by trade, not a diplomat. As such, he wasn't particularly prepared to handle aggressive overtures from the British and their offspring-turned-enemy, the Americans.

He had gone along readily enough when the British demanded he allow them to patrol his waters along the Gulf and land a force in Pensacola. Technically, he knew, his country had declared its neutrality in the war between Great Britain and the United States, but only a fool could not recognize the power of the British military – the same which had defended his own country against Napoleon.

On the other side he resented the way the Americans had pushed their way into Mobile and taken it without a fight. It was an important port, and the brash and brazen way in which they had maneuvered their way into its possession offended his Spanish sensibilities. This was not how diplomacy was accomplished. These upstart Americans needed to be put in their place. He could not technically do it on his own, but he saw no reason why he could not help the British. Perhaps if they won, Spain could reclaim their rightful place all along the Gulf of Mexico, including the port of Mobile.

But then the British started recruiting an army of warring Indians and dangerous groups of ex-slaves, out for revenge against their old masters. This gave him pause. The people he governed were frightened of the mass of armed misfits. They complained night and day. What was he going to do about it, they asked? Who was in charge – the Spanish or the British?

And then, the threatening letters from Jackson had started. Somehow, he had learned of the Spanish perfidy – of his allowing the British almost free rein within the colony of West Florida – how the native tribes and runaways were being armed. How he found out, Manrique could only guess. Perhaps he did have spies in the town – the Americans who lived among them were passing along information. He had no way of knowing.

But he felt safe enough in his snug, tight harbor and the forts manned by his five hundred men. There was no way the Americans could enter the harbor and attack – not with the British ships that patrolled along the Gulf. They did not possess the ships nor the manpower to accomplish such a task. And what could Jackson do other than that to reach him? There were thousands of acres of dark treacherous forests, swamps and bogs, deep rivers and gullies that lay between him and Jackson in Mobile. How could he possibly make his way to Pensacola without Manrique knowing about it in advance?

And so he sat. He was troubled, of course, by the arrogance of Colonel Nicholls and his bullying ways. The armed mobs that surrounded his small city were also of concern. It was frustrating to deal with the unhappy citizenry, but he kept assuring himself that all this would pass in time. Surely the British would win the conflict. They had marched and burned the capital buildings of the foolhardy United States in Washington City. They'd beaten them along the border of Canada. Although the Americans had managed some victories at sea, it was only a matter of time, he reasoned, before the English put the Americans in their place. They were upstarts and little but a nation of ruffians who didn't understand the niceties of running a country. Jackson himself seemed to be a man of some intelligence, as he gleaned from their ongoing correspondence, but he was only one man. There was little he could do by himself to change the tide that was sure to come and sweep him and his faltering nation off the pages of history.

Meanwhile, Governor Manrique would play the game. He would placate the British, while also doing his best to keep the impertinent Jackson at bay. After all, Jackson had no power to tell the great nation of Spain how to conduct business. They were free to allow the British into the port of Pensacola, and there was very little Jackson could do about it.

At least, that's what the governor believed.

CHAPTER 23

PENSACOLA

Jacob was most assuredly hungry that morning as he and his fellows followed General Coffee around the curve of Pensacola Bay to the east of town. He tried not to think about it, as he knew the day he faced would be long and hard, and that it might even be his last one on earth. It wasn't as if he was the only one who suffered – the last few nights, when they had camped for the evening, had been filled with reminiscences from his fellow soldiers detailing some of the fine meals their wives and mothers had prepared for them in the past. He reasoned this was probably how many men who found themselves facing an enemy with empty stomachs handled their situation. He would do his best to ignore the grumbling sound. There were more important matters to tend to.

Solomon, who rode confidently beside him, had a look of satisfaction and contentment on his face. He was smiling broadly and his hat was tilted at a jaunty angle on his head.

"Do you think they even know we're coming?" he asked.

"Well, we heard the news last night. No pickets out to speak of. You heard it yourself, Solomon. Doesn't appear they do."

"This might wind up being the easiest battle we've ever won!" was his response.

205

"Don't get too cocky, fellers," Sam interjected. "Them Spanish are tricky weasels. It ain't over yet."

"Don't be so glum. Jackson knows what he's doing."

"He usually does. But I can't fer the life of me figure this one out. Surely these fellers knew Jackson wasn't gonna just leave 'em sittin' over here causin' trouble."

"They don't know him as well as we do."

Sam sighed. "That's true. But I still can't figure it."

"It's to our advantage that they take us for granted," said Preacher. "If there's one thing you can be sure of, the British always reckon they're somehow smarter and wiser than we are. We saw that in the last war. And it's kind of comforting to know they haven't changed their low opinion. In the end, it will be their undoing."

Jackson himself was half amused at the lack of preparations the enemy had made. It was obvious as they approached Pensacola that his arrival would be a complete surprise to the Spanish and British forces holed up in what they considered a safe haven. It wasn't as if he hadn't issued more than a few veiled threats in his correspondence to the governor. They had refused to take him seriously. Just as well, he thought. They would soon learn he had meant business.

His spies and informants had kept him supplied with information about the troops he and his army would soon face. The many years of inactivity at the post of Pensacola had taken their toll. The Spanish were ill-prepared to face an enemy who earnestly desired to confront and defeat them.

As for the British, they were woefully undermanned. If they wanted to believe they could rely on the untrained warriors and motley assortment of disaffected blacks to shore up their defenses, that was strictly their own fault, he reasoned. The men under his command had been through the Creek War and had soundly defeated the Red Sticks at their height. They were hardened, battle-tested troops. Moreover, his forces greatly outnumbered theirs. How they could have taken for granted he would rest in Mobile while they continued to sow havoc in the United States, including their attack on Fort Bowyer – well, they would have to answer for that to their own superiors.

There were four British ships in Pensacola harbor when they arrived. They were a concern, but a surprise attack might just mitigate their effectiveness. The British were planners, and did not often react with speed when their stubborn insistence that they were always correct was challenged. So Jackson did not view them as a serious threat.

He had, of course, not gotten permission to invade Spain and take on the British who had ingratiated themselves into West Florida. He knew that if he were to somehow lose, there would be hell to pay from President Madison. But he was supremely confident that his decision to confront the enemy here and now was the right one.

The British had camped on the west side of the city. To throw the enemy off, Jackson left five hundred of his men there and led the rest in four columns around the curve of the bay to surprise the enemy from the east. A simple maneuver, but one he hoped would confuse and confound.

The Spanish troops, who had the most firepower, were confined in their forts, San Rosa and San Miguel. They had heavy guns within those walls, mainly facing west. He was hoping their lack of preparation would leave them in such a fluster that their efforts to impede him would be minimal.

To the east, his men would face the firepower of the British ships in the harbor. But the speed and maneuver of a surprise attack would deny the ships the chance to swing their broadsides into position in time.

Jackson sent a soldier with a flag of truce into the city to begin negotiations. He would take the city, either by force or by capitulation. It was up to the Spanish to decide.

His first messenger was fired upon by the cannon in Fort San Miguel.

Cursing at the shortsightedness of the Spanish, he withdrew his troops on the western approach a mile further out. The forts opened up with heavy fire in their direction, but with little effect. The balls whistled overhead, harmless. He could almost hear his men jeering at the ineffectiveness of the Spanish defense, and rightly so. Despite their short supplies, he knew he and his troops could wait them out, if need be. The enemy was in no position to get reinforcements, and they were outmanned, eight to one.

After consulting with his officers, the idea was broached to send a Spanish soldier who had been captured the previous evening toward the fort with a dispatch for Governor Manrique. Surely the enemy would not be so foolish as to fire upon one of their own.

Jacob and his comrades found themselves at the rear of the four columns to the east, on the outskirts of the city. The British ships in the harbor had begun firing upon them, but blindly after their first salvo. They, too, had been surprised by the appearance of the ragtag army, composed of a large number of Lower Creek and Choctaw warriors, Regular Army, and a mass of volunteers from Tennessee.

He scanned his surroundings, eager to fall upon any enemy that might pop their heads out and make themselves known. His rifle remained silent. There was no resistance to be found.

As they crept into the city, he heard a burst of fire from two cannon to the front of them. They had been placed in the center of a street to protect and defend the citizenry. The loud booms did not dissuade the troops ahead of him, however. The cannoneers were overwhelmed by the mass of men Jackson had placed in the lead for just such an occasion.

Soon, he realized that the British ships in the harbor had ceased firing at them. They lay like silent witnesses, with wisps of smoke still clinging to their bare masts and rigging, as if they were mere observers and had no interest in what took place among the small huts and houses that comprised the town they had just been trying to defend.

"Well, look a' there!" Sam exclaimed. "I guess they done give up!"

"Strange. You'd think they would've given more of an effort," Preacher said.

"Whoever is in charge out there seems to have taken stock of us and decided we aren't worth the powder," Solomon chuckled.

"Perhaps he has bigger plans."

"That's what I'm afraid of," Preacher said.

"What does that mean?"

"We all know their desire to capture New Orleans. I have a feeling they are willing to sacrifice this place in order to prepare for what really matters to them, and that's the city that guards the Mississippi. There's a bigger fight coming, boys. You can bet on it."

Jackson's men poured into the small village of Pensacola and began routing out Spanish soldiers hidden among the populace.

Jacob kept a sharp eye out for any signs of Red Sticks but could find none. Where they were hidden, he had no way of knowing. He poked and prodded at the dejected soldiers he came upon with his rifle, but since he didn't speak Spanish – at least, not enough to count – his queries on the whereabouts of the horde he suspected to be present somewhere went unanswered.

The people of Pensacola seemed happy enough to see them. A few of the women brought out their kettles from over their fireplaces with cooked victuals and fed the men who gathered around. Some of the Spanish only nodded and smiled at the American soldiers. Some spoke English and expressed their gratitude at their presence.

It wasn't long before Governor Manrique came forward waving a huge white flag as a sign of surrender. He was not alone but was backed by a few Spanish officers, their gaudy uniforms in disarray, their shoulders slumped and their faces glum. They hadn't put up much of a fight, and they seemed reconciled to their humiliating defeat.

Jackson accepted the surrender in person. While he bargained over the capitulation of the two forts, his men began setting up camp in the square and among the small houses that made up the town. There were a few small garden squares nestled among the cross streets, and these were fully taken advantage of.

"This here town seems nice enough. Would be better, though, if we had some food," Sam grumbled as they staked their tents.

"We'll wait for our rations," Preacher firmly replied.

"They ain't enough a' those to fill my belly."

"Maybe not. But you know the rules as well as anyone, Sam. The General will not tolerate any looting. These folks don't look prosperous enough to have much to spare."

"Maybe them Spanish fellers got extra."

Solomon laughed. "I doubt it. Did you see them? Most of them look like they haven't had any more to eat than we have."

As satisfying as it was for Jackson to accept the surrender of Manrique and the Spanish with such little resistance, there was still the matter of the British ships stationed just outside the bay. At the narrow point of the harbor was Fort Barrancas, which sat like a brown, brooding dog, heavily fortified, with an array of long guns that posed a real threat to the town itself, as well as Jackson's army. As the scuffle over Pensacola ended, he knew this fort remained under British control. He cursed silently at the thought of having to storm it, since he knew it would cost the lives of men he could not spare. But then, a certain amount of satisfaction could come from taking British prisoners.

As his men settled around their campfires for the evening, he and his staff took stock of the situation. Plans would have to be made to overcome the threat, and he let his feelings known vociferously to the men gathered around him. He would do whatever it took to drive the British off. He could not allow them to remain in Pensacola, as it would provide a jumping off point for the ultimate goal of the enemy – control of New Orleans.

He dismissed his staff and then placed his lap desk on top of his thin, long legs and began to write the letters he knew must be written about the situation he found himself in. Letters to Washington, to the Governor of Tennessee; and letters to the men in New Orleans who, even now, were preparing for his arrival. And last of all, a letter to his wife Rachel, whom he dearly missed.

As Jacob lay under his threadbare blanket before the fire that evening, he glanced upward at the stars that blinked down at him and wondered aloud, "I'm surprised we had so little resistance today."

"Me, too," Solomon replied.

"We've been told the lousy lobsterbacks had a whole army of Red Sticks to back them up. Did any of you see any signs of them?"

"Not a one," Sam replied sleepily.

"I imagine they have them safely tucked away somewhere, saving them for an emergency."

"That doesn't make any sense, Preacher," Jacob said, testily. "They didn't consider today an emergency?"

"Why would they? This is Spanish territory, after all. Looking at the response we got from the townspeople today, their presence here wasn't particularly welcome. Angering Spain would not be in their best interests," Preacher replied.

"Don't worry, boy. You'll get another crack at 'em before long, I imagine," Sam piped in.

Jacob wrapped himself tighter in his blanket. The night air had turned cool.

"I certainly hope so."

"Revenge is sweet, but we can't let that deter us from taking care of what is right before us, Jacob. We have to keep our eye on the prize."

"And what is the prize, Preacher?"

"It ain't the Red Sticks. It's the lousy British who started this fuss from the beginnin'. Now let's get some sleep, boys. We don't know what will happen tomorrow, but it might be more than what we had to deal with today," Sam said.

Not long after the sun had risen the next morning, the air around Pensacola was ripped apart by a huge explosion. An immense plume of dark, black smoke billowed skyward from the entrance of the harbor. Jackson's men rushed to the waterfront and gazed south. The fort protecting the harbor was no more. In its place was a smoking rubble, still hurtling red brick from what remained of its thick walls.

A ragged cheer erupted from them as they gazed at the conflagration.

"Those fools have done made our job much easier!" Sam cackled. "Now we don't have ta storm the place! They took it out for us!"

Jackson immediately sent a force of a hundred men out around the curve of the bay to assess the situation. As they moved out, the crowd of townspeople and soldiers watched as the British ships weighed anchor, let loose their sails and headed east, leaving the people of Pensacola with an undefended harbor.

The Spanish citizens were in shock as they watched them sail away. Then the shock turned to anger. The British had made promises. They said they would help defend them from the Americans, and yet they had abandoned them without so much as a fight. Not only that, they had destroyed the bastion of Fort Barrancas, which had guarded and protected them for many years.

The men Jackson sent out returned with their report. The fort was completely demolished. The British had packed their ships with their men and their Indian allies and left the town to defend itself as best it could.

This left Jackson with a dilemma. Pensacola was now virtually defenseless. Yet if he tried to keep control of the city by leaving a force there to defend it, he would dilute the strength of his own army. If he did so, he knew it would cause an international incident – one the nation he defended could not afford. His other choice was to make haste back to Mobile with his army and prepare for the battle he knew was on the horizon.

He confronted Manrique and demanded answers. What were the British plans? Where were they headed? Had they divulged their future intentions?

The governor grudgingly answered as best he could. He could not read their minds, any more than Jackson could. But he did confirm what Jackson already knew – they would move against New Orleans, and it would happen soon.

With that, Jackson's mind was made up. He quickly called his men and prepared them for the march back to Mobile. He would leave Pensacola in the hands of the Spanish. He would station a few hundred of his men a safe distance away, just in case the British attempted to return and use it as a base of operations. How the Spanish could defend Pensacola without a protecting fort at its harbor was their problem. Perhaps they had learned their lesson – allying with the British had been a fool's choice.

Chapter 24

Return to Mobile

Jackson and his army had marched from the northwest on their roundabout approach to Pensacola in order to ensure their attack would be a surprise. Now that the town was conquered and no longer a threat, he and his troops returned on the direct route – straight west on the Spanish Trail.

It was a well-worn path, having been used for more than a hundred years by groups of Europeans traveling between Mobile and Pensacola, and as a trade route by the Indians for far longer. It was a straight shot to Mobile Bay, where the triumphant army would then be loaded on boats and moved back to the city.

Despite the trail's frequent use, the size of the force it now carried was far larger than any it had seen before. Four thousand men, plus all the accouterments of an army, slogged along the road, which had turned into a quagmire from recent rains. The supply wagons got stuck in the thick, red mud, and the small artillery pieces the army carried also caused the column to slow. The path widened from the burden of so much traffic.

As the men marched through the sludge and muck, churned by the thousands of horse's hooves that carried the cavalry, they looked with glee at the fat, sleek herds of cows that occasionally showed themselves along the thoroughfare. There were large fields covered with the stubble of the last corn and cotton harvest, interspersed with towering forests of pine and oak and magnolia. Despite the hurried pace enforced by Jackson, they hooted and hollered at each other. There would be fresh meat tonight. The General would see to it!

Just as they had hoped, each man received a portion of beef that night for his supper, along with a handful of flour. They ate it hungrily, grateful for the fresh meat – something they hadn't seen in many a day.

There commenced a cold drizzle which seemed to soak through the tents the men had erected. Yet they were in good spirits. They had defeated the Spanish with very little loss of life. Their bellies were satisfied. They bantered and catcalled each other as they huddled over small fires they managed to kindle under the limbs of the large pine and oak trees under which they camped.

Despite Preacher's sage advice to keep focused on the matter at hand, Jacob still felt the sting of regret that they hadn't encountered any Red Sticks in the scuffle at Pensacola. As he lay under his damp blanket, he wondered whether he would ever get the chance to get the revenge he so desperately desired at that moment. Yet he also wondered if seeking it was what his uncle would have wanted.

He thought back to the life he had known before. Before war and turmoil, death and devastation, had interfered. It suddenly occurred to him, as he lay staring at the sky, that the life he had known would never return. Too much of it had been torn away. Why he had not thought about it before, he had no idea. Perhaps it was his youth – he was still only eighteen. Or maybe the stubbornness he had inherited from his father. But as he fell asleep, he felt a yearning for what had been, and the inescapable knowledge that life, for him, would never be the same.

Pierre Durand was awakened by clattering sounds that beat down from above the bluff. His eyes squinted in the early morning sunshine, and he could hear the soft slapping of the waters of Mobile Bay along the shoreline, not far from his head.

He arose from his prone position carefully and grabbed the sides of his pounding head. Where was he? And most importantly, how did he get here?

It took a moment for his mind to clear, and then he remembered.

His employer, Mr. Allard, had discovered the secret he had tried to keep hidden. He had suddenly entered the room where Pierre used to work on the books, just as Pierre had lifted a small canteen to his lips. The odor of the rum he kept in it was unmistakable.

"Here, here! What have you got in that canteen?" he asked sternly, as he snatched it from Pierre's hand. He put it to his nose and winced.

"Are you drinking while taking care of my business?" he shouted.

Pierre remained silent but dropped his head in shame.

"I hired you out of a sense of duty to your father. He and I have been friends for many years. I knew he was having trouble with you, but I took you on despite it. Is this how you repay my kindness to him, and to you?"

"I'm sorry, sir," Pierre gulped. His eyes remained lowered, as if studying the figures on the pages before him.

"I cannot rely on a drinking man to take care of my accounts. You understand that, don't you?"

Pierre nodded.

"You cannot be relied on. I demand you leave my employ. You have until the morning to clear out your things and be gone." He turned on his heel and huffed out of the room.

As Pierre, dejected, left the main house and walked to the small shack he called home, he heard the sounds of a large group of men on the move. Curious, he walked to the edge of the clearing around the plantation and peered through the surrounding border of trees.

He saw a long line of dusty travelers, hundreds of them, descending on the open spaces around the boundaries of Mr. Allard's property. He heard the sounds of marching feet, the whinnying of horses and the grumbling and groaning of heavy wagons as they moved into his view. The men who hove into sight all carried muskets but were clothed haphazardly. Some wore homespun, with hats jammed onto their heads, others were in buckskin, while a few marched in good order, clad in some sort of uniform, well worn, but still recognizable as blue. As he watched, orders were barked out by the men who seemed to be in charge. Tents and shelters were ordered to be erected, and the gathering men began to stake them out neatly in rows.

This must be Jackson's army, he thought. They had heard rumors they were on the move. Jackson's desire for secrecy about his plans against Pensacola had been openly discussed among the populace. Try as he might, even Jackson had no power over the gossip and speculation of the people around Mobile.

Pierre watched curiously for a while. But then his dire situation returned to his mind. What was he supposed to do now? He was without a place to lay his head as of tomorrow morning. Where was he to go? What was he to do?

He left the scene of the industrious men setting up camp and entered his shack. He had very few possessions to worry about – only his razor and soap, two extra shirts and another pair of breeches, and the clothes he had on his back. He looked around at the meager furnishings of his room – the small bed shoved into the corner, the cushionless straight-backed chair, the small washstand and cracked mirror above it. His father's house had been well appointed. He'd had all his needs taken care of, and even two servants to tend to his needs. Now he could not even maintain this simple, humble dwelling. How far he had fallen, he thought.

As he sat dejectedly in the rickety chair, he wondered to himself what to do. Come morning, he would have no place to live. He could not return to his father's house, that much he knew. If he returned, it would be as a beggar. Word would spread quickly that he had lost his position with Mr. Allard, and the reason for it as well.

He did remember, however, that he had a few coins in his pocket. Recklessly, he thought, he had nothing to lose at that point. He would walk the few hundred yards to the only place he could find refuge at the moment – to the ramshackle buildings and huts clustered beside the bay at the Villages. There he could drown his sorrows. He would worry about his future in the morning.

He passed by the shouting men and the bustle around them as they worked at building a temporary camp to house the army. He climbed down the bluff and proceeded to his favorite drinking spot.

He remembered very little after that. He had not even managed to make it to his bed, but had found himself splayed out on the sandy ground with an empty bottle in his hand.

Painfully, he climbed up the bluff, shaking and brushing the clinging sand from his clothing. As he got to the top, he observed the camp he had seen being erected the afternoon before. There were sentries posted, and the campfires before the tents were being kindled, hundreds of them. They stretched as far as the eye could see. Neat and orderly, he would have been impressed if it weren't for the splitting headache that blocked all logical thought from his mind.

He entered his shack and went immediately to the washstand, where he proceeded to splash the lukewarm water still in the bowl onto his face. As he gazed at himself in the cracked bit of mirror that hung over it, noting his thinning, black hair and the stubble on his face, he sighed. The puffy red eyes that stared back at him jolted him into reality. His life was a mess.

With shaking fingers he attempted to shave without much success. He cut himself on the curve of his pointed chin and then cursed and put down the razor.

The alcohol he was using to dull the pain of Rosa's loss was the root of his problems, he knew. If he were to have any chance at straightening out his life, he would have to give it up. At twenty years old, he was at a crossroads. But the temptation of losing himself in the bottle was a strong one.

And then it occurred to him the answer might be right outside.

He grabbed a blanket from the bedstead – Mr. Allard surely would not begrudge him that – and used it to wrap up his few possessions. The only way out, as he saw it, was to join the army that was camped right outside. It was said General Jackson frowned on the use of alcohol by his men. Perhaps that sort of discipline was what he needed to keep him from himself.

There was a great stirring of the soldiers when he entered their camp. They were gathering around a huge live oak, its limbs spreading out dozens of feet in every direction. Pierre noted a tall, thin man who had climbed up on one of the lower limbs, and using a hand to balance himself on a branch directly above him, was getting ready to address the men that were clustered around.

The man in question was neatly uniformed in a dark blue coat, white breeches, and tall black boots. He had an air of command about him as he patiently waited for the assembly before him to quiet. He spoke with a high-pitched voice that seemed to reach across the audience before him with little effort.

"Men, I must commend you for the bravery and fortitude you displayed before our enemies in Pensacola. I, like many of you, was disappointed that we didn't have the opportunity to give to the British what they deserved – a thorough thrashing on the battlefield."

A ragged cheer broke out.

"Nonetheless, I could not have asked for a better group of soldiers to lead. Your courage and resilience has been duly noted. We will have our chance against those who have chosen to attack the country we love.

The country we are proud to serve. The country that was forged by our forefathers." He paused while the soldiers murmured and nodded.

"Even now, our enemies are regrouping from their poor showing in our last encounter. But your General has plans, men. Even now, friendly forces are gathering together in New Orleans. Patriots, one and all, who wish to repel the scourge of British tyranny!" He raised his fist in defiance. The lusty cheers that greeted his words reverberated loudly. He raised his hand for silence.

"The British must not be allowed to take New Orleans. It will take you and I, and the good people of that fair city, to see to it that does not happen. We will return to Mobile, gentlemen, and once there we will gather what is necessary for a very difficult march. A march that must be made quickly. The very lifeblood of our country depends on it. So I ask, are you prepared to take that journey with me?"

The men cheered and yelled as Jackson climbed down from his perch. Pierre watched as they dispersed and began to disassemble their camp. He looked around to see if he could spot someone who might help him with his mission. He spotted a man with a uniform who was imperiously directing a group of soldiers gathered around a supply wagon.

"Here, you men, be sure take this wagon down below the bluff. There will be barges arriving to take it across the bay."

Pierre stepped forward. "Excuse me, sir."

The man stopped and looked at him. "What do you want?"

"I want to join up with Jackson's army."

"Well, I can't help you with that." He looked around huffily. "Do you see that man over there – the one in the forage cap? He might be able to help you." He waved Pierre away.

Undaunted, Pierre approached the man in question. "Excuse me sir. I want to join the army and was told you might be able to help."

"Maybe. Maybe not." He eyed Pierre up and down.

"Say, are you a Frenchie?"

"Yes I am."

"Well, I suppose we can sign you up. But it will have to wait till we get to Mobile. I'll have a table set up inside the fort. See me there."

Pierre persisted. "But . . . "

The man patiently explained. "I don't have the paperwork handy, son. Just ride along with us across the Bay and I'll take your signature once we arrive."

Pierre found himself jammed onto a shabby barge overloaded with a rowdy group of Tennessee volunteers, who raucously jeered at the jampacked boat immediately behind them.

"That old tub will never make it!"

"Hope you fellers can swim!" one cackled.

"Look out you don't get throwed overboard! The gators might getcha!"

Jacob and Solomon were wedged into the bow of the boat. Jacob noticed a young man clinging desperately to the side a few feet away. His face had taken on a greenish shade, and his hands were shaking uncontrollably as he held on for dear life. He could see he was not a soldier. He carried no weapon, and he seemed intimidated by the group of men who surrounded him.

He didn't know his situation, but at that point he didn't care.

He had listened intently to Jackson's speech back at the old oak tree. It had been stirring, no doubt. The men had responded with great gusto at his words.

But Jacob wasn't sure. He knew the route they would need to get to New Orleans was a difficult one. There would be numerous obstacles in their path. He, more than most of the men, understood that.

And yet, he had made his mark on a document in August that committed him for almost three more months. As the sultry cool breeze that skittered across Mobile Bay ruffled his hair, he resigned himself to following through on the promise he had made. He would be marching to New Orleans with the rest of Jackson's army. As with all soldiers, the prospect of facing the unknown was grim. A soldier's life was never his own. He and his comrades would have to trust the man who commanded them and hope he was not leading them to disaster.

CHAPTER 25

PREPARATIONS IN MOBILE

The man Pierre had spoken with across the Bay sat at a table, a bottle of ink and a quill poised above a sheet of paper. They were inside Fort Charlotte, and all around them were the sounds of barking orders and the clanking and cursing of men as the tents they had recently taken down before they left for Pensacola were now being resurrected, as if from the dead.

"Your name?"

"Pierre Durand."

"Where do you hail from?" The man didn't look up as he carefully wrote down his name.

"Mobile."

The man looked sharply up at him. "You French?"

"Yes I am."

"Speak any other languages?"

"I speak Spanish as well. And I have a good understanding of Creek and Choctaw."

"Wait here." The man arose from his seat and hustled off to a group of officers who had gathered to oversee the men as they worked.

Pierre glanced around. He had always been in awe of Fort Charlotte. Its thick red brick walls had always given him a sense of comfort and security. It had stood as a bulwark against the unknown in his mind. But he had never envisioned himself as a soldier stationed within it.

His path in life had been determined at the moment of his birth. His father had prepared him to follow in his footsteps, to take control of the family business once he was gone. Pierre thought about the hours he had spent hunched over ledgers and books, learning the trade his father had built over many years. The instructions he had received from the priests at the Church of the Immaculate Conception, although not a full-blown education, had been geared toward learning the ways of his faith. He had even learned Latin at their behest.

He began to have second thoughts about his rash decision to join the army. What, exactly, did he have to offer?

At that moment, a short, squat man, stuffed into a too-small blue jacket with dull gold buttons, hurried up to him.

"Sergeant Thompson," he crisply said.

"Yes, sir."

"I've been told you hail from these parts."

"I do. I was born and raised here."

"So you know most of the people in Mobile, then?"

"I suppose so."

"Well, I'm with the quartermaster department of this here army. Once you've signed your paper, report to me. I have a use for you. You can find me over at Jackson's headquarters."

"Yes, sir," Pierre replied.

The man returned and dipped his quill into the bottle of ink on the table and handed it to Pierre. He signed. He hoped he wouldn't live to regret it.

Jacob and his companions returned to their old campsite just west of town. They strung up their tarpaulins on the same trees and dug out the pit they had previously used for a campfire. Once accomplished, they relaxed before the roaring fire they had kindled and contemplated what their next steps would be.

"Boys, I think Jackson made it pretty clear. We're going to be moving out as soon as he can gather the supplies we'll need for the march. I'm wondering how difficult it will be," Preacher said.

"It won't be easy, that's for sure. There are a few trails between here and New Orleans, but it's an absolute wilderness out there. Lots of bogs and swamps and pitfalls between us," Solomon replied.

"Well, I don't plan on starvin' to death. Look here, between the four of us we should be able to git enough meat to tide us over," Sam interjected.

"Hunting will not be particularly good right now."

"Maybe not. But if we split up into two groups, we should be able to do all right."

"We should get to work immediately. Jacob, you know this area best. Any suggestions as to where our best chances are to get hold of fresh meat?" Preacher asked.

"My uncle and I hunted west of here and had good luck. I know of a few places where deer like to graze. We might even be able to smoke out a bear or two if we look sharp."

Before darkness fell, they had formed two teams. Solomon and Sam comprised one, Preacher and Jacob another. They had barely left their campsite when shots rang out from both. A couple of rabbits and a raccoon were soon roasting on spits over the fire.

Before the firelight that evening, Jacob got to work fashioning a couple of traps, like the ones his uncle had taught him to make. At first light, they set them on the banks of a nearby bog and then headed out, one group to the southwest, the other to the northwest.

They ranged the woods for two days. Solomon and Sam were able to find a black bear, hibernating at the edge of a dense growth of tangled shrubbery on the banks of a clear creek. Instead of shooting it, they used the butts of their guns to club it to death. There were other hunters in the woods now, and they didn't want their location to be revealed by firing off their weapons.

Jacob and Preacher managed to drop a couple of deer. They dressed them where they fell and then carried their carcasses to the camp. They wielded their knives and cut the meat into thin strips and placed them before a second fire, to begin the drying process immediately. The jerked venison would be needed in the future.

The small traps Jacob had fashioned yielded their own rewards, with a few raccoons and rabbits. These were consumed immediately, either roasted over the fire or cut up into chunks and boiled with a few wild greens.

Each afternoon, one of the four would make a trip into town, to report in at the fort and inquire as to when they would be called into service.

On the third day after they arrived, Solomon came racing into camp, shouting excitedly.

"We're on the move, boys! At first light! We're to move out with General Coffee!"

"Where we headed?"

"Jackson's sending us to Baton Rouge. Quick, lets gather our supplies and get into town. We don't want them to leave without us!"

Pierre met Sergeant Thompson on the stoop of Jackson's headquarters. There was a flurry of activity along the street in front, with riders on lathered horses racing up and jumping off their mounts, while others burst from the front door and grabbed hold of the reins of their own steeds and galloped off.

Men, too, were boiling in and out of the building in a steady stream. Pierre tried to make himself inconspicuous as he waited to see the sergeant. He noted some familiar faces – townsmen he had known since his youth – leaving the building with deep scowls and grumbling loudly. As he observed the scene, he thought to himself that he had never seen such a sight in all his life. The sleepy town he knew as home was in an uproar.

Eventually, Sergeant Thompson appeared and waved him over.

"Pierre, isn't it?" he asked.

"Yes, sir."

"I will make this brief. This army will be heading out in a few days. We need supplies to get us to New Orleans. Your job is to beg, borrow or even steal anything that isn't nailed down from the townspeople. We need foodstuffs and gunpowder and balls, and any weapons that might be useful. If a home has two muskets, take one. We don't want to leave them defenseless. I am under orders from Jackson himself to do whatever is necessary to gather what we need."

"The people here will not be happy with that order."

"We've been made aware of that." The sergeant frowned. "It's a sad day indeed when a General has to threaten his own citizens with hanging to get what he needs from them."

"Most of the people in Mobile don't really consider themselves Americans."

"Like it or not, they are. A few have come forward to offer what they have. Of course, those that have are mostly Americans newly arrived here. It's the Spanish and French that are unwilling."

Pierre nodded.

"You are not alone. There are groups out already out banging on doors. Most of them only speak English, though." He glared at Pierre. "That's where you come in. I expect you to go behind them and see if you can talk these people out of the things we're sure they're hiding. Can you be forceful enough to handle this assignment?"

"I think so, sir."

"Fine. Go back to the fort and get a horse and cart. I want it filled as quickly as possible."

Pierre returned to the fort and managed to finagle a sorry-looking horse and cart away from an idle gentleman who, at first, questioned his authority. Pierre simply spoke the sergeant's name and told him it was in his best interest to let him have the rig. The man sighed and handed over the horse's reins.

Darkness was falling as Pierre left the fort. He had no idea where to start. His head was still pounding from the drunken stupor he had awakened from that morning, and his hands were shaking uncontrollably. He was in no shape, he decided, to knock on any doors that evening. He was hungry and thirsty, having had nothing to eat the entire day. He was tempted to go to the tavern right outside the gates of the fort – one he had often frequented in the past – to find some food, but decided against it. The pull of the rum bottle would be too strong. He must not give into the temptation. He believed in his heart this was his last chance. If he failed as a soldier, he had no other refuge.

He opted to park his cart along St. Joseph Street, already quiet for the evening, curled up inside it and fell asleep. Perhaps in the morning he would be better able to follow his orders.

When he awoke the next morning, his head was a little clearer. The faint, early morning rays had just peaked over the eastern horizon when he began knocking on doors.

Some of the homes he approached had already been visited, but the men who had pounded on the doors had been strangers. The people of Mobile were not particularly fond of strangers and had only grudgingly complied with the demands. Pierre knew they would have hidden stores, just as his family had, in case of emergency. It was those he was after.

Pierre had never considered himself much of a talker, but in the back of his mind was the thought that he must prove himself or be destitute. He found himself coaxing and cajoling, beseeching and even begging his fellow citizens to let loose the supplies the army needed. Because they knew him, or at least knew his father, they were more forthcoming.

He worked at it all day, and slowly his cart began to fill. There were a dozen or so small bags of corn and meal, a few small kegs of preserved meat, and even four muskets. The Rodriguez family had offered him a hot meal, which he gladly accepted. He wolfed it down, grateful to have something in his stomach after two days going without.

The weak, winter sun had started to descend when he returned to the fort. His cart was not quite full, but he felt confident enough that the sergeant would be satisfied. He left the cart at the fort and steeled himself for the most difficult visit of the day. He must present himself at the door of his family's home.

He drew a deep breath before he knocked on the door. He closed his fists as tightly as he could to still the trembling of his hands. The maid, Alina, answered his knock, startled to see him.

"Is my father home?"

"He's in the sitting room with your mother," she said with a worried look.

Pierre entered the house. It smelled just as he remembered it. The soft aroma of the evening meal still wafted through the air, mixed with the odor of his father's evening pipe. When he entered the sitting room, both his parents looked up in surprise.

"What are you doing here, Pierre?"

"You haven't heard from Mr. Allard?"

"No." His father's face turned into a scowl. "This town has been in a turmoil all day."

"Jackson."

"Yes, Jackson. But you haven't answered our question. Why are you here, instead of across the bay, working?"

"I lost my job."

His mother looked down quickly at the bit of embroidery in her hands. His father gave him a cross look.

"I suppose I shouldn't be surprised. You have given yourself over to the work of the devil, son."

Pierre hung his head.

"If you are expecting me to hire you back, you are sadly mistaken. Until you get hold of yourself, I cannot use your services. You have gravely disappointed me." His voice raised. "And now, you've disgraced me with a friend and business partner. Soon, the whole town will be talking."

"I've not come to get my job back, Papa. I just wanted you to know I've joined the army."

A look of horror crossed his father's face. "Jackson's army?" he exclaimed.

"Yes."

"That man is destroying this town. It was bad enough when he billeted his men among us before he tore off to Pensacola. Now, he's returned with even more men. Thousands more. And he's stripping the town of the very necessities of life. He's taking the food right out of our mouths. And yet you've joined him?"

"Yes."

"Is that all you have to say?" His father stood, drawing himself up to his full height. A look of disgust crossed his face as he gazed at his eldest son.

"It's the only thing I could do. I know you won't understand, either of you, but I realize I have brought disgrace upon you and the family. I want to make things right."

"Don't expect us to support you in your decision, Pierre. I believe you've made a grave mistake. You must leave now. May God have mercy on your soul."

Darkness had fallen when he returned to the fort. There was no place to rest. Even the surrounding grounds were covered with neat rows of tents. He found a small spot at the base of the fort and curled up into a ball, his blanket wound tightly around his body. He was exhausted but had difficulty falling asleep. Images of his past life flashed before him. Safely ensconced in Rosa's parlor, her mother looking on with a smile. Walking along Royal Street with her small, trusting hand in the crook of his elbow. Sitting at dinner, with his smiling parents praising him for his good head for figures. The images eventually faded, and he fell fast asleep.

He awoke with a start the next morning, right before daylight. The soldiers that surrounded him were beginning to stir, sleepily emerging from their tents.

As the sun began to rise, he entered the fort, looking around for Sergeant Thompson to see what assignment he would have for that day. He found him at a rude table, made up of a couple of boards placed over two barrels. There was a sheaf of paper before him, and he watched as the sergeant fumbled with the quill in his hand, softly cursing.

Thompson looked up at him sharply. "Are you ready to resume your duties for the day?"

"Yes, sir."

"Get your cart, then, and get back to work. Today the south side, near the docks."

"Before I go, sir, may I inquire as to what you are doing?"

"I'm trying to take account of the supplies that were brought in yesterday."

Pierre went around the makeshift desk and looked over his shoulder at the jumble of numbers and letters the sergeant had painstakingly written down.

"I am a bookkeeper by trade. Perhaps I could help you."

"You know how to write?"

"Yes, sir. In fact, I can write in several languages. French, Spanish and English."

"A bookkeeper, you say?"

"I'm used to taking account of merchandise. I worked for my father in his trading business, and for a plantation across the bay, where I kept track of incoming and outgoing supplies."

The sergeant looked at him coolly. "Do you think you can count and record the stock we have on hand?"

Pierre didn't hesitate. "Yes, sir."

"Some of my figures might be off. You may need to correct them."

"I can do that."

A look of relief came over the sergeant's face. "I will leave you to it, then. My writing looks like hen scratches. Besides, I have other duties to perform. The General is in a big hurry and we have to finish gathering up what we can. He plans on us leaving in the morning."

Pierre took the quill from the sergeant's hand, leaned his tall thin body over, and got to work.

CHAPTER 26

JACKSON'S DILEMMA

Andrew Jackson was not a military man by trade. He had pursued a career as a lawyer in his youth and had been good at it. He had trained while still in North Carolina, where he grew up, and passed the bar by the time he was twenty. He had moved to Tennessee and established a very successful law practice there.

In the early years, he had traveled the back country of the state, plying his craft. It was here that he began to understand the character and resilience of the hardy souls that called the rugged wilderness their home. He would never forget those lessons, even after he moved to Nashville and involved himself in local politics.

Perhaps it was in the courtroom that he learned the importance of preparing for any contingencies that might arise. There, one had to be quick to make decisions and be able to absorb all the circumstances of the matter at hand. Facing a judge, a man had to be able to think on his feet and have a ready answer for any problem or challenge. The courtroom was about winning, and he enjoyed winning very much.

When he and his men had returned to Mobile after soundly trouncing the feeble resistance in West Florida, he had decisions to make. He had to be prepared for anything the British might throw at him, and the possibilities were numerous.

He knew, and had always known, that New Orleans was the prize the British most sought. His spies and informants had only reinforced this knowledge. With the war in the north not going particularly well for America, the capture of the city that rested in the heart of the Mississippi delta would be a serious blow to the struggling young nation that he loved so much.

And yet, despite all the information that flowed to him daily, he had no knowledge of how the British planned to capture what they sought.

He knew they had a fleet of ships sitting in the Caribbean, waiting to pounce. Which direction they would choose to take, he could only speculate.

There were several possibilities. They could storm Pensacola or Mobile in full force and then march overland to New Orleans, or head to Natchez or even Baton Rouge, where they could choke off the city from the north and then march south. Or they could storm the city directly with their fleet. He thought it was most likely they would choose one of the overland routes, as a direct assault, in his mind, would be more hazardous.

The dizzying array of pitfalls that surrounded New Orleans – bayous and jungles, reptile-infested bogs and streams – were well-known. Traversing the Mississippi upstream would be impossible for sailing vessels, aside from the mud and sandbars. To try and land troops directly from the Gulf into the delta would be a foolish endeavor. Overall, an overland route would make the most sense.

And so he went about preparing for any of the possibilities that might occur. He had left a small force near Pensacola to keep watch and buy time in case the British decided to use that city again as a base of operations. He reinforced Fort Bowyer at the mouth of Mobile Bay. That garrison could provide at least some resistance and give warning if the enemy decided Mobile was their destination. He would also leave a few men in Mobile for the same purpose – stall the British if they decided to attack from that direction.

Yet, he would need a strike force to protect his rear. If the British decided on an overland route, he would have to be able to counter it to protect the bulk of his army.

He decided the best solution for the problem was to send General Coffee and his cavalry to Baton Rouge, which sat eighty miles northwest of New Orleans. He could depend on the ability of the cavalry to get itself quickly to wherever they were most needed. From the confines of Baton Rouge, they could quickly return to Mobile or Pensacola to confront the British if necessary. They could also saddle up and come to his aid if the British were foolish enough to try and take New Orleans directly.

To have men stationed at Baton Rouge also helped with another pressing problem. He had received word that reinforcements for his army were being sent downriver from Tennessee and Kentucky. They were raw recruits, unlike the battle-hardened men already under his command. He could depend on Coffee to see that the new arrivals were prepared for the coming conflict.

The correspondence he was receiving from the people of New Orleans had grown increasingly frantic. There was no force to speak of there to protect them. They understood clearly the danger they faced, and they begged him to make his way to their city to protect them.

And so, on November 22, 1814, after only three days in Mobile, and despite a debilitating bout of dysentery that would have kept any other man sick in bed, he sent Coffee and his cavalry to Baton Rouge. He himself commanded the rest of his troops, two thousand of them, and they headed west.

Jacob and his fellow part-Creek Solomon, with Preacher and Sam, went west with Coffee's cavalry. Most of the men they traveled with were well known to them, having served with Jackson during the Creek War.

Since they had left Mobile in a hurry, the four men had not had time to properly cure the meat they had hunted while at their campsite on the edge of town. To keep it from going to waste, they shared it with some of their old comrades. It was happily accepted.

It was a tiresome slog to Baton Rouge, two hundred miles to the west. There were trails and a narrow road, to be sure, but they were not large enough to accommodate the more than a thousand men that comprised Coffee's cavalry. The rowdy Tennesseans cursed as they thrashed through the thick underbrush that dragged at their horse's hooves.

They brought with them a few wagons with supplies, but it wasn't enough to feed them all. General Coffee sent out hunting parties to help supply his men. As they were short on ammunition, those who were proficient with the bow and arrow were utilized. That meant that Jacob and Solomon, who both had the equipment and skill necessary for such an endeavor, were kept busy throughout the journey.

As they tracked through the wilderness, the beauty and majesty of the fields and forests, the clear running creeks and streams and the mysterious swamps and bogs they encountered left Jacob with a sense of awe. The lush landscape in which he found himself brought him a sense of peace, and he thought he heard whispers of home.

He traveled alone most of the time as he hunted down the deer and other forest creatures to help feed his comrades. Having honed his skills with the bow while living on his own before rejoining Jackson's army, his proficiency could not be denied. He never came back to camp emptyhanded. At times, his burden was so heavy he wondered if his horse would be able to carry it all.

Once back in camp he would drop off his catch at the quartermaster's tent and then find his comrades. Sometimes he would hide away a rabbit in his saddlebag and present it to them, at which time Sam would grin and whisk out his knife, skin it, and add it to the bubbling kettle before their fire.

"I'm shore glad they're sendin' you out, Jacob. We'd all be a sight thinner if it warn't fer you!" Sam would say.

"I don't mind. I like the solitude. It gives me time to think."

"Think about what?"

"Oh, I don't know," he replied vaguely.

"Maybe women!" Sam snickered.

Jacob shrugged his shoulders.

"Leave him alone, Sam," Preacher interjected. "Jacob seems to have much on his mind these days. I completely understand. Sometimes spending time by yourself draws your mind to bigger things. I know I do my best thinking when I'm alone on the hunt, deep into the Blue Ridge mountains back home." He paused. "You're a young man, Jacob. Thinking and pondering life's big questions is good for you."

The fighting men of Coffee's cavalry were happy when they finally reached Baton Rouge. It was a small city of about a thousand souls, yet bigger than the one they had just left. Like Mobile and Pensacola, it had swapped hands between the Spanish, French and the English, finally overthrowing Spanish control in 1810. Within two years it was annexed into the new state of Louisiana. The citizens were happy for the stability obtained by becoming part of the United States. Perhaps, at last, their future would be stable and secure, without the influence of far-off European powers. They welcomed the weary men of Coffee's cavalry with open arms.

The Mississippi River runs broad and deep past the city, its brown waters flowing smoothly toward the sea. It brought commerce and prosperity to Baton Rouge, with barges loaded with goods gathered from towns, cities and farms to the north headed to the city of New Orleans, where they would be traded and loaded onto the numerous ocean-going ships anchored at the mouth of the river. The citizenry were grateful for the bounty it brought. A brisk trade was established with the men who manned the barges, and the city looked forward to a prosperous future. Yet, that future could not be secure without peace, and peace could not happen without expelling the British, who had promised to return the area back to the control of the Spanish if they were to win the present conflict.

There was also the matter of the Indian tribes that still surrounded them. If the British were to win, there had been pledges made to the tribes that would not be beneficial to the people of Baton Rouge. Native lands would be returned, and restrictions made on the expansion of American settlers. Of even greater concern was the promise to carve out a nation for the tribes from lands that bordered the Mississippi and Ohio rivers. The prosperous trade along the muddy river that flowed before their town would be brought almost to a standstill.

And so, it was in their best interest to welcome General Coffee and the hard-charging Tennesseans under his command. Despite the cramped quarters and the desperate need to help feed the thousand or so men that had descended on them, the people of Baton Rouge were grateful for their presence.

The troops hadn't been in town very long – just a few days – before the barges full of new recruits began arriving at the docks. Soon, there was a virtual flood of them, including several hundred volunteers from Kentucky. Most of them were without weapons or horses, and they were boisterous, loud and demanding when they were unloaded onshore. General Coffee, with the urging of General Jackson, who was still on his way to New Orleans, would have his hands full trying to get them ready for the fight he knew was coming.

The most pressing issue was the lack of weaponry. Although muskets had been promised, there were few to be had. That, and a lack of ammunition, could hamper the fighting potential of the army. The lack of horses was also a problem. Coffee sent search parties out far and wide to acquire what horses they could.

Despite the shortages, he began instilling the military discipline needed to control the new recruits. Although all could shoot, they needed to learn how to march and to heed the commands of the officers among them. He relied heavily on the men who had served under him for so long to help teach them the hard lessons they would need to survive in battle.

Jacob watched, bemused, as Sam went about ordering and

reprimanding the new groups of soldiers that had been assigned to camp around their spot.

"See here, you fellas got a lot to learn about fightin'! You cain't just lay around waitin' for someone else to do somethin' for ya. You there, fetch some wood fer our fires! And be quick about it! An' don't leave your weapon out like that! Don't you know someone'll come snatch it if'n they get the chance? We got folks here with itchy fingers and no gun. Ain't you got no sense?"

Every once in a while, as he groused and complained, he would sneak a sly look in Jacob's direction and wink. Jacob would nod in reply.

It took twelve days for Jackson and his foot soldiers to reach New Orleans from Mobile – days of marching through swamps and fording streams, of bivouacking on what solid ground they could find, pushed unmercifully by their commander. Jackson continued to receive desperate messages from the citizens of the city, expressing fear of what they knew would surely come.

Pierre struggled as much, or more, than the rest of the troops. He had never been part of an army and was unused to the grinding physical labor of getting the carts that carried the food for them through the dense groves of pine and hardwoods interspersed between what seemed like an endless swamp. Through the pouring rain that fell day after day, he heaved from the rear of those damnable carts, and yanked and tugged at the reins of the draft animals that pulled them. Because their supply unit was at the rear of the column, they were always the last to arrive at camp. Then, once camp was made, he and the others in the quartermaster's department were in charge of dispersing food to the soldiers, who would send one man from their fires to pick up their allotment for the day.

When he wasn't busy handing out supplies, Sergeant Thompson had Pierre keep a running total of what foodstuffs had been handed out and what remained at the end of the evening. A simple task, really, but it seemed particularly arduous at the end of a day filled with the physical demands and the overwhelming labor that was required to reach camp in the first place.

And yet, he was grateful for it all in the end. It kept his mind from thinking about the bottle. The urge to satiate his need for rum began to lesson as the days went by. His head began to clear now that it was free from the alcohol he had depended on to keep him going. Instead, he had to concentrate on placing one foot forward, through the muck and mud of the churned-up trail they were following. And then, instead of rest, he had to help disperse food and keep the books.

On the eighth day of the march, Sergeant Thompson approached him just as he was helping remove one of the carts from a deep mud hole, made deeper by the thousands of marching soldiers in front of him.

"Pierre!" he called. "I need to speak with you."

Pierre straightened himself up and said, "Yes, sir?"

"I don't know how those bastards in Jackson's staff figured out you can read and write as well as you do, but they're requesting you meet with them. They may have need of your services," the sergeant said gruffly.

Pierre tried to straighten his jacket and adjust his breeches to make himself more presentable, but he could do little about the splatters of mud that covered him from head to toe.

"I imagine they will keep you, once they learn you can speak all those languages. I'll miss you. Now I'll have to keep the books myself and I don't look forward to it."

Pierre nodded at him and headed forward until he came to the huddle of people surrounding the general, all on horseback. A few of them eyed him suspiciously, and one haughtily asked, "Who are you?"

"My name is Pierre Durand. I'm with the quartermaster's department. Sergeant Thompson said someone here has asked to speak with me."

An affable looking man turned when he heard him.

"Are you French?"

"Yes, sir."

"I hear you have a clear hand."

"So I've been told."

"Can you communicate in English as well as French?"

"Yes. And Spanish too. I grew up in Mobile."

"Ahh," the man replied.

"The sergeant informed me my services may be needed by the general's staff."

"My name is Lieutenant Cleveland. We always have a need for more interpreters. Once we arrive in the city, there will also be a need for extra hands for correspondence."

"I'm a bookkeeper by trade, sir. I am used to working on paper."

"I'll look to find a horse for you. Try and keep pace with us until I do."

Pierre did his best to keep up with the group until a horse was secured for him. He spied General Jackson ahead. He was hard to miss. His shock of gray hair was uncovered, and his ramrod back spoke volumes. He was undeterred by the numerous roadblocks that had been placed in his path for months on end. Despite his illness, the lack of supplies, and the shortage of men, guns and ammunition, he was determined. He would rescue New Orleans from the imminent invasion, no matter the cost.

CHAPTER 27

JACKSON ARRIVES

There was much rejoicing within the city of New Orleans upon the arrival of Jackson and his troops. The citizenry watched as the General entered town, in a carriage rather than on horseback. His bout of dysentery had left him in a weakened state, and he was thin and drawn as he struggled to wave to the crowds gathered along the streets as he passed by.

He was immediately taken to a building on Royal Street that his staff had arranged for his headquarters. A flag was hung from the third floor to identify it. Crowds gathered outside, waiting. After a brief respite, Jackson rose and strode out onto the balcony to address them.

The people of New Orleans were a mixture of many cultures. There were the French, of course, descendants of the original founders of the city in 1718, buttressed over the years by refugees from Acadia, St. Domingue and elsewhere. Blended in among them were those of Spanish descent, as well as a numerous free people of color, who had escaped their bondage from the islands of the Caribbean and had found their way to the city. Creoles, people born in the region, often with a mix of black and European blood, were also numerous. There was an increasing number of Americans in the city since the Louisiana Purchase in 1803. Divergent groups with different perspectives, there were cultural and political strains between them.

As he gazed across the crowd, Jackson knew the only hope he had of defeating the British was to somehow bring these diverse peoples together. He needed to convey to them the dire ramifications should their city fall to invasion, and they had to work as a team to defeat the enemy of them all – the British.

French was the common language of these people. Therefore, as he spoke, an interpreter conveyed his words to the crowd. As he began his address, his body straightened. He spoke with feeling, with power and an air of defiance.

"I have heeded your call and your concerns over the fate of New Orleans. I and my men have come to defend this city. A great city, and a great people, who deserve the protection afforded to you by your fellow countrymen. My goal is a simple one – I will drive the British back into the sea, or perish in the effort. People of New Orleans, we must put aside our differences and be united in this effort. If we do not, I fear the consequences for you will be severe. Among you are people who disagree with my goal. Let me be clear – any of you who are against this effort will suffer serious repercussions. In order for this city to survive, we must unite." He paused as the crowd gazed at him rapt, hanging on his words.

"Let's us join together now in this effort. Let us stand firm in our resolve. If we do so, victory will be our reward!"

Standing at the front of the crowd, Pierre noted the effect this man had on the people who surrounded him. His flashing eyes and resolute voice had stirred them. His demeanor – one of obstinate defiance – seemed to invigorate those gathered around, and they cheered him wildly. It seemed the people of New Orleans had accepted this strong-willed man as their leader. As he thought about it, Pierre could see why. It would be hard to find a man more willing to bend the will of the people to his own. Jackson exuded the confidence of a man so convinced of the rightness of his cause that it was contagious.

Pierre's cramped quarters were in a house near the headquarters. The small family that owned it graciously allowed he and five other men of the staff to move in. It was a tight fit, and Pierre found himself on a pallet in the kitchen. For the time of year it could have been worse, he decided. The warmth of the glowing embers in the fireplace at night helped fight off the damp cold. There was nothing worse than the frigid winds that blew off the Mississippi River and infiltrated the city at that time of year. Coupled with the almost constant rains – rains that managed to find their way into every nook and cranny of the town – they were a continuing reminder that nature had more control over the plans of mere men than he would have liked.

Now that the General had arrived, the people of the city could breathe a sigh of relief – and also get to work. The bars, saloons, restaurants and brothels in town were soon conducting a booming business. Pierre did his best to avoid such places. He kept his head down whenever he found himself on the muddy streets. He had gone without alcohol for a few weeks now, and he desperately wanted to avoid the trap such establishments represented.

While at work, he was one of several gatekeepers, whose jobs were to filter out the citizens who appeared at headquarters demanding to see either the General or someone else with influence. He was amused by some of them – regular citizens who requested the General's plans so that they could make their own. A few were more serious – either offering particular goods for the needs of the army or veiled threats as to what would happen to Jackson and his men if they didn't protect them from the British as he had promised. Most of those who approached spoke French. Some spoke Spanish. Pierre, being fluent in both, was in high demand.

He would return to his kitchen nook as late as possible, often being the last to leave headquarters, mostly because the men who were housed with him were freely using the bottle to pass the time, and prone to goading him into joining them.

Daniel Forwood from Nashville, who worked as a runner for the General, was the worst.

"Ho, Pierre! You should try this new bottle of wine! Best I've ever had!"

"No, thank you."

"Ain't you French, though? I thought French folks loved wine. They do here in New Orleans, anyways."

Pierre shook his head. "I'm sorry. I've had a long day. Sleep is my only interest."

He very rarely saw Jackson those first weeks, as he was out inspecting the city's few fortifications and redesigning them to be of the most use. Whenever he did appear, haggard and thin, he was always surrounded by hordes of aides and citizens, vociferously expressing their opinions on one thing or another. Jackson paid them little mind. He would go into his office and immediately begin working on his correspondence. Letters to Washington. Letters to his contacts in Mobile; to his men stationed near Pensacola and to General Coffee. Letters to anyone and everyone who could help supply the army with what it desperately needed – guns and ammunition. Once at his desk, he would work far into the night. Pierre, who preferred to remain and avoid the prodding of his fellow boarders, would stay inconspicuously in the outer foyer. He admired Jackson's drive and determination and came to believe he definitely could save the city. Maybe he was the only man who could.

Jean Lafitte walked the streets of New Orleans with impunity. He was a handsome man, with dark hair and a swarthy complexion. He most certainly understood the importance of appearance, and presented a dashing figure whenever he was out and about.

The people of New Orleans loved him. He and his smugglers provided the luxuries they craved, and on which they'd come to rely. Cinnamon and spices, fine linen and clocks, crystals, perfumes and other goods were nearly impossible to come by. Without his keen sense of business and trading, they would have to do without. If he was a pirate, that was of little importance to them. He provided a service and they were grateful for it.

The authorities, however, had taken a dim view of his operations. He had done his best to avoid the embargo on British and other goods that had been imposed on the city since the war had started. His smuggling operation, situated fifty miles south of the city on the islands of Barataria, had become a sore spot to a few of the merchants in the city. He consistently undersold them and avoided paying taxes on the goods he provided.

His operation had flourished since the start of the war. Hidden within the bayous of south Louisiana he had giant warehouses with docks and numerous ships that plied the waters of the Gulf, capturing whatever vessels they could. The number of ships under the command of Jean and his older brother Pierre had grown steadily.

He preferred, of course, to call himself a privateer. He held letters of marque from some of the islands in the Caribbean, and in his mind that made him a privateer. How others chose to view him was their business.

Although of French descent, he had a soft spot in his heart for Americans. He sensed the United States would prevail in the conflict in which they were now embroiled. He most certainly hoped so. For his operations to continue, it would be much easier to evade whatever forces the new country would try to muster against him and his little enterprise. If the British were to prevail, their Royal Navy would greatly impede the business he and his brother had worked so hard to build.

The British had contacted Jean in September and offered him a deal. If he would join forces with them and employ his ships against the Americans, they would grant him British citizenship and land grants in either their Caribbean possessions or Canada. Included in the correspondence was a handwritten note from Colonel Nicholls, the man responsible for the shameful British defeat at Fort Bowyer, and who had cut and run from Pensacola when Jackson attacked. If he refused, they promised to capture the small city he had built for his operations in Barataria and put an end to his smuggling.

It was an offer worth considering. Yet, he had a problem. His brother Pierre sat rotting in jail in New Orleans, having been convicted of piracy.

And the Governor of Louisiana, William Claiborne, held the key to his freedom.

Being a man of intelligence and cunning, Lafitte thus put off the British and told them he would think about it. He talked to the men under his command, and they had no desire to become part of the British navy. They were cruel and exacting taskmasters, the British, and his freewheeling men had far more to gain if they continued under Lafitte. Jean quickly sent the letters with the British offer through back channels to the Americans, and at the same time he volunteered his assistance in resisting the forthcoming British invasion.

Perhaps this gesture would have an impact on their views of the Lafitte brothers and their unique form of commerce. Within two days, in fact, his brother Pierre managed to escape from the jail in which he was being held.

But later in September his warehouses, stores and ships were attacked by an American expedition led by Commodore Daniel Patterson. There was a short battle, in which ten of his ships formed a battle line across the bay, but his men soon abandoned their position. They set some of their own ships on fire and fled into the swamps. Once ashore, the American expedition captured eighty of his men, eight of his ships, and twenty cannon. Again, Pierre managed to escape.

But his forwarding of the British letters asking for his assistance had an impact on Governor Claiborne. Pierre had offered his services in the defense of the city, and the shortage of manpower and equipment lay heavily on the governor. He immediately asked the American authorities for leniency for the Lafitte brothers and their men. He even went so far as to write Jackson, saying the destruction of the pirates and their conclave in Barataria had been a mistake. Their services were needed. They could provide a strong line of defense if the British attacked by sea.

Undeterred by the raid on the small city he had created in the swamps and bayous of lower Louisiana, Jean knew he would still benefit more from an American victory than a British one. He would wait and see if the Americans would come to their senses. He had something to offer them. It would be up to Jackson to recognize it.

The men stationed with General Coffee in Baton Rouge were growing impatient. They were cavalry, after all, and the tedious, anxious waiting for orders to move south to New Orleans meant that tempers were short.

Sam spent much of the time grousing about everything imaginable – from their rations to the weather to the wearisome ineptitude of the new recruits. Preacher tried to reason with him but with little success. Jacob and Solomon did their best to just leave him be. In their minds, life was easier without the added stress of listening to his complaints.

With any free time he had, Jacob would leave camp and head to the river. He would sit on the bank and gaze across the broad, deep water. It was a moving sight, that brown water of the mighty Mississippi, with eddies and swirls slowly moving past him, heading south to freedom from the constraining banks that held it.

Sometimes he was able watch the sun set over the western shore. The orange, yellow and reddish rays that glanced off the forest across the way seemed to him to hold a promise. Of what, he was not quite sure. But those quiet moments brought him a sense of peace, despite the tumultuous activity that had engulfed him ever since he left Mobile with General Coffee. He soaked it in as best he could. There was a real storm brewing, he knew, and felt sure it would be unlike anything he had yet experienced. As he watched the sinking rays of the sun against the western horizon, he would sometimes close his eyes and recollect all that had transpired since that dreadful day at Fort Pierce, when he heard the sound of the fierce battle that had taken so many lives at Fort Mims. In his mind's eye he could also picture his Uncle John, smiling and nodding at him. Whatever happened, he hoped he could prove one day to be half the man his uncle had been.

Along with the many new enlistees, Coffee had been blessed with a shipment of muskets and ammunition that had stopped off in Baton Rouge, enroute to New Orleans. He had immediately seized it. Jackson would depend on him to be fully armed and ready when he summoned him south. As his regulars taught the new recruits how to properly fire and maintain their weapons, Coffee patiently waited for word from his commander. He had to be prepared to move at a moment's notice. When the call came, he was determined to be ready.

CHAPTER 28

PREPARATIONS

When Jackson arrived in New Orleans, he hoped the city would have made a real effort to prepare for the coming onslaught. For months he had fielded letters from the citizens and officials of Louisiana, begging for his help. So he assumed the city had known enough to begin stiffening its defenses. He was none too happy with Governor Claiborne when he discovered it had not.

There were at least a thousand men who had volunteered – a mixture of Creoles, Frenchmen and American citizens – but they had not been organized properly. Furthermore, there had been no effort to fortify the city for defense. It was rumored that the enemy had somewhere between ten and twenty thousand men aboard the ships that had already sailed to the mouth of the river. Jackson had no time to waste. He must immediately set about preparing the city for battle.

He first set off south, into the delta to Fort St. Philip, and was angered at what little work had been done to prepare for the coming storm. He immediately ordered it to be upgraded with heavier cannon and instructed that the interior barracks, ramshackle affairs that were falling in on themselves, be torn down and new batteries placed above and below it along the banks of the Mississippi. He spent some time reconnoitering the river, as it flowed between its muddy banks, to see if there were any other places that could be fortified.

As there was no time to build brick or wooden fortifications, the only material available was the thick mud along the river. Earthen works would have to do. He wrote to Governor Claiborne and asked that the planters, who had grown rich with the use of slave labor, be called upon to provide the use of their slaves in the construction of the works. It wasn't much to ask considering the bleakness of their situation.

There were other issues that had to be resolved. New Orleans was the center of a spider web of bayous and streams that fed into it – a delta of tremendous size. He had called upon the Governor to block those waterways to prevent the enemy from using them as avenues of attack.

The army was also in urgent need of guns and ammunition. The call went out among the populace to willingly offer whatever they had, so that the volunteers from the city could be properly armed. His direct, forceful manner was not always received well, but desperate times called for desperate measures. If the city wanted to be saved, each and every citizen must do his part. He relied upon the men of the 7th and the 44th infantry, who had come with him from Mobile, to help organize the volunteer units from New Orleans.

On the thirteenth of December he was informed by Commodore Patterson, in charge of the meager American naval forces, that the enemy had anchored off Ship Island, to the northeast, close to the entrance to Lake Borgne, with thirty sails, including at least six ships of the line, heavily laden with cannon. But Jackson knew these heavy ships would be useless, as they needed deeper water to operate. The shallow water that surrounded the city would be to his advantage.

But Lake Borgne led directly to New Orleans. It lay almost due east. If the British captured the lake, it was a backdoor entrance straight into the city.

Lieutenant Jones did his duty with all the vigor he could muster. His five small gunboats and 182 men formed a defensive line of battle across the entrance to Lake Borgne. He stared uneasily at the forty-two barges and gigs with over a thousand British seamen and Royal Marines as they advanced on him. He knew it was an impossible task that he faced, but behind him lay the city of New Orleans. His orders were to do all he could to safeguard the city.

It was a brief but intense skirmish, and the men under his command fought valiantly. The first American gunboat was attacked and fiercely repelled the onslaught. Two of the British barges got stuck in the shallow waters of the lake, and a lusty cheer went up from his men. The rest of the enemy's watercraft briefly withdrew to regroup, but then forged ahead.

In the ensuing battle, his forces were overcome by the sheer numbers of British. Jones himself received a severe wound and was captured, along with the rest of the Americans who had survived the attack.

They were subjected to intense questioning after their capture. The British wanted to know the strength of the enemy they faced. How many men did Jackson have to defend the city? Without missing a beat, the reply was the same. The Americans told their captors Jackson had an army composed of eight thousand men. This was a lie, of course. Jackson's force at the time was less than half that. But what was a little lie among enemies?

Jackson's headquarters received a copy of a proclamation made by Admiral Alexander Cochrane, commander of the British fleet tasked with capturing New Orleans, and Major General John Keane, commanding the land forces. It was dated December 5, 1814.

To the Great and Illustrious Chiefs of the Creek and other Indian Nations:

The Great KING GEORGE, our beloved Father, has long wished to assuage the sorrows of his warlike Indian Children, and to assist them in regaining their Rights and Possessions from their base and perfidious oppressors.

The trouble our Father has had in conquering his Enemies beyond the great waters, he has brought to a glorious conclusion; and Peace is again restored amongst all the Nations of Europe.

The desire therefore which he has long felt of assisting you, and the assurance which he has given you of his powerful protection, he has now chosen us his Chiefs of the Sea and Land to carry into effectual execution.

Behold the great waters covered with our Ships, from which will go forth an Army of Warriors as numerous as the whole Indian Nations;

The same principle of justice which led our Father to wage a war of twenty years in favor of the oppressed Nations of Europe, animates him now in support of his Indian Children. And by the efforts of his Warriors he hopes to obtain for them the restoration of those lands of which the People of the Bad Spirit have basely robbed them.

Come forth, then, ye Brave Chiefs and Warriors, as one family, and join the British Standard – the signal of union between the powerful and oppressed, the symbol of Justice led on by Victory.

If you want covering to protect yourselves, your wives and your children, against the winter cold – come to us and we will clothe you. If you want arms and ammunition to defend yourselves against your oppressors – come to us and we will provide you. Call around you the whole of the Indian brethren and we will show them the same tokens of our brotherly love.

And what think you we ask in return for this bounty of our great Father, which we his chosen Warriors have so much pleasure in offering you? Nothing more than that you should assist us manfully in regaining your lost lands – the lands of your forefathers – from the common enemy, the wicked People of the United States, and that you should hand down those lands to your children hereafter. And you may rest assured, that whenever we have forced our Enemies to ask for a Peace, our good Father will on no account forget the welfare of his much loved Indian Children.

Again then, Brave Warriors and the Indian Nations, at the mandate of the Great Spirit we call upon you to come forth arrayed in battle, to fight the great fight of Justice, and recover your long lost freedom. Animate your hearts in this sacred cause. Unite with us as the sons of one common Father and a great and glorious victory will shortly crown our exertions.

Pierre Durand spent every waking moment at headquarters. There was much to be done – mainly letters to write in answer to the barrage of correspondence from citizens demanding the attention of the General, or at least a high-ranking member of his staff. There was often a crowd gathered outside, watching in silence as the numerous couriers and runners continuously brought in new information, or were sent out, rushing off with new orders to the troops stationed in and around the city.

The mood of the citizenry had changed. Upon Jackson's arrival, there had been celebrations as they welcomed the man they hoped would save them from the attack they knew was coming. The saloons and bars had been crammed with customers and the streets filled with dancing and jubilant people, black and white, Creole and French. As the days passed, they grew more somber as their plight became more obvious. As he walked the streets to and fro from headquarters to his boarding house, Pierre noticed the difference. The people he spotted late at evening and early in the morning were silent and pensive. The hour, they felt, was almost upon them.

Jackson was desperate for men. Once the attack of the gunboats on Lake Borgne had occurred, he realized he must bend a little. The courageous actions of Lieutenant Jones and his handful of men at the lake were very much appreciated. Despite the tragic loss of the lieutenant and his men, they did provide a benefit. He now had an understanding of the British army's plan of attack. He had not expected them to attempt to reach New Orleans via the lake, and so he had to adjust his own strategy.

Governor Claiborne had encouraged him to make use of the free blacks who were clamoring to take part in the city's defense. They were willing and could be depended on to fight well, the Governor insisted.

So, as he viewed the state of his small army, Jackson authorized the inclusion of a battalion of one hundred and fifty black soldiers. In return for their services, they would receive the same pay and considerations as the rest of his troops.

This, of course, set off a firestorm among the slaveowners of New Orleans. They pelted Jackson with letters of outrage and stormed headquarters, demanding that the decision be revoked. Arming black soldiers would encourage a slave rebellion, they insisted. What could he possibly be thinking?

The outrage grew as Jackson toured the plantations on the outskirts of New Orleans and freely recruited slaves to bolster his ranks. He boldly promised them their freedom if the battle was won.

Pierre was kept busy writing letters and engaging in heated exchanges with the outraged white citizenry. They bombarded him with demands to see the General, or at least an insight as to where he could be found. He, of course, felt no compunction to give out any information. It wasn't his place to question the decisions of General Jackson. In his mind, it wasn't their place, either.

All in all, he was thankful for the distractions of his work. It kept his mind off Rosa and the stress and strain of his relationship with his parents. His life in Mobile now seemed a distant memory, even though he had only been gone a little more than a month. His contribution to the war effort might not be much in the eyes of some, but life for him had taken a favorable turn. As long as he could keep his head down and focus on the tasks before him, he could avoid bad memories and bad habits. That, he decided, was a very good thing.

It was now more than obvious that the British would not be using the ports of Mobile or Pensacola as a jumping off point to attack New Orleans. The battle at Lake Borgne revealed they would attempt to overtake the city from behind. Therefore, Jackson sent an urgent message to General Coffee, stationed in Baton Rouge with his cavalry, to immediately make his way to the city.

The men under Coffee's command were eager and ready. They were fully armed and most of them battle-hardened. Many had been with General Jackson during the Red Stick War. They had been tested and proven they had what it took to face an enemy. Although the new recruits that had been sent south from Tennessee and Kentucky were still green, they were buoyed by the opportunity to fight with such men. Men who had a notion of what it was like to withstand the fire of battle. Men who had seen the death and destruction of war but were still willing to sacrifice for their country.

The road between Baton Rouge and New Orleans was a thin, straggly one. Most of the traffic between the two cities in the past had been by way of the Mississippi. Certainly it was not one that was used to the pounding hoofs of two thousand horses, accompanied by wagons to supply their riders. Yet the men who traversed it that rainy, dreary December were undeterred. They had forged paths before, in the deep, dark forests of the country of the Creeks, and from Mobile to Pensacola. The trek through those swamps and bayous between Mobile and Baton Rouge had also been a serious challenge. Surely the journey between the two cities that both lay upon the muddy banks of the river could be overcome quickly after their past experience.

As they sat before their campfires after a hard day's ride, the men were boisterous and loud as they exchanged catcalls and challenges between the fires.

"Them redcoats ain't gonna know what hit 'em!" was a common theme.

"Yup! It'll be like pickin' off turkeys!"

"I'll lay a bet that us boys from Fayetteville will git more than the rest of ya!"

Jacob wasn't so sure of their bravado. These men, dressed in homespun and buckskin, hardly looked like an army. He had never seen regular British troops, but imagined they did not look anything like he and his comrades.

"I don't know, Preacher. We may not be ready," Jacob voiced to the older man.

Preacher nodded at him. "It will be a different sort of fight. I imagine the redcoats will line up in neat rows in their shiny uniforms and march straight at us. At least, that's what they've always done in the past."

"Are we ready for that, do you think?"

"I don't know. But I have the utmost confidence in General Jackson. He's a smart man. I imagine he will figure something out."

"And if he doesn't?"

Preacher laughed. "Well, I'm not going to speculate on that. But I do know one thing – the British will do what they always do – decide we are unworthy opponents. It will be up to us to prove them wrong once again."

CHAPTER 29

DECEMBER 23, 1814

When General Coffee and his men arrived in New Orleans on December 19 they found the city in turmoil, the streets filled with frantic citizens and aimlessly rambling soldiers and volunteers. The shopkeepers were bravely trying to conduct their business among the throng, but without much success. The nearness of the British and the realization that what the city had feared for months was now upon them had sent the populace into a tizzy. Coffee and his men got busy situating themselves within the city and awaited the commands of their leader.

Pierre did his best to navigate the crushing hordes on his way back and forth to headquarters. He was uneasy at the thought of facing the enemy in battle. He had been issued a musket and given practice how to use it, but the idea of firing it in the heat of battle made him worry. Could he hold up under the strain? He decided he must. He would attempt to do what every good soldier did – follow the orders given him without question. By now, he had grown to trust Jackson. He was a force of nature, the General. His ability to demand and persuade and cajole were well known. Pierre was definitely under his spell.

Jackson himself decided, after much persuasion from Governor Claiborne and his aides, that he would have to bend himself once again and accept the services of a group of men with whom he had no affinity – the pirate soldiers under the command of Jean and Pierre

Lafitte. Although he held these men in contempt, they had possession of things he most desperately needed to protect the city – men, cannon and ammunition. His spies had reported the British had far superior numbers and plenty of supplies to conduct their attack. With misgivings he agreed to meet with the pirate Jean Lafitte. He would have to bite his tongue and accept the services of men he considered seaborne jackals, the dregs of society.

So as his forces gathered, Jackson found himself at the head of a most unusual army. There were regular American infantry troops, volunteer horsemen from Tennessee and Kentucky under General Coffee, and frontier militia units from Tennessee under Generals Carroll and Morgan. Then he had units of Creole and white volunteers from New Orleans, with a smattering of French toffs, as well as a unit of free blacks alongside hundreds of slaves. There were also Creek allies and a group of Choctaw warriors that had recently arrived from Pensacola. Added to the mix toward the end of December was a group of pirates. By any standard, it would take a miracle for such a motley band to work together against a well-trained and armed enemy – soldiers of the same army that had defeated Napoleon. It would take a very special man to unite this disparate group together to defeat the powerful force mobilized against them.

Having been in New Orleans for but a few hours, Jacob decided city life was not for him. The press of people, and the smells and the sounds of the town were almost more than he could bear. A cold dampness pervaded the area, ringed as it was by the Mississippi River on its edge and the delta at its feet. Why on earth so many people would crowd together to live in such a small space was beyond his understanding.

He and his companions camped where they were told, and it was a cramped space indeed. It was an open square in the heart of the city, and there was not a spare inch within it to be found. There was much grousing and complaining over the lack of space.

"There ain't even enough room to turn around if'n your elbow is out," Sam sputtered. "Here, you get off'n my spot!" he would shout if anyone encroached on the small patch of ground he had designated his own. "You fellers need to find yer own spot! This here's been taken!"

Without much enthusiasm, Jacob and Solomon explored the city for a short time on their own. They did stare with a certain amount of awe at the impressive bawdy houses and ornate saloons that dotted the city. But that awe could not overcome their sense of horror at the cramped quarters and throngs of people rushing through the rain-soaked streets.

"Well, this certainly is different from home, isn't it?" Solomon mused.

"Yes, it is," Jacob sighed.

On December 21, a cold wind began to blow. It swept off the water of the Mississippi and chilled the soldiers huddled over their campfires – small ones as there was a decided lack of firewood. Many of them did not possess the necessary clothing for the cold, and they rubbed their fingers together over their fires and grumbled.

On the next day, Jackson met with the corsair Jean Lafitte for the first time and they came to an agreement. The pirates, with their cannon and ammunition, would join the fight against the British invaders. Despite their different backgrounds, they found a sense of commonality. Jackson found the brash, courageous Lafitte to be an intriguing fellow. He had braved the possibility of being arrested in order to meet with him. That was the type of thing Jackson respected. And he welcomed him to the fight.

By the evening of the 22nd, the winds and cold had taken a bitter turn. The mud in the streets of New Orleans was now hard and crunchy from the blasts of frigid air. A thin layer of ice had formed over the puddles and pools, deposits from the recent rains.

When Jackson's army awakened on the morning of December 23rd, they were thoroughly frozen and miserable. Although their tents had shielded their bodies from the frost that had formed the night before, there was little to protect them from the freezing wind that whipped through their campsites.

They arose and went about their daily duties despite the weather.

In the early afternoon, couriers went pelting out of headquarters, scattering throughout the city. The news they brought to Jackson's army was urgent – the British had been spotted due east of New Orleans. They had managed to find a route along a bayou that led out of Lake Borgne and had snuck down a side road. According to the informants that had rushed to headquarters, their intent was clear – they were heading straight for the city.

Jackson's orders were specific and precise – each unit that was able would immediately march out of the city to meet the threat. They were to gather as silently as they could a short distance away from the enemy army and await the signal to attack.

Jacob and his comrades raced through the streets of New Orleans – streets filled with throngs of wailing women in carriages and men, their eyes wide with fright, rushing headlong every which way. He was relieved when they reached the city's outskirts and left the madness behind.

They moved straight east, not far from the piles of mud and dirt that formed the levee along the river, built to keep the Mississippi in its place. While they moved, he and his companions checked their pouches and powder horns to be sure they were well supplied with ammunition.

"Do you think this is it, Preacher? Do you think this is what Jackson has been waiting for?"

"I don't know, Jacob. I'm surprised those lousy redcoats were able to sneak up on us. But I wonder how many men could have easily traveled down from the lake without us knowing about it. I'd be surprised if this was the main force of the army. Probably just a feint to feel us out."

As darkness began to fall, the army halted. An eerie fog began to drift off the river and gave a ghost-like appearance to the men as they waited for the signal to attack.

Out on the river, the USS *Carolina* and a small gunboat had managed to silently come down from the city, under the command of Commodore Perryman. It was a schooner and bristled with cannon and men who knew how to use them.

When the darkness was complete, the *Carolina* opened up on the lead British contingent, which had made its way down the bayou and made camp. The redcoats were easily spotted by the hundreds of campfires they had lit, seen even through the foggy, damp frigid air.

Taken by surprise, the British had nothing to counter the barrage of cannon fire. It was at that moment that the troops sent from the city by Jackson attacked them with a tumultuous yell.

Stumbling through the night's darkness and fog, which was soon mixed with acrid smoke belching from the shipboard cannon in the river, Jacob wondered if any of his shots rang true, or even if he was firing on the British and not his fellow soldiers. He fumbled with reloading when he couldn't see. The officers in charge shouted orders but he paid little attention. Aim, fire and reload. Aim, fire and reload.

He struggled to make out the figures of men before him. There were shouts of panic as some discovered they had been firing on their own comrades. With the overcast sky and moonless night, even the bright red uniform coats of the British were hard to spot through the dense clouds that enveloped the combatants. The familiar smell of gunpowder burned his nose and made his eyes water.

The firing from the ship in the river stopped, as it was too difficult to gauge who exactly they were firing upon, as the lines of struggling, gasping men merged together. Jacob found himself using his rifle butt as a club to counter the thrusts of bayonets that jabbed at him, by leering faces that seemed to all look the same.

At the start of the battle, Solomon had been at his side. Within minutes they were separated, and added to the stress of the struggle to survive at that moment was the memory of his separation from his Uncle John all those months ago at Horseshoe Bend. He would never forgive these murderous, marauding soldiers, who had come to take away the lives of those he held dear, who had traveled thousands of miles to interfere with a people of whom they knew nothing, if anything happened to Solomon.

He loosened the hatchet at his belt and lowered his rifle. The familiar handle of it felt good in his grip. As a boy, he had been well trained in its use. His uncle had seen to it. He began to swing it now at those faceless British soldiers who lunged at him with their bayonets. He parried those long blades with forceful swings, arcing his weapon and slashing at the strangers who had come to do him harm.

He could feel his hatchet hit bone and saw the spurts of blood that burst forth from the men who met up with its whirling weight. He dodged and swerved and deflected those jabbing blades. He was angry now, angry at the need for such violence. He had not asked for this fight. It was not one of his making. But survive it he must.

After the frantic flurry of hand-to-hand fighting, the battle devolved into a musket duel at more of a distance. Minutes dragged by as neither side wanted to give, and the struggling mass of men fought on. Finally, after more than two hours, the bugle sounded. Jacob heard it above the groaning of the wounded and dying men that lay all about. It was the sound of retreat, and he reluctantly withdrew with the rest of the men in his unit.

It was with relief that he spotted Solomon as they left the field. He was none the worse for wear, though he did have a slash on his left arm. He had lost his hat, and his face was grimy with powder burns, but he was alive.

"Are you all right? Are you hurt?" Jacob called to him.

"I'm fine," Solomon replied cheerfully. "It isn't much of a cut."

Jackson removed his men about half a mile east of the battlefield, where they immediately plopped to the ground, exhausted from the bitter struggle they had just endured. There were a few wounded among them, and a doctor was busy making the rounds to see who needed to be carried off to the city and who could be tended to where they lay.

Jacob and Solomon searched until they found Preacher and Sam. They, too, had managed to escape any real harm. Their greetings were muted. Wearied to the bone, the four huddled together and somehow managed to get a small fire going, over which they tried to warm their frozen hands.

"Preacher, what do you think we will do now?" Solomon asked.

"I don't know. I suppose it all depends on what the General decides."

"Ain't no tellin'," Sam piped in. "You can't read the mind of Old Hickory. I bet, though, he's already made his plans. It ain't like him to not be prepared."

"He wasn't prepared for this, though," Jacob said.

"Yeah, but he saw it got took care of, didn't he," Sam declared with a tinge of anger in his voice. "He got us where we needed to be, and in a hurry at that."

"The British would already be in New Orleans if he hadn't acted quickly, Jacob. That's the mark of a good leader. He has to be quick on his feet and respond as fast as he can when circumstances occur beyond his control."

"They'll be back, though, you can count on it. Them lousy lobsterbacks haven't taken the beatin' they deserve. Leastways, not yet," Sam said.

"I just hope we are better prepared for them when they come than we were tonight," Jacob replied.

They had left the city in such a hurry that most of the men had failed to bring their gear with them, and it was a cold and miserable night. Despite being without their blankets there was very little grumbling. The fancy uniforms and the smart maneuvers of the enemy had not dissuaded them. They had managed to hold their own against the empire's Regulars, and they felt a sense of pride in that.

Chapter 30

The Battle

The men rested for a short time after their first skirmish with the British on December 23. Jackson, who had spent hours in the saddle during the previous weeks scouting possible locations where he could make his stand, withdrew them further, another mile and a half to Chalmette Plantation. There was a canal there – or to be more precise, a large ditch – that looked like a very favorable position to receive the enemy.

It was called the Rodriguez Canal, and at some time in the past had been used to bring in water to the plantation from the river to power a sawmill. By now it was defunct and no longer in operation, its shallow waters useless. But it would be a good start for the trench and earthen battlements necessary for the defense of the city. There was also a large plantation house there that would serve nicely as his headquarters, at least temporarily.

As the men moved behind the canal, its defensive potential was obvious to all. To the right lay the Mississippi River and the levee. To the left, a large cypress swamp. Beyond the swamp was the bayou that the British had used to move down toward the city the day before. In order to get to the American lines the British had two choices. They must either forge a road through the jungle of tangled roots and jagged tree stumps, large cypress trees and muddy water of the swamp – a herculean task that would take weeks – or skirt the swamp along the path they had used on the 23rd and march straight down the open field in front of Jackson's fortifications between the swamp and the river. Even with a favorable wind, attacking up the Mississippi was no longer a possibility, at least anytime in the near future. They had unloaded their ships at Lake Borgne. To use the river, they would have to reload their men and materiel back onto the ships anchored at the mouth of Lake Borgne and then sail south, enter the Mississippi and follow the river upstream a full hundred miles, navigating the twists and turns and sometimes shallow waters of the body of water that was the lifeblood of the city of New Orleans.

Pierre Durand had remained at Jackson's headquarters in the city on December 23rd, but once the General had determined he would fight the British at Chalmette Plantation, he and all the staff were commanded to join him on the 24th. He quickly packed his writing materials, gathered his few personal belongings and moved to the plantation house. By the time he arrived it was already jammed with men.

He knew at some point he would be ordered to the lines. His role at headquarters was pretty much finished as the citizens of New Orleans were now hunkered down in the city, six miles away. There would be no petitions or pleas from them now. Their very lives were at risk and their survival was uppermost on their minds. He busied himself as best he could with some of the ledgers and books, his clear hand noted by his superiors.

Jackson ordered his men to begin enlarging the long, straight line of the canal. At first, it was only the slaves he had borrowed from nearby plantations who jumped into the watery muck at the bottom, using shovels to toss the mud upwards to form a sort of breastwork. When Jackson noticed that, he berated his men.

"I meant for every one of you to put your hands to the work!" he shouted. "You, there!" He pointed to some white recruits from the city. "Get into that ditch! I expect every single one of you to do your part!"

Jackson placed General Coffee's men at the very left end of the line, leading into the swamp. They were also expected to dig out the trench before them, and it was not an easy task, as their part of the line extended into the muck and mire of the swamp.

Jacob sweated and cursed at the task when it was his turn to take a shovel. The stench of the mud he dug up was overwhelming at times. It reeked of the long dead animals that had their final resting places there, and the rot of the dead trees and underbrush that helped create the ooze that he stood in, knee deep.

While he worked, he looked down the straight line of the ditch and saw others were busy with the same task. There were hundreds of men sweating and cursing and shoveling and tossing their laden shovels upward, and the mud breastwork they were forming began to take shape. Others were hauling bales of cotton and downed trees to help reinforce and give structure to what they built.

Behind him, the men of Coffee's regiment were attempting to build structures upon which they could rest, as their portion of the defensive line was nothing but soggy sludge. They used their hatchets to slash at the cypress trees around them and then tied the branches together to form platforms on which they could lay. Some fortunate men claimed the few spots of high ground as their own, and God help any other man who tried to infringe on their claim.

The weather had eased somewhat since the bitter cold night of the 23rd, but fires were still necessary to warm the cold fingers of the men huddled around the small flames they had managed to light. Rations were few, but there were no real complaints. They had already faced the British once and they knew other attempts would be made to dislodge them and take the city. The usual bravado and boisterousness of the men from Tennessee was now muted.

When Jacob left the trench, covered in grime from head to toe, he saw that Sam had managed to build a sort of platform large enough to hold two men. He handed his shovel off to Solomon and hailed him.

"Is it sturdy enough?"

"I reckon so. Leastways we can take turns, the four of us, when we have a chance to rest."

"It's Christmas day tomorrow."

"We won't be celebratin', Jacob."

"I suppose not."

"I will be happy to recite some verses from the Bible for us," Preacher interjected.

Sam looked at Jacob sharply. "Didn't know you celebrated Christmas, you bein' an Indian."

"I know about Christmas. I was well versed in the Christian faith."

"It doesn't matter, Sam. I will be sharing verses for any and all here who would like some comfort from the Good Book," Preacher said quietly.

As Jackson and his men were busy building their fortifications, the British worked tirelessly moving men and cannon down the narrow path along the bayou and to the east of the vast swamp that stood between them and the American line. They worked methodically at the task, day and night. Major General Sir Edward Pakenham pushed them, convinced he had Jackson's ragtag army exactly where he wanted them.

As they worked, they were continually peppered with shots fired by snipers and scouts, hidden in the swamp. There were not enough Americans in ambush to prove to be more than a nuisance, but there were brief skirmishes that broke out between the two sides as the British prepared to put a stop to the arrogance of this fledgling country that thought it could defeat the greatest army in the world. The British had defeated Bonaparte, after all. Many of the men who found themselves in the humid, fetid jungles of Louisiana had fought against Napoleon's finest. For the Americans to believe they could face off against them was pure foolishness.

Aside from the short sermon from Preacher, Christmas came and went without much notice. On the 27th, the British sprung an attack on the USS *Carolina*, the ship that had been used so effectively against the redcoats on December 23rd. As it sat on the Mississippi, British cannon, secretly dragged up to the riverbank during the night, opened up on it, and the vessel was soon no more than a burning hulk. The gunboat *Louisiana* managed to escape the onslaught, although badly damaged. The guns aboard it and the *Carolina* were salvaged, thanks to their crews, mostly composed of Lafitte's pirates, and were placed on the far right of Jackson's defensive line.

On the morning of December 28th, enough British soldiers had gathered between the swamp and the river for Pakenham to attempt a reconnaissance to test the strength of the American line. Two columns were sent forward – one along the levee road that ran beside the river and one on the edge of the cypress swamp on Jackson's left.

The largest British force, along the levee, carried with it a few small cannon among its marching units. The American guns from the river, placed the day before, and a few field pieces already planted on the breastworks, caught the British cannon in a crossfire and soon made short work of the enemy, forcing a retreat. Jackson's line on his right had held.

On Jackson's left, though, things had not gone as well. Using a small trail along the side of the swamp, a British force had advanced, headed right for Coffee's regiment of Tennessee volunteers.

Jacob sighted his rifle, propped upon the top of the five-foot-high breastwork he and his comrades had so recently completed, aiming at the scarlet-clad troops as they marched forward. This was the first time he had seen attacking redcoats in daylight, and despite the chill in the air, he could feel the cold sweat dripping down his back. At the yelled command, shots rang out all along the line, with the British troops returning fire. Jacob was soon enveloped by the bitter smoke that filled the air and heard shouts from his left. The British were attempting to flank them. If they could make their way around Coffee's men they could roll up the whole army from the rear.

He and others shifted to their left and began pouring fire into the foremost British troops. They, in their smart red uniforms, with crossed belts and bayonets that gleamed in the sunlight, began to fall as the accuracy and dependability of the long rifles of the Tennessee men took their toll. The British bore as much of the punishing fire as they could before pulling back.

Immediately after the smoke had cleared, Jackson sent word that the line on the left must be extended further into the swamp. He had watched as Coffee's troops came under fire, and the British had come too close to flanking his army. This would never do.

So Jacob and his comrades picked up their shovels once again, to endure the backbreaking task of extending their breastworks further into the jumbled roots and vines and cypress trees.

When the new year dawned on January 1, 1815, Jackson's defenses were set.

On the opposite bank of the river he had placed two batteries of cannon, manned by Louisiana and Kentucky volunteers. These were meant to enfilade the British when they ventured to attack the Americans' main position, which everyone now called Line Jackson.

Anchoring the main line immediately on the levee was a redoubt called Battery 1, manned by regular troops and a company of volunteers from the city of New Orleans. Next came Batteries 2 and 3, where Jean Lafitte's pirates and some of the crews from the *Carolina* and the *Louisiana* would make their stand. To their immediate left were more volunteers from the embattled city, including a company of free blacks.

Battery 4 came next, which included the largest American cannon, a huge 32-pounder that had been salvaged from the *Carolina*. To the left of that were more militia troops and free men of color. Batteries 5 and 6, with Regular Army gunners, were flanked to the left by volunteers from Tennessee and Kentucky under the command of General Carroll. Batteries 7 and 8 had been hastily constructed after the British attack on December 28 and were defended by the hardy souls of General Coffee's Tennessee volunteers, along with a band of Choctaw Indians.

The British had managed to haul some of their own cannon down the narrow, winding path beside the bayou, and began pounding at the American line. One of their first targets was the plantation house Jackson had been using as his headquarters, heavily damaging it. He and his staff would switch to the open field from then on.

To Pierre Durand, the screaming sound of the British cannon and the answering American salvos were unnerving. Each cannon blast caused him to jump, and the earsplitting sound of it almost overcame him. Musket in hand, he had positioned himself between Batteries 3 and 4, with volunteers from the city. They, too, were jumpy at the artillery battle that had begun.

He mostly kept to himself those first few days of the new year. He was a stranger to the men beside him. Even though many of them seemed as anxious as he, there was little they had in common, other than a desire to see this through to the end.

As cannon balls crashed against the sturdy breastworks, and the night sky was sometimes lit with the trails of British rockets fired in their direction, he and his fellows rested when they could, ate what was supplied them, and waited, tense and worried, for what was inevitable – an all-out assault on Line Jackson.

"This here battle is shapin' up just fine fer us, fellers!" Sam exclaimed, as Jacob and his companions huddled over the small fire they had managed to kindle, their fingers extended to soak up what warmth they could.

"Doesn't seem that way to me," Jacob replied. "I never knew there were so many cannon in the world. A man can't rest with all this racket going on."

"We're on the better side of the line, Jacob. Just think about all those other men closer to the river. They're taking the brunt of it," Preacher said. "Those men stationed closer to the batteries are most probably deaf by now!"

"I don't see why Sam thinks we're at an advantage."

"You don't see the genius of it?"

"No, can't say as I do."

"Look," Preacher explained patiently. "The redcoats are making the same mistake here that they did during the last war. They've decided that they, being British, are superior human beings. They've fallen into a trap, yet they still don't know it."

"What trap?"

"They've got a dense cypress forest on the right and the Mississippi River on their left. Their only option now is to march straight up that empty field in front of us and attack us head on. Their ships are still anchored at the mouth of Lake Borgne. They are of no use to them."

"So it's kinda like a cattle chute," Sam chuckled.

"But they have heavy artillery!"

"As do we. And we won't be marching across an open field."

"Their cannon ain't doin' 'em no good, Jacob. Can't you see? These here breastworks is as fine as you'll see anywheres. Their cannon ain't gonna breach 'em. I'd bet my life on it!"

January 8 dawned, and General Pakenham began his assault.

It had two phases. First, he launched an attack on the batteries Jackson had placed on the opposite side of the river. The idea was to overwhelm the batteries placed there and turn the cannon against the flank of the American line across the river. The British attack ran late but was successful – the Americans were forced to flee, but not before spiking their cannon, making them useless to the British. There would be no American guns used against Line Jackson.

The main phase was to march upon the American line in a massive frontal assault. It was still dark when their advance started, and the British had the advantage of a thick, murky fog to cover their approach. But just as they got within range of the Americans, the fog gave way to the early morning light. As soon as they were spotted, the batteries all along Line Jackson opened up with a ferocious fire that mowed down rows of British troops.

The hardy men of the American line, safely ensconced behind their earthen breastworks, spied the enemy, lined up in perfect formation, marching toward them with muskets and bayonets glinting in the sunlight. None of the defenders had seen such a display before, and for many it was a sight they never hoped to see again.

Pierre's hands shook as he fired his musket and reloaded, fired and reloaded. Because of the billowing clouds of choking smoke from the hundreds of muskets and roaring cannon around him, it was nearly impossible to train his eyes on a particular target. But fire he did, into the redcoats' own cloud-shrouded lines.

Despite the confusion that surrounded him – the sweating, shouting men and cacophony of gunfire, and the screams and hurrahs of his fellow soldiers – he wondered what his father would think of him if he could see him now. As he wiped at the sweat that poured down his forehead, he could not guess. At this moment, he decided, it really didn't matter.

The British saw some success by the river, overrunning a protruding part of the American line, but nowhere else were able to reach the main breastworks. At one point a regiment of Highlanders crossed the field at a slant, making themselves a broad target for half of Jackson's army, particularly cannoneers firing grape. They bravely stood, though much of the British army was now lying on the field, dead, wounded or ducking from the unrelenting fire.

At the far left of Line Jackson, Jacob and his comrades were using their rifles to great effect. The superior accuracy and range of the long rifles used by the volunteers could not be denied. Despite the swelling clouds of gray smoke that surrounded them, they could still spot flashes from the enemy, as well as glimpses of scarlet uniform, and their aim was true.

"Got another one!" Sam would exclaim after his rifle jerked.

"How can you tell for sure?" Jacob shouted.

"A feller just knows these things," Sam replied. "I told ya it would be a cattle chute!"

General Jackson stood behind his line, shouting orders and directing fire as he spotted threats in the lines of the advancing British. He stood straight and tall, despite the missiles whizzing around him, focused on the display of thousands of British troops before him.

The bright trails of the cannon balls being fired in both directions lit up the battlefield in the early morning light. He could see the struggling batteries of field artillery deployed by the British, even though they were often surrounded by thick clouds of smoke. He watched as the withering fire of his own batteries battered and hammered them. The accuracy of the pirate cannoneers at Battery 2, there by the command of Lafitte, could not be denied. As he stood there, watching, he decided he had made a good bargain with that scoundrel.

After two hours of incessant pounding by the American artillery, the British began to withdraw their troops from the field. Jackson didn't know it at the time, but their commander, General Pakenham, had been killed in action, hit twice by grapeshot.

As he watched them withdraw, he was satisfied. As he viewed the field in front of him, littered with the bodies of the dead and dying and the crushed remnants of the artillery pieces that had been employed against his line, Jackson knew he had won the day.

CHAPTER 31

THE AFTERMATH

After the British withdrew from the field, the Americans viewed the savage panorama before them. The dead and wounded lay in great heaps on the ground, their bright red jackets splotched with the darker red stains of their life's blood. They heard the anguished cry of the wounded, begging for help and pleading for water as they lay prone and helpless.

Shattered cannon and the carriages that had transported them were tossed here and there among what remained of the once fine, neat and orderly lines of British soldiers that had marched so determinedly just a few short hours before.

Some parts of Line Jackson happily took into custody British soldiers, who, upon spying the retreat of their army, raised their arms high and gave themselves up.

As Jackson and his staff toured his troops, he was met by the loud cheering and hoorahs of the men he had led to such a stunning victory. They shouted their approval, and their satisfied general gladly accepted it.

The British were allowed to retrieve their dead and wounded. Pierre was happy for it. To gaze on the carnage that had been inflicted by him and his fellow soldiers was such a ghastly sight it nearly turned his stomach. It was amazing, he thought, what men were willing to do to others. But he had done his duty as he saw it, and although he did not have the heart to be as gleeful as the men who surrounded him, he knew no man could fault him for his actions that day.

As Jacob watched the British hauling off their casualties, he felt a deep satisfaction over his day's work. These men in scarlet coats had fueled the fire that had taken so much from him and his people. Without their prodding and pushing, their needling and cajoling, their supplying and encouraging the Red Sticks who had turned his world upside down, his life would have been different.

He did not hold anything but contempt for these men, and did not regret the suffering he and his fellow soldiers had inflicted on them.

If the men thought that once the battle was won they would be relieved of duty on the line they were sorely mistaken. The ever-cautious Jackson insisted they remain on high alert. He could not know whether the British would return to attack them again. Until the enemy had left the area for good, his men would stand guard and be prepared for another assault.

There had been strict instructions handed down by Jackson that liquor was forbidden while the men remained on guard. However, some of the men encamped around Pierre had managed to slip in a few bottles, and they discreetly made use of them each evening as they warmed themselves before the fire. Pierre did his best to ignore them and steer clear of any temptation, but the strain and stress of battle ate at him. He argued with himself each evening – maybe just one drink. But he fought his urge as best he could and avoided the men who offered him refreshment from their forbidden stores.

Jacob and his comrades, still stuck in the muck of the cypress swamp, grew restless as the days went by. Their conditions were nearly intolerable, and they could see little relief on the horizon.

They worked at bettering the racks they had made for sleeping, slightly raised above the filthy mud, but that did little to ease their discomfort. It rained intermittently, and the pieces of canvas they used to try to keep the cold drizzle off while they attempted to sleep were sometimes inadequate. The damnable rain soaked the canvas, and water dripped incessantly down on them when they tried to rest.

With difficulty, a few fires were kept going but weren't large enough to give much warmth to the hundreds of miserable soldiers who attempted to huddle around them. They were barely large enough to cook the meager rations the men were handed, and as the days ticked by their grumbling grew louder.

"It just ain't right, I tell ya. We should be chasin' them filthy redcoats right back up the road they come in on," Sam complained.

"That makes no sense. Why leave these fortifications, where we know we can defend ourselves, and put all our lives in jeopardy? Didn't you just see what happens in a battle on an open field?" Preacher replied, a bit testily.

"Yeah, I saw it. But look here – we done killed heaps of 'em. I bet they got hardly anyone left to fight back."

"You have no way of knowing that. I think the General has everything in hand. He knows more about their situation than you do, my friend."

"Maybe so. But I sure am tired of sittin' in the mud, Preacher. It's time fer somethin' to happen, one way or another."

"Perhaps. Patience is called for. After all we've been through, we can handle a few more days of discomfort."

It took nine long days for the British to depart. Nine days of hauling what was left of their cannon up the trail on which they had come, back to their ships anchored at the mouth of Lake Borgne. Nine days of dragging their wounded up the same trail, nervously looking over their shoulders to see if the Americans would pursue. Nine days of half-starving men, their once proud uniforms now in tatters from weeks of campaigning, struggling through the swampy terrain. Nine days of realizing they had just suffered a stinging defeat at the hands of people for whom they'd had little regard.

They had attempted to build a road through the swamp back to the lake to make their exit quicker, but with little success. The British troops who had defeated the great Napoleon were now in such dire straits they didn't have the manpower or supplies to accomplish such a feat.

As the days passed, Jacob grew silent and contemplative. Now that the British were defeated, what would be his next move? His enlistment would be up in a few days and his life was now at a crossroads. He could choose to reenlist, or he could leave and strike out on his own. But where would he go?

He had no desire to return to his father's house, back to the people who had rejected the part of him that he had no control over – his Creek heritage. That very heritage was now in jeopardy, thanks to the agreement Jackson had made with the Creek people. He had stripped them of most of their lands at the Treaty of Fort Jackson, and with it a way of life that would now be almost impossible to maintain. Was there any point in returning to his mother's people, now that his Uncle John was dead?

And yet, he had no desire to continue fighting. He had seen enough of war and deprivation and death.

He did remember viewing the land west of the Mississippi River while he and the rest of Coffee's command had waited for Jackson's order to move south to New Orleans – the hours he'd spent contemplating the beauty and mystery of the deep forests on the other side of the muddy, whirling waters, a sight that had captured his interest and imagination. Perhaps there was a place for him, to the west. Perhaps he could forge a new direction for his life. Maybe he was meant to live alone, dependent on no one but himself.

"You know our enlistments are up in a few days," Solomon said to him one day.

"Yes, I know."

"Do you plan on signing back up?"

"No. I have made other plans."

"Heading back home then?"

"No."

Solomon looked at him. "Why not?"

"There isn't much there for me anymore. My father and stepmother made it quite plain to me at our last meeting that I was not particularly welcome there."

"Yes, I remember you telling me that."

"They find my Creek blood abhorrent, Solomon. I have no place there anymore. What about you? Will you rejoin?"

"I'm not sure. I haven't decided yet. Where will you go, Jacob?"

"I'm thinking of crossing the river, heading west. Finding my own path. I'm not as fortunate as you. You have a family and a place. Your Pa has already decided to give you part of his land, hasn't he?"

Solomon nodded. "Yes, he has. The thing of it is, I don't know that the life of a farmer is what I really want. After all we've seen and done, I don't know if it suits me to go back home and pick up where I left off."

Jacob nodded.

"Perhaps I could go with you!"

Jacob looked at him squarely. "It most probably will be a difficult existence, my friend. I'm not sure what is west of here, but it will be wild country. It will be tough going."

"I'm sure. But two guns are better than one, Jacob. We could help each other. Whatever is out there will be easier to handle if you aren't alone."

"What would your Ma and Pa say about you leaving?"

"I'm not worried about that. They have my brothers Henry and Nathan to help them out. They would be just fine without me, I believe."

"I'll be heading out just as soon as Jackson relieves us from duty on the line."

Solomon grinned broadly. "I'll get Preacher to write a letter home for me."

Once the General made the decision that his troops were now free from duties along Line Jackson, there was great rejoicing among the men. The British were gone, hopefully for good, and the city of New Orleans exploded with reveling celebration.

The very next morning, bright and early, Jacob and Solomon said their goodbyes to Preacher and Sam.

"It's been a real pleasure serving with you two," Preacher said. "May God bless you and keep you safe."

"Thank you, Preacher. We pray the same for you," Solomon replied.

They gathered their horses from the corral and headed north of the city. Lake Borgne was still under the watchful gaze of American troops, on high alert in case the British decided to turn back, so they decided to cross Lake Pontchartrain, on the far eastern edge of that body of water. Once the barge dropped them off, they found the ruts of the road heading west, and decided to make camp near it. They built a roaring fire and settled in.

Pierre Durand woke with a start. Through his blurry eyes he spied the comrades who had induced him to take part in the celebration over the British departure. They lay together in a jumble, close to the dying embers of the fire they had danced around the night before.

Some of the men had family members from the city smuggle in small kegs of wine and spirits as soon as the news broke. He had done his best to avoid imbibing, but the pull had been too strong to overcome. He vaguely remembered these men who had convinced him to partake in the revelry, and his head dropped in shame at the memory.

He nearly wept as he looked around him. How could he have let this happen? Where was his resolve? His head ached so as he cradled it in his hands. What was to be done now?

He could not stay. The city of New Orleans was not the place for a young man like him, prone to use the bottle to hide his feelings of loss and sorrow. It was a city that enjoyed its celebrations and festivals, fueled by fine food and strong drink.

Desperately, he thought of what he could do and where he could go. His enlistment was up in just a few days. Could he return home, perhaps? Could his father forgive his failings and take him back into the position he had held before drinking had taken control of his life?

He raised himself up and tried to straighten his clothing. He could smell the stench of rum on his jacket. He shuddered as he vaguely remembered the previous evening's debauchery. He went to his tent and gathered what few things he possessed and made his way to the corral where the horses were kept. The camp was a beehive of activity, and there were no questions asked when he requested a horse and saddle.

He headed north of the camp. When he approached Lake Borgne, it was obvious he would not be able to cross there. Patrols were along the lake, and there were boats out upon it, ever watchful for a British return. He turned his horse west and found a group of skiffs and barges heading north on Lake Pontchartrain. He begged a ride, and as he bounced across the rough waters of the lake, his stomach churned and his hands trembled.

He stumbled off the barge he had ridden and spied the ruts of a road, heading both east and west. Beside it, he saw two young men sitting before a roaring fire with a spit of salt pork roasting over it and a kettle of some sort that gave off a pleasing aroma. He had not eaten anything since noon the day before. His hunger pangs forced him to approach.

"Excuse me, gentlemen. Do you mind if I share your fire? It has been a very difficult day and I could use a rest."

Jacob and Solomon looked up to see a rumpled young man in obvious distress. Not only was his clothing askew, but there was a tinge of yellow in his complexion that spoke of some sort of illness. As Jacob looked closer, he had a feeling he had seen this man before.

"You're welcome to sit a spell with us," Solomon replied. "Our victuals are almost cooked and we'd be happy to spare some extra. You look as if you haven't eaten lately."

"That is true," Pierre replied as he sat down next to them. "My name is Pierre."

"You're French, I take it. What brings you out here? You from New Orleans?"

"No, I've been with the army. My enlistment is about up and I'm thinking of returning to my home in Mobile."

"I'm Solomon, and this here is Jacob. We hail from the Alabama River, not far north of Mobile."

"Are you gentlemen heading home as well?"

"No," Jacob replied. "We've decided to head west of here. We don't know where, exactly." It was then that he recalled where he had seen Pierre before. "Say, I think I remember you. You rode along with us in the same boat across Mobile Bay, right after we marched from Pensacola."

Pierre nodded. "Yes, I remember crossing the bay. I'm sorry to say I don't remember you, however." He changed the subject. "Why are you heading west?"

"We've had enough of war. We've been with the army since before Horseshoe Bend. On the loose since Fort Mims, in fact. Our enlistments are up and we have decided to go our own way, unencumbered."

"You are aware that the Spanish still hold territory west of here, right past Louisiana. It's called New Spain. Do either of you gentlemen speak Spanish?"

"Not much," Solomon replied.

"Perhaps I could be of service to you."

"How so?"

"I have very little to go home to. My father and I have had a disagreement, and I fear going back to Mobile will not be of any benefit to me. I am fluent in Spanish as well as French. Perhaps I could go along with you and be an interpreter."

Jacob looked at him balefully. "I'm not sure about that. It will be a difficult journey. We can't afford to take along anyone who cannot pull their own weight."

Pierre leaned closer in. "But I have a musket and a pistol and I know how to use them. I did my part in the battle we just won. I am experienced at buying and selling. You will be hunting and trapping, correct? I have experience in the fur trade."

"Well . . ." Jacob mulled.

"We should let him come along," Solomon said. "An extra musket can't hurt, Jacob. If two guns are better than one, then three would be even better."

As Pierre looked hopefully on, Jacob grudgingly nodded his head.

And so, the next morning the three arose, saddled their horses, and headed west.

———

Author's Note

Throughout American history, there have been pivotal events that today garner only a sentence or two in the textbooks that review our past. One such event was the Fort Mims Massacre.

When it occurred, the news of the horror inflicted on the settlers of the southern frontier were blared across the headlines of all the major newspapers in the country. The goriest details were not spared, and the outrage they engendered was real and intense.

Without the massacre, there would have been no Creek War. What had been a simple tribal dispute erupted into a full-blown war after Fort Mims was attacked. The Battle of Horseshoe Bend, an impressive military victory during the conflict, catapulted Andrew Jackson into the national spotlight.

Without the Creek War, Andrew Jackson and his volunteers from Tennessee might not have had the military experience needed to win such a decisive victory at the Battle of New Orleans. And without that victory, would Andrew Jackson have ever been able to win the Presidency?

Jackson was not always a man of his word. The freedom he promised to the black slaves who helped seal his victory at the Battle of New Orleans never materialized. The men were simply returned to the plantations from which they had come.

He also made promises to the many Creek warriors who fought by his side throughout the conflict. After the Battle of New Orleans, he did give some of those faithful soldiers grants within the lands he had obtained from the Creek Nation at the Treaty of Fort Jackson. They returned and settled just north of what is today Atmore, Alabama. They named their settlement Poarch.

When the Indian Removal Act was enforced in 1831, this handful of Creeks was allowed to stay, as they had received their land grants directly from Andrew Jackson. They were joined by a few others who managed to escape from the city of Montgomery, where members of the Five Civilized Tribes were being held before removal along the Trail of Tears.

And so they remained. When the Civil War broke out, some of their descendants fought for the Confederacy, as they were slaveholders, just as their white neighbors were.

As the 19th century progressed, they stayed put, wedded to the land that had been granted them decades before. Untethered as they were from their Creek brethren who had been forced to settle in Oklahoma, some of the ways and knowledge of their people began to wane. By the time the 20th century dawned, the ties were thin, but the knowledge of who they were never died.

Subjected to the same racial prejudice as their black neighbors, they struggled to survive. They were denied even a basic education, yet there remained a hope that could not be dimmed. They renewed ties with their own people out west and determined they would be recognized for what they were – Creek Indians. They began an intense campaign to receive federal recognition of their tribal status, and it was finally granted in 1984. They are now proud to be called the Poarch Band of

Creek Indians, and have become an integral part of the culture of south Alabama.

I would like to give special thanks to the following people, who were of tremendous help to me as I did the research for this book: Charles Torrey, Research Historian at the History Museum of Mobile, and Angelica Tilton and Kristin Parrish at the Pensacola Museum of History. Their assistance was invaluable and very much appreciated.

I scoured through dozens of books and many articles and websites for the information I used to write this story. For those who would like to know more about the times and people I covered, here are some books and materials that might help you to further understand the period:

For more information on the Poarch Band of Creek Indians, I highly recommend a visit to their website at https://pci-nsn.gov.

To learn more about the Creek Indians and their culture, *Creek Country: The Creek Indians and their World* by Robbie Ethridge is a good source.

For more details about the Battle of Horseshoe Bend, see *Tohopeka: Rethinking the Creek War and the War of 1812*, edited by Kathryn E. Braund.

To get a good perspective on the volunteers who followed Andrew Jackson, including personal testimonies of individual soldiers, I found some great information in *Tennesseans at War 1812–1815* by Tom Kanon.

For a good overview of the entire struggle along the Gulf Coast during the War of 1812, I suggest *Struggle for the Gulf Borderlands: The Creek War and the Battle of New Orleans 1812–1815* by Frank L. Owsley.

To get an understanding of Mobile in the early years, there is *Colonial Mobile: An Historical Study* by Peter J. Hamilton. This particular book can be found on the internet archives at https://archive.org.

There are, of course, numerous volumes on the life of Andrew Jackson. The one I found most helpful for my purposes was *Andrew Jackson Vol. 1: The Course of American Empire, 1767–1821* by Robert V. Remini.

There are dozens and dozens of scholarly works about the Battle of New Orleans. *Patriot Fire: Andrew Jackson and Jean Laffite at the Battle of New Orleans* by Winston Groom I found to be most helpful.